ABOUT KILLER MOVES

He's a hacker. A high-tech hitman. And now...a daddy?
When Matteo skips prison with a clean record, his conscience is anything but. Guilt hits him like a sack of marbles when he spots the woman he jilted. The clincher? Her child who looks like him.

Renee's son may have Matteo's eyes, but she won't say who fathered AJ. She's also mum on what sent her into hiding or why guys with guns are after her. But when Matteo blocks an attack, he persuades Renee to appoint him their protector.

Keeping them safe means faking they're a normal family road tripping with s'mores and snuggles and possibly a sniper rifle. Toss in a potty-training toddler and temptation from the woman he still craves, and it's officially Matteo's toughest mission.

But with danger nipping their heels, the only way to save his family may be to leave their lives for good.

2
ASSASSINS
in Love

KILLER MOVES

USA TODAY BESTSELLING AUTHOR

TAWNA FENSKE

KILLER MOVES

ASSASSINS IN LOVE BOOK #2

TAWNA FENSKE

THE ASSASSINS IN LOVE SERIES

- Killer Looks (free prequel novella)
- Killer Instincts (Dante and Jen)
- Killer Moves (Matteo and Renee)
- Killer Smile (Sebastian and Nicole)

KILLER MOVES

Assassins in Love book #2
Matteo and Renee's story

For Paxton.
The coolest three-year-old I know.

CHAPTER 1

*M*atteo always said his first stop after prison would be Saucy Buns for a burger. Extra pickles, no mayo.

Turns out ground beef can't compete with his sisters.

Tech World barely could.

He only stopped for computer gear. His offshore accounts have plenty for a new laptop, plus an external hard drive and six burner phones because that's just good business sense. Out front, he gives a homeless guy hand warmers from aisle six. Cookies from checkout, plus two hundred in cash. "Stay safe." He gets in his car without looking back.

Now Matteo's on I-5 in his 1973 Alfa Romeo Spider, headed for Miss Gigglewink's Daycare. Not a normal post-prison stop for a felon, but Matteo's hardly normal. Besides, his conviction's overturned. He's a free man.

He's got the top down, windows open, though it's fifty degrees and drizzly. Thank God his sisters brought the car. They wanted to pick him up, but Teo needed the closure of watching those concrete walls fade in his rearview mirror.

Needs his sisters not to see him detour past the home of the

1

shady cop who stuck him behind bars. Detective Reggie Dowling doesn't even own the brick rambler anymore, but Matteo needs to see. Needs to know where the bastard landed after Teo's pals twisted his arm. The twisting might've freed Matteo, but it also sent Dowling underground.

He shouldn't care. He's free, and that's what matters.

Errands complete, Matteo's killed enough time to be sure all the students are gone from Miss Gigglewink's. It's farm show-and-tell day, so both sisters should be there.

Hitting his signal, he turns onto the road he knows like security code for a Unix operating system. Two more blocks and he's on the leafy street where his grandma's craftsman bungalow sits in the swoop of a cul-de-sac. His chest gets tight as his brain brews a memory of sitting on that curb with a grape soda.

"Tenants left this behind." Grandma Nondi wheeled the bike from the garage. "Looks your size. Almost new."

He'd never had a bike. Never dreamed of riding one. All the way home, he cried fat, quiet tears, smearing his face with a sleeve so she wouldn't see. They took it to the farm where he taught himself to ride. Taught Nic and Jen, hovering when they wobbled.

Nic got the bungalow when Nondi passed, and Jen got the farm. Matteo got the beach house, and he's glad about that. Maybe he'll buy a bike. A red one with a black seat so he can pedal to the shore with the sun on his back and his grandma's memory perched on his shoulder.

He parks at the curb and scans the dental clinic across the way. Sebastian LaDouceur, DDS. *The Dentist* swears he's going straight. Just a dentist now, not the kind that makes bad guys go away for money. Matteo will believe that when he sees it.

At the front door of the daycare, he hesitates. They expect him at the farm by five, but that's three hours. He needs to hug his sisters sooner.

"Matty!" Nic flings the door open and throws herself at his chest. "You're here! I hoped you'd come early."

"Hey, kid." Hugging hard, he wonders how the girl with pigtails and a lisp became a business owner. Not just any business. A daycare for folks fleeing bad situations. Pride floods his chest as he hugs her harder.

Pride and concern. "Is it okay if I'm here?" He sets her on the steps. "I can leave if—"

"No, you're good." She grabs his hand and hauls him inside. "Students are long gone. We're just cleaning up so we can load the lambs."

"Matty!" Jen wipes her hands on dirty blue jeans. "I shouldn't hug you. I'm covered in lamb poop, but I really *want* to hug you and—"

"Then we hug." He squeezes the girl whose diapers he once changed. All grown up and living with his best friend. Jesus. How did that happen? "Missed you."

"I missed you, too." She pulls back and laughs. "I know we saw each other three days ago, but this feels different."

"Damn right it does." If she only knew. "How's Dante?"

"Good." She wipes her hands again. "He'll be at dinner tonight."

"He's *making* dinner tonight." Nicole slaps a hand to her heart. "If Jen doesn't hurry and marry him, I'll bang the man silly for his elk chili recipe."

"Jesus." The throbbing in his head is new. "Can we maybe not talk about banging?"

An eye roll from Nic. "You just got out of prison. I'd worry if you didn't have banging on the brain."

More throbbing, mostly in his temples. "Let's also not say the *P* word." He scans a shelf lined with kids' board books. "Not here."

"P word?" Nic's grinning as she moves through his periphery

to straighten a stuffed animal. "Penis? Prick? Piss? Pussy?" She's enjoying this too much. "Or did you mean pris—"

"That."

"You're like a mime with his tongue yanked out." Nicole looks at Jen. "Let's load the lambs and get out of here."

"Actually, we kinda need you." Jen sidles over with her sweet little sister smile. "Think you could help for a sec?"

His gun hand slips to his belt before he remembers he's not carrying. Also, helping at a daycare doesn't require firepower. "Sure."

Nic points at a pen of bleating lambs. "One of my sweet little angel students broke the latch."

Jen mutters something like "demon child," but she's smiling. "The second we open that gate, the lambs will run for it. We need someone to hold it shut."

"Only until we get the first ones in the truck." Nic's already walking to the pen. "With five lambs, Jen and I can each get one on the first run, and then with the three of us—"

"I follow the math." He's got dual degrees in mathematics and computer science. He can figure out how to count sheep. "So I'm on guard duty."

"Not with brute force." Nic lifts an eyebrow. "We just need your body to block them from darting out."

He's done worse with his body for a lot less payoff. "Let's do it."

They get into position. Jen's got a hand on the gate, while he squats beside Nic as a human blockade.

"Let 'er rip," Nic calls.

Jen swings the gate open, and three lambs bolt. Nic snags the first one, while Matteo grabs the second, spinning so his back shoves the gate shut.

"Got you!" Jen scoops up the third lamb.

Behind him in the pen, two lambs bleat in protest. The one in his arms is a wriggling wad of fleece, baah-ing in his ear. "No complaining." He shifts so his back's firmly at the gate. "You're well fed, I'm positive. My sister's the world's biggest softie."

"Hey." Jen pretends to glare. "Who kicked ass on a kidnapper when—"

"We're not talking about it." Picturing his kid sister in danger has his head throbbing again. "Hurry up."

"Come on." Nic starts for the door. "You sure you're okay holding down the fort?"

"Positive." His lamb squirms some more. He scratches its ears, and the animal relaxes.

"We'll be quick." Jen shoves the front door as her lamb bleats. "It might take a sec to get them situated."

"Got it handled."

"Thanks, bro." Nicole follows her out the door calling, "Glad you're back!"

"It's good to be back." He says it to empty air, or maybe the lambs. Brown eyes plead for freedom.

"Sorry about the cage." He's a sucker for brown eyes. "If it helps, I relate."

The smallest lamb bleats and rears behind the bars. Adjusting his hold on the one in his arms, he scans the classroom. Miss Gigglewink's. The cuteness hurts his teeth.

Bright plastic chairs march miniature rows around the room. The wall above the whiteboard holds paper cutouts of numbers formed by cartoon animals. A caterpillar three, a spider eight. There's a bookshelf with titles like *The Wonky Donkey* and *Never Ever Tickle a Turkey.*

Through the window, he scans the playground. Can kids really fit down that plastic slide? It resembles the trunk of an elephant, with steps up the back. So damn adorable.

And so far from where he's been. God, this is weird.

Stroking the lamb, he kicks his legs out in front of him. "My sisters are great, huh?"

The lamb bleats and wiggles.

5

"Smart," he continues. "Tough as hell." His throat's tight all of a sudden. "For a fuckup, I've got great sisters."

Another bleat from his fleecy friend. He shouldn't swear at daycare.

"Whoa!"

A child's squeal swings his eyes to the doorway. Matteo stares as a boy in red sneakers rockets toward him like a missile in overalls. "*Lambie Lambie Lambie Lambie!*"

The kid's red shirt ripples as his sneakers squeak the vinyl. There's a gleam in his green eyes, and Matteo's not sure if it's joy or budding psychosis.

"Hey there." Matteo shields the lamb with his body. "Can I help you with something?"

The kid skids to a stop. "*Lambie!*"

"Yes." He looks down and confirms. "Correct."

Clasping his hands together, the boy grins. "My hold?"

"Um." What's the protocol here? "You can pet, I guess."

The kid drops to his knees and sighs with joy. Eyes wide, he strokes the lamb's neck. "Gentle." He looks at Matteo and smiles. "*Gentle.*"

"That's right." Cute kid. Looks like Jen as a toddler with those ocean eyes and sandy hair and a dusting of freckles. One strap of his overalls looks twisted. Should he fix it?

Better not. His arms are occupied anyway. "You like lambs, huh?"

The kid nods at the dumb question. That's the great thing about kids. No judgment. Kinda like Nic when he gave her a haircut. He was twelve, and she was six, and their parents were dead, and what the hell did he know about girls' hair? She wasn't even pissed about the bowl cut. "You did your best, Teo."

Like that's enough.

Anyway, this kid has hair like that. Tiny Tic Tac teeth that gleam when he smiles.

"Soft." He watches Matteo with his fingers raking fleece. "Sooofffft."

"That's right."

Footsteps approach the door left creaking in the wind. Matteo looks up and feels his heart stagger.

Her.

"AJ!" Renee scans the boy, and for six breathless seconds, Matteo scans her. The lush curves he knows by heart. The dainty fingers, the gold-brown hair to match her eyes.

Eyes that'll turn cold in five, four, three, two...

"AJ, we've talked about you running off and—*oh God.*"

The color leaves her face. A face framed with curls shorter than last time he saw her. She gapes with a look that's half stunned, half horrified, and a hundred percent unhappy to see him.

"Renee?" His voice comes out rusty, so he tries again. "Renee Lorenson?"

Three years, two months, and nineteen days. That's how long it's been. The buzz in his brain says he's missing something. That he'd already know it if his heart wasn't sucking all the blood from his brain.

"Don't call me that!" She bolts with a hand outstretched.

For an instant, he thinks she's reaching for him. He'll give her anything she wants. A handshake? A kidney? The keys to his car?

She snags the kid's hand instead. "We're going home."

"But Mama." The boy swings sad eyes to Matteo. No, not him. The lamb in his arms. "*My hold.*"

He sounds so pitiful, Matteo's ready to hand over both the lamb and his PIN number. "Another time, kid."

"No." Renee's voice snaps like lightning. "*Not* another time. Not ever. Not—"

"Wait." The buzzing spreads to his ears. Numbers whirl, dates and memories and a jumble of history. His brain's firing now.

The kid senses something because he tugs Matteo's sleeve. "Who you?"

"AJ." Renee's voice sounds strained.

Matteo swallows. He needs to know. "How old are you, AJ?" The kid lifts one sticky, starfish hand. "This many."

One finger, two, three.

Realization dawns like a kick to the head. He's dizzy and dumbfounded and, above all, sure of one thing.

"Renee." He gulps and drags his eyes to her face. "Were you going to tell me?"

CHAPTER 2

*R*enee's heart pumps so hard she's sure it'll squirt through her ribs. Sweat soaks her palms as lunch sloshes sideways in her gut.

But she keeps it together because she's a mom.

"Matteo." Her voice creaks, and she hates it. Hates *him* for looking this good for a guy who's been behind bars.

"Wait." She's not sure she wants the answer to this question. "Did you escape?"

He frowns. "Cleared of all charges." His eyes don't leave hers as the lamb he's holding starts to wiggle. He soothes it with a stroke of his palm. "Just released."

Knowing him, there's a story. A huge one he won't share because he's Matteo freakin' Bello, and God forbid he clue her in about anything.

The less you know, the better.

His favorite phrase. One she still hears in her dreams. Dreams where she's grabbing him by the balls and twisting until he—

Well. She's got bigger issues now. AJ's looking between them, and she prays he won't ask questions. "Lambie." He breathes the word with reverence, eyes moving to Matteo's face. "Who you?"

9

Oh, God. How's he going to answer?

"I'm your f—"

"Fa-la-la-la-la-la-la-la-laaaaah." She shouts the next stanza, "Deck the halls with boughs of holly, fa-la-la-la-la-la-la-la! 'Tis the season to be jolly, fa—"

"Santa?" Her son scrunches his face at Matteo. "You're Santa?"

Damn, she's made it worse.

Matteo's staring like she's lost her mind. "I'm your *friend*." He gives her a pointed look. "And a friend of your mom's."

She should argue they're not friends, but that's petty. Pettier than ignoring the question dangling between them like a flaming disco ball.

"Were you going to tell me?"

He's going to ask again, and she needs an answer. A better one than the truth. Her brain's pulsing, struggling to keep pace with her heart. Does he have to be so damned handsome? That dark hair always slayed her. Like a man has any right to have such a thick, glossy mop. She used to run her fingers through it, trailing them down his neck and over broad shoulders as he—

"Sorry, Matty!" AJ's teacher runs in, eyes aimed down as she scrapes something off her shirt. "That took longer than we thought because Jen's lamb shit all over the—*oh*." She blinks at Renee. "Sorry. I didn't see you come in."

"Bad word." AJ gives her his wide-eyed stare. "You said swears, Miss Nicole."

"You're right, buddy." The teacher, God bless her, knows not to use names. "Sorry about that."

Her son nods wisely. "The F-word?"

"Uh, no." Nicole casts a glance at the alphabet on the wall. "We'll cover that one later. *Much* later." She looks at Renee. "I'm sorry, did we have an appointment?"

"No." Renee clears her throat, since they're all staring. "AJ forgot his backpack." She tries to keep her voice tuned to Mom

Lite. "We saw the lamb truck, and he took off running before I could stop him."

Matteo looks from her to Nicole and back again. A furrow forms between his brows. "Wait. You go *here*. To my sister's daycare?"

No one answers. Even the burble of the aquarium seems quiet.

Her sweet boy steps up. "Miss Nicole reads me Blue Truck." He pats Matteo's knee and the lamb squirms. "Know what Blue Truck says?"

They're all struck mute. Even Nicole's sister—Jennifer?—doesn't speak as she slips through the door wiping hands on her jeans.

Matteo clears his throat. "What does Blue Truck say?"

"Beeeeeeeeep!" AJ twirls, sneakers squeaking. "He says *beep!*"

"Huh." Matteo digests that, watching with an expression Renee can't read. "Can't say I know that one."

"Or horse?" AJ stops dancing. "Know what he says?"

Matteo again. "Neigh?"

"Yes!" AJ's bouncing, bumping the lamb in Matteo's arms.

Jennifer hurries to take it from him. God, he's got great arms. And hands. And—

"Blue Truck." AJ snatches a book off the shelf and dives for the empty spot in Matteo's lap. Her boy snuggles in like he belongs there and looks up. "Story?"

Oh, God.

Matteo stares like his lap is full of strawberry jam. "Um."

Her son scrunches his face. "You read?"

"Yes." Matteo's throat moves. "Yes, I can."

AJ lifts a hand. "You gots an owie."

The tiniest flinch from Matteo as the boy drags a hand down the scar at his throat. "Yeah," he says softly. "It doesn't hurt."

"Okay." AJ pats the book. "You read now."

Her old lover meets her eyes. She expects more questions, maybe accusation.

What she sees is—regret?

"I, uh." Matteo clears his throat again. "I don't think I should read right now."

A grudging wave of gratitude gets her in the gut. But her boy doesn't give up easily.

"I help." AJ—forgetting all about stranger danger—flips open the book. "A duck," he reports. "What does he say?"

Matteo hesitates. "Quack?"

"Uh-huh." He flips a page. "And the cow?"

"Moo?"

This shouldn't hurt her heart. Shouldn't make her ovaries ache. Her feet feel stuck to the floor, and there's not enough air in the room. She's not sure if she should laugh or grab her kid or duck under a desk and cry.

"There's a pig." Her son flips the page and shifts in Matteo's lap. "What's a pig say?"

"Oink." He's getting the hang of it.

She wants to hit him. Or fall into his lap because she's a shameless hussy with horrible taste in men. Three ex-cons and a guy who turned up married. Them, plus Matteo Bello. That's only a small sample of her dating roster.

Does he have to look so edible? Her heart's a Hershey's kiss in the sun, and she can't see a single way to make him go away.

"And a sheep." AJ bounces, making Matteo wince. "Like lambie! Baaaaaaa!"

The real lamb wriggles in Jennifer's arms. "I'm taking him to the truck." She steps back as Nicole flicks a glance at Renee. Her lips form soundless words.

Need help?

Yes, but not the kind she's thinking. Renee nods.

Nicole claps her hands. "Okay, gentlemen!" She claps again,

the one-two-three rhythm for getting kids' attention. "Time for a break."

It's the moment Renee finds her voice. "Your b-brother." Her tongue twists up the word, so she licks her lips. Sees Matteo's eyes on her mouth. "You never mentioned a brother."

Something clouds Nicole's eyes. "Yes, well." She swallows. "He's been away for a while."

"I see."

Nicole's gaze swings between them. "I'm sorry, do you two know each other?"

Renee can't look at him. If she does, she'll spill it all. "We really need to get going."

AJ pretends not to hear as he turns a page in the book. "Toad's name is Toad and Goat's name is Goat and my name is AJ."

"AJ." Matteo repeats it with a reverence she shouldn't love.

Her boy bounces some more. "What's your name?"

"Matteo." There's a catch in his voice she's never heard before.

AJ squints. "My Tail?"

"I—sure." Matteo looks at her. One shoulder lifts in a helpless half shrug, and her heart grabs the bars of the cage it's kept in.

She sees the signs now, plain as day. The pale green of Nicole's eyes. So much like Matteo's. All three Bellos have those eyes. Renee shuts hers and tries to breathe. She changed her name. Cut her hair. Moved two hundred miles from Seattle.

Then she picked a daycare owned by her ex-lover's sister. It's official. She has the worst luck in the history of humankind.

Opening her eyes, she squares her shoulders. "Okay." She sticks on a happy mom smile. "Sweetie, we need to go."

AJ clutches the book. "No, Mama."

Another big breath draws steel to her voice. "I'm counting to three." Nothing like numbers to strike fear in a three-year-old. "One."

"Nooooooo!" His howl splits her heart in half. AJ clings to the bottom of the book. "Bluuuue Truck."

TAWNA FENSKE

Matteo looks from her to the squirming child in his lap. "In addition to reading," he says slowly, "I also count."

AJ stops howling. "Count?"

"Two comes after one." He gets to his feet, arms enfolding her boy. Sets him on the ground like he's fragile. "Pretty sure you don't want Mom to get to three."

Matteo's so close. Too close. The heat from his arms makes her magnetized, like she can't step back. Can't stop recalling how those arms felt wrapped around her.

"Two." She hates her voice for quivering.

AJ holds the book like it's a life raft, but at least lets go of Matteo's leg. "One more page, Mama." His little lip quivers. "Please?"

Nicole murmurs low. "Keep the book if it'll make this easier."

Nothing will make this easier. Not one damn thing.

"Three." She scoops up her son and pulls him to her chest. It's like he's on fire, and she's smothering the flames. The book hits the floor, and as Matteo bends to grab it, his hand skims her hip on the way down.

More flames, these ones licking up her torso. Belly, arms, breasts. She shifts her grip on AJ and steps back.

"Bluuuue!" AJ throws his head back and clocks her in the chin.

Renee doesn't flinch. Doesn't release her hold.

Nic's uneasy gaze skates over her. "Are you okay?"

She's not okay. There's a geyser of emotion gurgling in her chest. She needs to get out before it blows.

"I'm sorry, he didn't get his nap. We're fine. Better than fine." It's her happy mommy voice. She can't look at Matteo.

"I'm so sorry." Nicole's whispering over AJ's howls. "I didn't know you'd be coming back. My brother—"

"It's okay, really." She shifts her boy's weight and feels him go limp. He curls into her, seeking safety. How long until she can't protect him? "My fault for stopping by. I know the rules."

14

Chapter Two in the school handbook. *After-school meetings must be scheduled to avoid contact between families.*

She never guessed it might matter. Not like this.

AJ shoves a thumb in his mouth. "Lambie," he mumbles. "My Tail."

"We're leaving now." She sweeps past them, shoulders back, arms holding her child for dear life.

As she heads for the door, Matteo's eyes burn twin holes in her shoulder blades. She shivers and hugs her son tighter.

* * *

RENEE CROSSES the café and feels eyes following her.

It's nothing new, the sensation. She hopes it's someone eyeing her salad. Spring greens and juicy slabs of grapefruit, topped with smoked salmon. Her favorite. It's why she risked coming here twice this week when she normally shakes it up. She's always been cautious.

But Matteo rattled her. Days after seeing him, she's still not herself.

Darting a glance right, she checks her watch. Fifty minutes 'til her next Zoom meeting. Enough time for two chapters in her Susannah Nix book. Scanning the room, she spots the man in a corner booth. Her heart trips in her chest.

The stranger.

It's the second time she's seen him this week.

Paranoia, she thought the first time.

But she's been on the run long enough to trust her instincts. If she's being followed, she's been found. If she's been found, she has to move again. That's how it is.

She scans him in her peripheral vision as she walks to the other side of the café. Blonde mustache, big forehead, ugly square glasses. The glasses and mustache might be fake, but the forehead's not. Same guy as last time? Must be.

15

Or maybe she really *is* paranoid, because the guy's standing to greet a woman. They're embracing and laughing and God, she's a fool. That's definitely not a stalker.

With a sigh, she sinks to her booth. Her back's to the wall, and she's got a good view of the café. She sets her salad on the table and paws through her purse for the e-reader. When she looks up, Matteo's across from her.

"Hello, Renee."

"Jesus Christ!"

She throws the Kindle, and he catches it in one hand. The edge of his mouth quirks. He hands back the tablet without comment. Without smiling, which is good. She doesn't have to see the dimple. The one that steals her breath each time.

"Afraid not." He lays his palms on the table.

"Excuse me?"

"Not Jesus." He kicks his legs out under the table, knee brushing hers. "I do feel a bit like I've risen from the dead."

"Go away, Matteo." She hates the quiver in her voice. The way she can't seem to drag her knee from his. "Why are you here?"

He doesn't answer. Not that question, anyway. "My sister never said your name."

"What?"

"At the daycare. She didn't address you by name."

"So what?" She picks up her fork and pretends her hand isn't shaking. Nic calls her Raina but knows it's not real. All the families use fake names. "Your sister's careful about privacy."

"School policy." He studies her face, her arms, her torso, like he's cataloguing parts of her. "Nic never names clients. Not their kids, either. She protects the students at all costs."

The ball in her throat makes it tough to swallow. She spears a bite of salad and tries to get it down. "Your sister's good at her job."

A flash of pride in his eyes. She chews her lettuce, hoping he'll move on. Hoping he doesn't. Hoping the floor opens up and swallows her.

It's Matteo who swallows, rippling the scar on his throat. A million times she asked about it. A million times he joked how it happened.

Grizzly attack.

Freak barbecue accident.

Got struck by a light saber defending the Death Star.

Talk about red flags. Closed-off men are her specialty. She should know better.

"So you're in hiding?" He studies her face. "Running from me?"

"I didn't have to, did I?" Crap, she said it out loud. "You took off running on your own."

He closes his eyes. Five seconds. Ten. When he opens them, green pools fill with regret. "Renee." He lays his hands flat. "I'm so sorry. I don't even know where to start."

"Sorry?" She shouldn't have this conversation. It's water under the bridge, but a dam bursts inside her. "Remember what you said the night you disappeared? Your last words to me, Matteo?"

He looks at his hands. "No."

Of course not. It meant nothing to him.

She hates what it meant to her. What it *still* means. "You said, 'I won't be gone long.' Said you were going out for ice cream."

"Potato chips." He winces. "Sorry."

"Whatever." She stabs the salad again. "You said 'See you in a few.' Remember that? It's been more than three years, Matteo. You went to Mars for those chips?"

Guilt joins regret in his eyes. "I'm a dick." He sighs. "Something came up, and I had to run. It wasn't safe to stick around. To put you at risk."

"No phone call, no email, no telegram." She pokes a wayward crouton, splitting it in two. "Not even a sticky note. We dated six months. I slept at your place nearly every night. If you wanted to split up, all you had to say was—"

"Renee, I'm sorry."

"Sure," she spits. "That would have worked." Or something. Anything to explain why he cut and ran like everyone else in her life. Her mother. Her father. A dozen foster families.

She should have known he'd leave, too.

"I thought I could get back to you," he's saying. "Thought if I just went into hiding for a bit—"

"I'd wait around twiddling my thumbs?" She shakes her head and stabs some more lettuce. "I was worried sick about you."

Sick over more than that. Hours she waited. Days. Weeks. How hard would it have been to give her closure?

I'm just not into you.

I'm not ready to commit.

Your house is gross, and I get why you never brought me here before.

"Where did you go?" She doesn't expect an answer.

Matteo measures his words. "Prison."

"Yeah, I got that." She looked up records. Knows exactly how long he spent behind bars. "Six months passed between you going out for potato chips and when you got arrested. You couldn't have called?"

He lets out a long breath. "It's... complicated."

Of course it is.

"I knew you had secrets." She looks at her salad because it's easier than looking at him. "I would have respected that. But I at least deserved a goodbye."

He drags a hand down his face. "It's hard to explain."

How many times did she hear *that* from her dad?

"Sorry, sweetheart." He'd give her sad eyes as a social worker stood by the door. "Daddy's going away again. Maybe they'll let you come see me?"

Matteo sighs. "I didn't want to burden you with that. Knowing how you grew up, I couldn't put that on you."

18

"Knowing you're a *criminal*?" She snorts and stabs her salad. "News flash: I figured it out."

"I'm sorry, Renee." He's shaking his head, struggling for words. "I thought if I just kept you out of it, I could clear my name and come back and—" The ice in her eyes stops him. "I guess it doesn't matter now."

"It really doesn't." She spears another hunk of lettuce, attention darting to the corner table. The stalker's still there. He's scrolling his phone, pausing to sip from a white mug. No sign of the hugging woman, who might've been an actress for all she knows. Not hard for a criminal to pay someone to build his cover. Dear ol' Dad taught her that one.

Not a criminal. Just a guy drinking coffee. Your imagination's gone wild.

She shivers.

"You okay?"

She looks at Matteo. "I'm fine."

He leans close and lowers his voice. "You can talk to me, you know."

"No, thanks."

There's nothing to say. Three years ago, she told him all about her life. About the teen mom who ditched her with a deadbeat dad. About growing up in foster care and her lousy taste in men and her hope she'd finally found someone good and strong and kind and—

Well. Look how that turned out.

Renee picks a cherry tomato off the edge of her plate. "If you're going to sit here, at least change the subject."

"All right." He rolls both hands on the table, and she tries not to look at them. "What brought you here from Seattle?"

"I like Oregon farm country." There. She can do evasive, too. "We've moved around a lot these last couple years."

Matteo doesn't push. "How long have you lived here?"

"None of your—" Hell. He'll find out anyway. "Six months."

"You like it?"

She studies him warily over her iced tea. "Is this where you grew up?"

"Yes." He blinks with surprise. "Did I not mention that?"

"You said you were born in Italy, lived in Dovlano, moved to Oregon as a kid. If I asked for more, you changed the subject." That should have tipped her off. If he'd named his hometown, she'd never have moved here.

He folds his hands on the table. "How's your father?"

"Dead."

"Oh, shit." The sympathy in his eyes seems real. "I'm sorry."

"We weren't close." He knows this. Knows way too much about her, while she knows squat about him.

"How's your—"

"No." She sets down her fork and looks at him. "You don't get to show up out of nowhere and interrogate me."

He looks at her for a long time. "You're right." Hesitating, he draws a breath. "Is there something you want to ask me?"

Is there? It's her chance to get answers. To open this can of worms instead of letting sleeping dogs lie. Why do all these idioms have animals? Her mind's a freakin' children's book.

She picks up her fork to give her something to do with her hands. "You were running from the law. I got that much. But I want to know why you just vanished. How you could just get up and leave without a trace not ten minutes after—" She stops as her cheeks warm. "Never mind."

"After what?" He sits up straighter.

More heat fills her cheeks. "Nothing."

"After the best sex of our lives?"

"After the first time you came to my house." Okay, the sex thing's true, too. "Six months we dated. We always went to your place or a hotel. The one time I showed you where I lived—" The hand-me-down furniture, the lumpy couch from a grandma she never knew "—*that's* when you decide to leave without a trace?"

This time, he doesn't look away. "I didn't think of it like that. I just knew I needed to get gone fast."

"Because the cops were after you?" It doesn't take a genius to guess. "They questioned me for weeks, you know."

"I didn't know."

"So, that was fun." He knew damn well how she felt about police. A childhood spent dodging them with her dad left quite an impression.

Matteo draws a breath and flags a waitress. "Coffee, please," he says. "Black. And a refill for her iced tea. Thank you."

"Coming right up."

He waits 'til the server slips out of earshot. When he looks at Renee, his eyes soften. "I went to MIT."

Hardly a secret. "That's one of the first things you told me about yourself." One of the few things, actually.

"I never said how I got there." He pinches the bridge of his nose. "Raising my sisters, I couldn't go to college out of high school. I was twenty-three when recruiters called me again out of the blue."

It's more detail than he's ever given, though she's not sure what it has to do with anything. "Okay."

Another sigh. "Someone had to watch my sisters. Our grandma was—"

He stops, and she waits for the rest. She's still waiting when the waitress brings the coffee and iced tea. "Thank you." She takes a sip as the server leaves. Matteo's not restarting his story.

"Your grandma was *what*?"

"Flighty," he says carefully. "Not always around. Given our family history—"

"Which was what?"

He frowns. "I don't like talking about that."

Renee rolls her eyes. "Fine."

Not like he'll start opening up now. From what little she knows, he raised his sisters himself. Their grandma—she had some kind of nickname, didn't she? Renee never met her, never met the sisters, either—

"Nondi," she blurts. "Wasn't that your grandmother's nickname?"

He looks startled. "You remember?"

"You mentioned it once." All these scant details she squirreled away like nuts. "Wasn't it a mashup of the Italian and Dovlanese words for grandma?"

"Yeah." He still looks surprised. "Nonna and Disla—my younger sister, Jen—she came up with it."

The hurt in his voice makes her insides soften. "I'm sorry," she says. "Nicole said she passed last year." That would have been while he was locked up. "I know you were close," she adds softly. "I loved your grandma stories." He'd tell them when she needed to smile, those rare times Teo shared personal stuff. "She sounded amazing."

"She was." His breath leaks out like there's a balloon in his chest. "Never got to say goodbye." He looks at the ceiling. "Anyway, before that. She traveled a lot and for *reasons*, I couldn't leave my sisters alone."

Curiosity pokes her in the ribs, but she doesn't push. If he doesn't want to share his *reasons*, she won't pry. "They couldn't go with you?"

"To Massachusetts?" He shakes his head. "They were both still in school. And with Nondi gone so much, I couldn't just vanish."

She ignores the pinch in her heart. She knows damn well that he *can* just vanish. "What did you do?"

A muscle moves in his jaw. "Made a deal with the cops. They'd keep my sisters safe, and I'd help out on a contract basis."

Matteo working with law enforcement? She chokes on her tea.

"I know." He hands her a napkin. "They needed a computer geek. Someone off-the-books to help with tech investigations. Strictly confidential. I did it almost six years."

She's flabbergasted. "And you're telling me this *now*?" There are millions more questions, but she'll start there. "Wasn't it confidential or—"

"Should have been." His expression hardens. "Right up until I got double-crossed and wound up in prison, and I'm done talking about this now, okay?" He huffs and drags a hand through his hair. "Sorry. I just—didn't want you thinking I left *you*."

"Okay." She's digesting what he told her. Crooked cops? A covert job with police? A deal to guard his sisters?

It's more than he's ever shared. "Thank you for telling me," she says.

"You're welcome." He sips his coffee and watches her. "My turn?"

She looks at him. "For what?"

"To ask questions."

"Depends what you want to ask."

One edge of his mouth twitches. "What does AJ stand for?"

She doesn't answer. Stabs a bite of salmon, conscious of the heat in her legs where his knee skims hers. The heat *between* her legs as he brushes her arm and smiles and says—

"Aardvark Juice?"

"What?" She pulls her arm back.

"AJ. Or wait, no—you named him Abacus Jones." His lips twitch. "Setting him up to be a mathematician."

"No." She tries not to smile.

He scrubs a hand over his chin. "Let's start with the A."

"Let's not."

"Abarcy," he tries. "Derived from a Greek word meaning bread. Someone who's abarstic has a voracious appetite. Does AJ eat a lot?"

She doesn't dignify that with a response. His charm is *not* what she needs.

"Altiloquious." He keeps going. "Someone who speaks loudly and with great enthusiasm and intellect. That fits."

Another bite of salad as she swallows a swell of pride. AJ's always the smartest kid in class. Leave it to her genius ex to notice.

"Aphercotropism." Matteo snaps his fingers. "That's when a plant encounters an obstacle and grows its way around it. Maybe you named him Aphercotropism James to be traditional?"

She stifles a laugh with a bored sigh, which doesn't work. It sounds like she's passing a hairball.

"Got it!" He points a finger. "Antipelargy. A seventeenth-century word for reciprocal love felt between parents and their children. You're clearly nuts about the kid, and he loves you."

Her heart hits her throat. She swallows it back and meets his eyes. "Matteo…"

"Antipelargy is derived from the Greek word for the stork," he continues. "*Pelargos*—which is traditionally said to be an affectionate bird."

"Matteo!"

"That doesn't start with an A or a J." He rubs his chin and looks thoughtful. "Rearranging the letters in Matteo gets you Atomet, or maybe Aeottm or Ametto or—"

"You're an asshole."

"That does start with an A." He grins. "Not a great name for our son, though."

Our son.

She hates how that sounds.

She loves how that sounds.

She needs a drink stiffer than iced tea. Snatching the glass, she downs the rest in three gulps. When she sets it down, he's watching her.

"Your mouth."

She blinks. "What about my mouth?"

"Always unhinged me." He sighs like that's not a good thing.

Watching him, she waits for more. Slides forward on her seat without meaning to. Something softens in her chest, and she says it without thinking. "Alessi."

He blinks. "Alessi?" Green eyes go wide. "Like my grandmother?"

"Like *my* grand*father*." She picks up her fork and stabs her salad again. "I never met him, but my dad talked about him all the time. A carpenter." She needs to stop talking. "He built the armoire in my bedroom."

"Okay." The smile in his eyes shouldn't hit her this hard.

"It's a unisex name, you know."

Leaning back on the bench, he spreads muscular arms across the booth. "And the J?"

She doesn't answer. Owes him none of this. Tapping her e-reader, she flips to the page where she left off. Another forkful of salad. Another stretch of silence where she feels eyes on her face. His or the stranger's?

His, she decides as her skin starts to tingle. Tapping the screen, she turns a page she's read three times. Movement tugs her eyes to the other table. The one in the corner where the stranger flips a page in his newspaper. He just looked over, touched a bulge in his jacket.

A gun? *Oh, God—*

"Renee?"

"What?" She swings back to Matteo. Knows before he speaks what he's going to ask.

Who is AJ's father?

He cocks his head. "Who are you running from?"

"Who says I'm running?"

He holds up one maddeningly huge hand. "One." He ticks a finger. "You're in a daycare for families fleeing bad situations. Witness protection, that sort of thing." He ticks another finger. "Two. You're impossible to find. No email. No phone numbers. No forwarding address. You wanted to vanish."

"I had the same contact info for six months after you left." There's that spark of anger again. If he'd wanted to reach her, he could have. A postcard or something. Anonymous email, for God's sake.

"Three," he continues. "You keep looking at that table."

"What table?" Oh, God. The man's staring. She feels it more than sees it.

"The table with the guy who keeps watching you. Creepy dude with a big forehead. He's standing now and—

"What?" Panic rips through her. She sees the man's hand slip to his coat pocket as he—

"Here." Matteo gets up. Moves around to plant himself on the bench beside her. His body's now wedged between her and the guy who's doing nothing more menacing than tipping his server. *Goddamn it.*

Matteo's heat soothes her, but she shivers anyway. Watches him stare the guy down. The man looks away, whistling as he tucks a dollar on the table. With Matteo beside her, she feels okay looking at the guy. She's definitely seen him before. Maybe she isn't crazy.

"Better?"

She's too tired to play dumb. "It's nothing."

"Doesn't seem like nothing to me." He watches the stranger walk out of the café. When the man pauses at the door, Matteo touches his own pocket.

Is he *armed*?

It should piss her off, not comfort her. Her idiot brain doesn't get that, and she ends up scooting closer. Matteo's warm and solid and smells like clean cotton and vintage books. A soothing combination for a man who looks this lethal.

They watch together as the stranger steps outside. He looks both ways, then crosses the street. Pulls out a phone, tapping the screen as he disappears around a corner. Renee swallows hard.

"You cold?"

She shakes her head. "No."

Her salad's almost gone. So is her lunch break.

So is her certainty she hasn't been found.

Sighing, she looks at Matteo. "Why did you come here?"

"Heard the salmon salad's good."

She stares and doesn't smile. Lifts the glass to her lips when she feels them start to twitch. When she sets it down, he's watching her.

"I wanted you to feel safe."

She blinks. "What do you mean?"

"It's why I came here to talk to you." He looks around, observing the lunch rush, the packed bar, the crowd by the counter. "Public space. No kid." His eyes flicker, but he keeps them trained on her. "No sisters or co-workers or anyone else listening. You can speak freely."

Her throat hurts as she swallows.

If only.

She clamps her lips together. If she doesn't, she'll blurt it out.

He sighs. "I thought it was me."

The words startle her from silence. "What?"

"Secret daycare. Untraceable address." He folds his hands on the table. "I thought you were afraid of me."

"No." Renee swallows hard. She might be angry with him. She might even hate him. But fear him? "Never."

"Really?"

His surprise catches her off guard and she laughs. "You might be a capricious sack of snot who's probably into all kinds of illegal things, but scary?" She shakes her head. "Not to me."

"Capricious sack of snot?" He bursts out laughing. "I watched you stomp a guy's foot in a bar and call him a motherfucking cocksucking sack of monkey shit who couldn't find his dick with both hands and a magnifying glass."

Renee's cheeks warm. "I'm normally a pacifist."

"Wasn't commenting on that. Just your new G-rated curse words."

Her face gets warmer. "I'm a mom now." A mom who's

pleased she used a word like "capricious," even though she never went to college. "I've cut out cursing. No violence, either. That night was an exception."

"You were magnificent."

So was he. She doesn't want to rehash, but— "You weren't so bad yourself."

His green eyes darken. "The asshole shoved his girlfriend." Matteo's jaw tightens. "I have zero tolerance for that."

She shivers. Recalls the snap of bone in the man's wrist as Matteo pinned him to the wall. From five feet away, she heard the words he growled in the man's ear. "If you ever, *ever* lay a hand on a woman again, I will eliminate you."

Another shiver as she looks at the door where her stalker disappeared. She swallows and looks at Matteo. "Someone's after us."

"Who?"

"I don't know."

"Why?"

"I don't know that, either." She sounds like a moron. "It started maybe a month after you left. Someone broke into my house and trashed the place."

"Jesus." His jaw clenches. "I'm such an asshole."

"You knew about this?" She wondered about that. The timing and all.

"What? No! I meant I should have been there to protect you."

Renee sighs. Now the dam's broken, and she can't stop it all from spilling out. "Someone started following me. Not always the same guy. Different men. Scary men." She swallows hard, hating this part. "I was coming out of my doctor's office one day, and someone grabbed me."

His knuckles go white around the coffee mug. "When?"

"I was seven months pregnant. He had a mask, so I never saw his face." She closes her eyes so she can't see pity in his. "I fought him off. Hit him in the face with my purse. That's when I knew it wasn't just a random thing."

"So you went into hiding." Matteo frowns. "Did you try the cops?"

She snorts and grabs her iced tea. Someone filled it again, and she's not sure when that happened. She's too distracted, too troubled by his thigh against hers beneath the table.

"The cops." She snorts again. "Because they're always so kind to the daughter of an ex-con."

Not just any ex-con. The most notorious thief in the Pacific Northwest.

"Yeah, I get that." He drags his hands down his face. "Guess I shouldn't be surprised you're self-reliant."

"I had to be, didn't I?" Her salad's almost gone, but she picks up half a crouton. "It's how I grew up."

He watches her face. "You have no idea who'd be after you?"

"I've dated plenty of losers." She gives him a pointed look. "Could be one of them. Maybe someone tied to my dad." A pause. "Maybe someone after *you*?"

It's a theory she had for a while. But once she looked him up and found his name among inmates at the State Pen, it made no sense. What would someone gain by coming for her?

He watches her face like he's trying to memorize it. "So you were pregnant when you went in to hiding."

"I'm not doing this with you." She stabs the last piece of salmon. "Bottom line, I got scared. I had more than myself to protect, so I took off."

He's quiet a long time. Too long. She can do this, too. Just sit and stare and not notice how the sunlight makes his eyes glow.

Matteo breaks first. "Let me help."

Her laugh chokes out bitter and sharp. "How?"

"Whoever's after you, he's found you. That's what you're thinking, right?"

A crouton sticks in her throat. She can't speak, so she nods.

"Let me help," he says. "Let me protect you. You and AJ. Please?"

"How do I know it's not you they're after?"

"You don't." At least he's admitting it. "All the more reason to let me watch over you. If it's me they want, they can have me and leave you alone."

It's a crazy idea. She'd be stupid to consider it. To trust the guy who abandoned her, alone and afraid, without warning or closure or—

"I'll think about it."

He nods. "Okay."

Beneath the table, she bumps his knee again. This time, he smiles. The dimple shoots an arrow straight through her soul.

"Jude." She blurts it too fast to think.

Matteo stares. "What?"

"AJ's middle name." She can't believe she's sharing this. "Alessi Jude."

"Jude." His voice floats with wonder. "Like the Beatles song."

Her cheeks warm. "I loved that song *before*. It doesn't mean anything that—"

"That it was playing in the bar the night we met?"

She nods, willing him to believe it. Willing herself to forget how he knelt before her like some courtly knight. "M'lady." He smiled and doffed his baseball cap. "They're playing our song."

Her heart rolled over, same as it's doing now. "We have a song? I've never met you."

"Matteo Bello." He held out a hand. "May I have this dance?"

She agreed, and he swept her off her feet. Wooed her again a month later when he sang it in bed. He'd never played guitar before, but won one in a poker game and stayed up all night learning chords. His voice wasn't great, but it rang strong and true as he belted that Beatles tune.

How could she not fall for him?

She just can't do it again. Too much at stake this time.

"Okay." She shoves aside the shadow of memory. "Okay. I need you." Not the right words. "For protection. I—thank you. I don't know where else to turn."

He slides a hand to hers. Covers her fingers with his. "I'm all yours."

"Strictly platonic." Her fingers curl beneath his. "Only because it makes sense. If it might be you they're after—"

"We'll get to the bottom of it. Promise."

She's heard his promises before. Why would this be different?

"I—should go." She checks her watch. "I have a Zoom meeting."

He releases her hand and sets a fifty on the table. Puts his coffee mug on top of it. "How will I reach you?"

The waitress runs over and clears Renee's plate. Blinks at the fifty, eyes sliding to Matteo. The man has faults, but he's generous. God only knows where he gets his money.

Renee draws a breath. Time to claim some of that generosity.

"I'll reach out through your sister." No way she's giving him her contact information. She's spent too long safeguarding it. "Later this week."

"All right."

She slings her purse over her shoulder. "If I see that guy again, I'll take pictures."

"Be careful." He's frowning as she shrugs on her sweater. "I mean it, Renee. Don't take chances. Let me take them for you."

Another shiver shakes her. "Thank you." She steps back from the table. "I'll be in touch."

She heads for the door, feeling his eyes follow. All the way to the car, the tingle trails her spine.

It's a feeling she hates herself for craving.

CHAPTER 3

*T*he boy is his. He's positive.

Almost positive.

His hacker skills turned up a birth certificate. Blank in the field that says "father." That hurts more than it should.

"Matteo?" The knock at his door has him slapping the laptop shut.

Holding his breath, he sits very still. His sister's bunkhouse has bonuses. Family time, homemade meals, a chance to feel useful rebuilding the Bello Vineyards website while he figures out his next career move.

"Matteo?" Jen huffs on the other side of the door. "I know you're in there. I see your shadow through the blinds."

He sighs. The bunkhouse has minuses, too.

"Hang on." Standing, he shoves in his chair.

A quick scan of the laptop ensures he wiped out his browser history. Not just the birth certificate, but his search for Renee's stalker. Nothing so far, but it's early days. He shuts it all the way down this time.

"Coming." He goes to the door and opens it. "What's up?"

"Ugh. Problem."

His fingers flex, feeling for a firearm. Jen rolls her eyes.

"Not *that* kind of problem." She jerks a thumb toward the tasting room. "I need muscle, and Dante left."

His hands ball in a fist. "He *left* you? I'll find the fucker and—"

"Jesus, relax." Her eye roll reminds him of junior high years. "He had a meeting. Something with Sebastian."

"I see." He sees more than he should. His buddies had a plan last night to eliminate a sex-trafficking ring and whisk the women to safety.

He misses whisking. The eliminating, too.

But he needs to keep his nose clean. Find ways to use his degree instead of raw talent. He shakes his focus back to Jen. "What do you need?"

She thrusts a Bello Vineyards T-shirt at him. "We've got a booth at Pairings this year. The wine thing at the Oregon State Fair?"

"I'm familiar."

"My winemaker just called. Our Pinot won silver, and we need seven more cases. Can you run to Salem? I have to stay here and keep the tasting room open."

"No problem."

"Here, take the truck." She hands him the keys to their grandma's '51 International and backs away. "The T-shirt should get you through the gate. I loaded all the cases in back. Thanks, Teo!"

"Next time, ask for help *before* lugging 126.006 kilograms of wine by yourself." He frowns. "280 pounds. Whatever."

She flips him the bird, plus a quip about geeks who tabulate the precise weight of wine. "Go be social, Matty. It's good for you."

With a sigh, he tosses the keys in one hand. So. He's going to the Oregon State Fair.

Stuffing the keys in his pocket, he returns to the dining room to change shirts and lock his laptop in the gun safe. It's the same model Dante uses for his arsenal, but tech is Teo's preferred weapon. A grenade couldn't get through this safe. He knows, he's tested it.

He also tests the truck's brakes before getting behind the wheel. There's no cause for suspicion, but that's what Jen thought before the brake lines got cut.

Confident it's safe, he cranks the truck's engine and the driver's side window. The drive to Salem takes thirty minutes. He spends each one gulping gusts of fresh air filled with good grassy smells. He's missed this.

Missed chasing bad guys, if he's honest. It's what got him caught. His inability to resist the chase.

Speaking of which, Renee hasn't called. Hasn't sent a message through Nicole, either.

"It's been two days, Matteo." His middle sister shoved her hands on her hips when he asked for the eleven-thousandth time. "Give the woman some space. She's been through a lot."

"Like what?"

Nic narrowed her eyes. "I never discuss clients' personal information. By 'a lot' I meant the crap *you* pulled."

Guilt grabbed him by the gut. "You didn't know her when we dated."

"No, but you talked about her all the time." It was back when he lived in Seattle. "Never said her name, but I knew you were seeing someone special."

"Text me if she gets in touch." He walked away, hating himself all over again.

Renee's face floats through his mind as he takes the turn to the fairgrounds. He doesn't like her story about the stalker. She's tough as nails. Always has been. If she's scared, there's a reason. Not a reason that leaves him sure about her safety.

It's four when he hits the fairground parking lot. The truck fills up with corndog smells and the perfume of fried cinnamon dough. His stomach growls. Maybe he'll treat himself once the wine's unloaded.

"You made it!" A blonde jogs over, and he recognizes her as the winemaker. Leslie someone? She unhooks the tailgate. "We're down to our last two bottles, and the event starts in ten minutes."

He hoists a case and looks around. "Where do you want it?"

"Right here." A woman with purple-streaked hair rolls up with a wheeled hand truck. "Thanks, man. We've got it from here."

Leslie flips a hand between them. "My wife, Cammie. Jen's brother, Matteo."

"Good to meet you." Cammie shakes his hand with a fast, firm grip and gets back to loading wine. "You sticking around for the fair?"

"Maybe." He pictures himself strolling like a normal guy. Scanning craft booths and livestock. He could ride the Ferris wheel. "Okay to keep the parking spot?"

"Yeah, but ditch the T-shirt." Leslie points at the Bello Vineyards logo. "That'll get you through the gate, but you'll have people hounding you about wine."

He didn't bring another shirt, but that shouldn't be a problem. He's hardly an approachable guy. "Thanks."

Leslie wheels off with the hand truck. "Have fun."

Fun.

When's the last time he did that?

He ambles through the gates, nodding to the ticket-taker whose gaze lingers on his chest. He catches her looking, and she blushes. "What's your workout routine?"

"Twenty-three months of hard time."

She laughs like he's made a joke, and he hates himself for saying it. He's not proud of his time behind bars. Doesn't like talking about it. His lunch with Renee pulled a plug on his dammed-up subconscious. He needs to get that fucker shoved back down.

He's gone ten steps when a guy grabs him by the arm. "Hey, man! Love the Gewürztraminer."

"Huh?" It's been years since he fired German artillery. That model doesn't ring a bell.

"Almost reminds me of a Müller-Thurgau from Southern Oregon, you know?"

"Right." What is he talking about?

"Lots of kick, I mean."

Teo drags a hand over his head, remembering Jen's tip about socializing. "Nothing kicks like a Howitzer, though."

The guy laughs and claps him on the shoulder. "Good one. Seriously, though—last year's Gewurz was on point. Perfect notes of apricot kernel and rose." The man makes a weird little fist and kisses the tips of his fingers. "Magnifique."

"Uh-huh." Fuck, he's talking about wine?

"Keep up the good work." He claps Matteo's shoulder and ambles off before Teo can say he's not the damn winemaker, and it's misogynistic crap to think he would be.

Time to fix the T-shirt. Spotting a booth with bumper stickers, he heads for the pile and grabs one. "Thanks."

"Thank *you* for supporting the Oregon dairy industry." The volunteer smiles at his chest as he slaps the sticker over the vineyard logo on his chest. "And for your service."

"My service?"

"You've got that military look about you." She winks. "Army? Navy? With guns like that—"

"Just the sticker, thanks."

Maybe he should go home. But no, this should work. No one's asking him about wine, so he follows signs that say "Hypnotist at 5:30." That sounds good. Slipping through a gate marked "Family Funland," he heads toward the main stage.

A pang of memory slugs him in the gut. Grandma Nondi bringing him here at thirteen when he felt way too old for kiddie games.

"Want to get your face painted?" She winked as they watched an artist brush Nic and Jen with matching butterflies.

His snort held all the coolness of a teenage boy. "Don't you think I'm a little old for that?"

He slid her a sidelong glance. A real question. He really wanted to know.

"What I think," Nondi said as she slid an arm around him, "is that you're a kid who had to grow up way too fast. And if you want your fucking face painted, go for it."

God, he misses her. Kicks himself every day that he wasn't there when she passed.

Shaking off the memory, he scans the crowd. He's by the petting zoo, a white pen filled with sheep and goats and calves and even a wallaby. Toddlers wobble beside parents poised with iPhone cameras. A tired-eyed pygmy donkey watches from a corner.

"Hi, donkey." He tries to recall a donkey in the story AJ read him. Was there one? He can't reach from here, but he'd love to scratch this one's ears. Petting zoos are just for kids, right?

"Hey, man—good one!" A teenage boy points at his chest. "That's, like—a breastfeeding joke?"

The kid's buddy laughs. "Nah, man—he's looking to get some titties."

"Huh?" Matteo looks down and sighs. *Got Milk* blares bright red from the sticker on his chest.

That'll teach him to read before slapping slogans on his shirt.

With another sigh, he peels off the sticker. "I support the dairy industry."

"Yeah, man. Me, too!" The first kid cracks up and grabs imaginary boobs on his buddy's chest. The two run off laughing like idiots.

Matteo shoves the sticker in the trash. Human contact is overrated.

With more grumbling, he peels off his shirt and yanks it inside out. He's tugging it back on when he hears her voice.

"Matteo?"

Renee.

He knows it's her, even with his face wrapped in cotton. "Yeah?"

"Why are you stripping by the petting zoo?"

Dragging his shirt down, he meets her eyes. They're almost gold, lit by sunlight and a smile he hasn't seen in ages. He tugs at his hem and pretends not to notice she's fucking gorgeous. "Got tired of drawing attention."

"And you thought taking off your clothes would help?"

He's teeing up a retort when something nails his knee. Not something. *Someone.*

"My Tail!" AJ hugs his legs. "You at the fair."

"I—yeah." He swallows the lump in his throat. "I am."

"You come see animals." Small fists grip one leg of his jeans. "Mama says we feed. You feed, too."

"Um." He looks at Renee, whose face goes pink. "I was leaving." He clears his throat. "If you want. Or I could stay. You did ask me to—"

"I was going to call." She rests a hand on AJ's head. "It's been a few days with no incidents. I thought maybe I imagined it."

They both know that's not true. "Maybe so."

"Come!" AJ tugs his jeans. "There's lambies, My Tail. And goats and chickens and moo cows and—"

"It's fine." Renee bites her lip. "If you want to join us, I mean. I could really use your hands."

"Oh?" He flexes his fingers and pretends there's no lecherous thought running through his mind. "Sorry. Not what you meant, right?"

"What?" Her eyes flick to his hands, and her cheeks go pink. "Oh—I didn't think—"

"Of course." God, he's botching this. Lifting both hands in surrender, he tries again. "I'm all yours. What can I do?"

She licks her lips and looks everywhere but at his palms. "Pellets."

"Pellets?" Another slang term he doesn't know.

"Farm animal feed." She points to the petting zoo entrance. "They sell wafer cones filled with food pellets. I need one hand to corral AJ and one hand to take pictures, but that leaves me with no hands for holding food."

"Done." He whips out his wallet, glad he can help. "Three, please."

An attendant in a red and blue shirt takes the money and hands him three cones of green pellet food. "Five bucks."

He gives her a ten. "Keep the change."

"Thanks." She swings open the gate. "Don't feed the donkey and watch out for the chickens." Her smile drifts to Renee as AJ pulls her through the entrance. The girl looks at Matteo and grins. "Your son's cute. Looks just like you."

"Thanks." He shoves the word past a lump in his throat.

Your son.

He watches Renee pet a brown and white llama. Watches AJ's wonder-filled gaze. Watches another dad—a real one—stoop to hand his son a fistful of pellets.

You can do this.

He's taken out a moving target in high winds at two hundred yards. How hard can a toddler be?

Drawing a breath, he strides through the gate, not believing a word of his pep talk.

CHAPTER 4

hat the hell is wrong with you?

Renee knew that sculpted chest before she saw his face. A sure sign she's messed up.

"Pet gently, like this." She's working to keep her eyes off Matteo, but she has to grab more food pellets. "Thanks."

"Sure." He's gentle as he pours a pile of green feed in her hand, then his own. A brown goat snuffles close.

"There you go." His voice sounds calm and soothing. *"Prendilo con delicatezza."*

Italian. That's her guess. He used to whisper in bed, breathing words against her throat, ears, breasts. Italian or Dovlanese? She'd try to guess, then forget everything but his hands on her body.

"Capra dolce." His voice is gruff and gentle, the pellets tiny in his big hands.

She's jealous of farm animals. That's what it's come to.

Pushing into mom mode, she catches her son's hand. "AJ, like this." She demonstrates, petting a pygmy goat from neck to rump. "Feel how soft?"

"Soft." His eyes light with wonder as he slides a single pellet to a baby deer. "Bambi."

"That's right! And what's Bambi?"

He strokes again, gentler this time. "Deer."

"Such a smart boy."

If she sticks with AJ, she won't see Matteo. Won't feel him moving beside her, the warmth of his arm brushing hers as he hands over more animal feed. She has to keep her wits, even with longing and lust staging a sword fight in her chest.

That's not even her biggest fear. When she saw Matteo, she nearly wept with relief. Maybe she's seeing things, but after several days of calm, she's sure she saw the creepy stranger lurking near Family Funland. Different clothes, different hair, different everything, really. But the forehead...

Or maybe she's imagining things. Still, she can't shake the feeling she's being watched.

"AJ, honey." She tugs him back beside her. "Stay where I can reach you."

"Okay, Mama."

Such a good boy. She should focus on him, not imaginary boogeymen. The stranger's nowhere in sight. The buzz beneath her skin has nothing to do with *him* and plenty to do with Matteo.

He reaches past her to hand AJ more pellets. "There you go." So big and broad and competent in this ocean of animals.

"My Tail! Look." AJ points to a sheep in the corner. "Going potty."

"Sure is." Matteo snaps a photo, because of course he does. Such a guy. "Look—they're cleaning it up."

"Oh." AJ gapes at a girl in red and blue maneuvering a two-sided scoop. The same attendant who said "your son" like it's obvious.

Swallowing hard, Renee sees it, too. Anyone would, whether

it's true or not. They *look* like a family. The sort of family she never had but always wished for.

"Hold your hand flat like this." Matteo splays a palm as AJ lays his own digits flat. "I'll put the food right in the middle."

"Okay, My Tail."

God, that's cute. She should correct him, but what would she say?

Call him Matteo.

That seems wrong, but the alternative—

"Mama, look!" AJ giggles as a llama hoovers pellets off his palm. "She's hungry."

"She is hungry." Matteo flicks her a glance, and Renee's belly flips. He clears his throat. "I'm hungry, too."

"Oh?" Her mouth goes dry.

"Thirsty, too." He's undressing her with his eyes, or maybe she's imagining that. They're at a petting zoo, for God's sake. He's doing nothing more lecherous than holding a wafer cone as a llama head-butts his chest.

She looks at her watch. "It is almost dinnertime."

"Can I get you a corndog?" He frowns and lowers his voice. "Sorry, is that okay?"

Her answer slides through gritted teeth. "Not if you meant it as a filthy euphemism."

Matteo snorts. "Cute, but no. Just wondering if you're one of those moms who avoids processed junk."

"Oh. No, we love processed junk."

"Then corndogs are my treat."

She nods, ready to thank him. For asking about junk food. For buying their dinner. For putting his shirt back on so she didn't sink her teeth into one rounded pec. As she opens her mouth, she spots him.

Him.

The stranger. The guy with the broad forehead.

Oh, God.

Chills rake her arms as she watches the man half hidden by the handwash station. The mustache is gone, and he's got dark hair now, but it's the same guy. She's almost sure.

"Renee?"

Her throat feels dry. "Do you—"

"Yeah." He steps so he's between her and the man, shifting so AJ's behind him. "I see him."

"I'm not crazy, right?" She keeps her voice soft, so AJ doesn't hear the shake.

"Not crazy." Matteo slips more food to AJ but doesn't drag his eyes off the man. Doesn't take his hand off the boy's shoulder.

Renee can't see the stranger's eyes behind dark glasses, but the man must feel them watching him.

"He's moving," she whispers.

"Heading into the 4H pavilion." Matteo frowns. "I'd follow, but—"

"No, stay." Her hand flies to his arm. "Please."

His eyes go soft. "Of course."

"Thank you." Her hand's trembling, so she draws it back. "We're out of pellets anyway."

AJ holds a hand out, immune to the whole exchange. "More?"

She slips on her mom smile. "I'm kind of hungry. Are you hungry?"

"So hungry." Matteo rubs the ridges of his abs through his T-shirt. "How about you, little man?"

"Corndog!" AJ bounces between them. "Mama—corndog now?"

She looks toward the 4H pavilion. Did they imagine the whole thing?

Or is the stranger watching?

"If he's watching," Matteo murmurs, "it's best if he sees you're not alone."

"Right." It makes sense. "Do you think he's, um…"

She can't say the words. *Armed. Packing heat. The kind of man to open fire on a pen full of preschoolers and livestock.*

"No." Matteo shakes his head. "I don't think so." He hesitates. "If I had to guess, he's a lookout. He's just...watching."

"For what?"

"Not sure."

AJ darts after a spotted calf. She follows, keeping her voice low as Matteo glues himself to her side. "If you were me," she whispers, "what would you do?"

"Leave the fair or play wait-and-see?"

"Yes." She watches her son hug a sheep's fluffy neck. "We only just got here. I'll leave if we have to, but—"

"No." He scans the pavilion. "Let him see there's someone guarding you. Someone who'd die before anyone laid a hand on you."

She shivers, but not from fear. "Okay."

AJ tugs her hand. "Corndogs, Mama."

"One second, sweetie." She points to the pen in the corner. "Did you see the wallaby?"

"Wawa-bee?"

"Right there. The one that looks like a kangaroo?"

"Oooh." He drops to his knees for a better view. "Hi, hoppy hoppy."

Matteo touches her arm. "You trust me?"

"Not really."

He laughs and draws his hand back. "Fair enough."

"But I trust you more than the guy out there." She doesn't let her gaze go to the 4H pavilion but feels him anyway. "I trust you to watch our backs."

"It's a start." He crouches beside AJ. "Ready to get those corndogs, buddy?"

He's instantly on his feet. "Corndog!"

"That's right." Rising, Matteo puts a hand on her back. "Is this okay?"

"Of course." Her body telegraphs something closer to "hell, yes," but it's steered her wrong before. "It's fine."

"Let's go." He guides them to the exit, then crouches beside AJ. "We're going to stay very, very, *very* close together, okay?"

AJ nods. "Follow-the-leader?"

"Exactly like that." He pauses to tie AJ's shoe. "Maybe closer."

"Okay."

He steers them to the handwash station, scanning the crowd so subtly it's an art. He catalogues everyone. The pack of teens pushing each other by the cotton candy booth. The couple watching their teen scale a rock wall. An old lady licking a snow cone by the fence.

At the wash station, he hoists AJ to a step stool. "Know what we get as a prize if we all wash our hands really well and then stick *close close close* together?" Matteo turns on the water.

"What?" AJ pumps soap and starts to scrub.

"Fingernails, too," she reminds him.

"More soap." AJ wobbles as he leans for it. Renee starts to steady him, but Matteo's there already.

"Careful, buddy."

"What treat?" The kid keeps his focus. "Good treat?"

Matteo looks at her. "I'll bet your mom knows a good treat."

It's not meant to sound sexy, so she doesn't react. Damp palms don't count. "Funnel cake." She cranks the taps at her sink. "A great big one, with strawberry syrup and whipped cream. How does that sound?"

AJ throws out his hands, flinging water everywhere. "Yummy!"

"Perfect." Matteo reaches for a paper towel, lips brushing her earlobe as he leans in. "As far as anyone sees, we're just a regular family having fun at the fair. A very *close* family."

She nods and scrubs her nails. Sees her hands shaking again. "Whatever you say."

* * *

THEY'VE HAD dinner and dessert and no more sightings of the stranger. Maybe she imagined him. Or Matteo did, too. He hasn't stopped scanning, eyes searing everyone who gets close.

Even under his watchful gaze, Renee can't relax.

"You good?"

She dabs her lips with a napkin. "That was tasty."

"Wasn't talking about food." He tears the last piece of funnel cake and nudges it to AJ. "You want the big piece or the little piece, buddy?"

Her son assesses the spread. "My Tail bigger." He shoves the large piece at him. "You have."

"Thank you." He picks up the big piece. "Very generous."

"Gen-russ." AJ shoves fried dough in his face.

"You're tense," Matteo murmurs to her.

"Always."

"No sign of our friend." He clears his throat. "I called my own friends. *Discreet* friends. When you were in the bathroom. They're keeping an eye out."

"They're here?" She scans the crowd. "I don't see anyone."

"Yep."

She waits for more, but that's it. Pawing through her purse, she finds a baby wipe to scrub AJ's face. "What now?"

Matteo wipes his hands on a napkin. "What else is on your State Fair list?"

AJ flings his hands and sends the wipe sailing. "Stuffie! My Tail win stuffie?"

"Stuffie?" He looks to her for translation.

"Stuffed animal," she says. "The plush kind you win at the games. Not taxidermy."

"Thanks for clarifying." He crumples the plate and tosses it at the trash ten feet away. It drops dead center as he stands to help her up. "Do you mind if I put an arm around you?"

"Oh." Heat floods her cheeks. "I guess not."

Her body buzzes as he draws her close and guides AJ to a spot between them. Something hard bumps her hip. Blushing, she sweeps a look at the front of his jeans. "Is that—"

"No." He lifts one brow. "I have a little self-control."

Now her cheeks are blazing. "I didn't really think—"

"You did." He grins and pulls her close enough to breathe against her neck. "And I'm flattered you think it reaches all the way to my hip."

Is there a hue beyond crimson in the color palette? She's sure her cheeks hit it. She orders herself to breathe as he guides them toward the games. He's keeping AJ close, shifting so the boy stays shielded.

AJ pulls ahead as they approach a booth. "Teddy. *Teddy!*"

"Good eye." Matteo moves to keep up. "That's a big bear."

Renee arrives at a battered wood counter facing a bored-looking teen. "Hey there."

The kid grunts and tips a black ball cap. Matteo grabs the toy gun tethered to the counter. "No scope on this thing?"

"What?" The kid slouches in his chair. "Oh. Nah."

Teo turns it over in his hands. "What sort of recoil does it have?"

The kid frowns. "I don't know, man."

"Trigger needs adjusting." He sets the gun back on the counter.

"Yeah, it sucks." Yawning, the kid pulls out his phone. "Doesn't even have live ammo."

Renee touches Teo's arm. "No guns, please. Not even fake ones."

She's braced for him to argue. His eyes shift to AJ and soften. "Right. Yeah, of course."

"Thanks." She squeezes his arm and regrets it. There's muscle layered thick atop muscle he already had. Multiplied muscle. She needs to stop touching him.

47

"Fishy." AJ points to a booth where they're giving goldfish to folks who toss rings around bottles. "Fishy fishy fishy fishy f—"

"Let's stay focused on stuffies." The last thing she needs is a pet to care for.

Matteo swoops to the rescue. "There's another booth with bears."

Her son looks where he's pointing. "*Big* bears."

"Bigger's better." Crap. *Don't look at Matteo. Don't look at Matteo.* "For bears."

Matteo puts an arm around her and guides them to the next booth. "Darts. Is that non-violent enough?"

"Depends." She sets a hand on AJ's shoulder as he stretches to touch a bright blue bear. "How are your dart skills?"

Matteo grins. "Pretty good."

Of course they are. Just like everything else he does.

Except sticking around when you need him...

"How does this work?" He hands cash to the teen attendant, who hands back a trio of frilly-tipped darts.

"Throw the darts." She shrugs. "Hit the balloons."

He turns one over in his palm. "Not very sharp."

"It's a family event." The girl looks at AJ singing to the bear. "Bad idea to give sharp objects to randos high on sugar."

"Fair enough." He studies the sea of balloons. Six or seven dozen, and she's sure he assesses them all.

Renee studies him instead. The coiled muscle in his shoulders. The tightness in his jaw. The concentration in his eyes as he draws back an arm and—

Pop!

AJ squeals as the balloon bursts. "Again, My Tail." He claps and stomps. "More!"

"Nice shot, man." The girl looks impressed.

"Again!" AJ hoots.

"All right." He shoots Renee a look that dives to her belly. "Do I get anything special if I hit two at once?"

She licks her lips. "What do you want?"

The girl hands him another dart. "You earned an extra for hitting a black balloon on the first try."

"Yeah?" He adds it to his handful and studies the board. "If I hit two more, we get the bear?"

"The small one." Renee points at a chart outlining prizes. "A small bear is good, right?"

"Yes, Mama." AJ touches the little bear, but his eyes sweep the large one overhead.

Matteo grunts and eyes the board. "Two more, huh?"

He throws again.

Pop!

And again, before she sees his arm move.

Pop!

"Nice one." The girl gives him a small bear, and he hands it to AJ.

"There you go, kid."

"Baby bear." AJ sinks to the filthy concrete and burrows his face in yellow fur. "Bitty baby bear."

Matteo gives her a look. "Bigger's better. You said so yourself."

Heat hits her cheeks again. "I didn't mean—"

"Three more darts, please." Matteo scans the board. "How do I get the big bear?"

"Hit more balloons," the girl offers.

"Thanks." Matteo takes a dart in each hand and looks at Renee. "Two at once," he says again. "Do I get something special?"

"How about my undying admiration?" She's trying for cool, but it comes out shaky.

"Worth it." He turns back to the board. "Yellow and pink."

His arms snap so fast they're a blur.

Pop! Pop!

One pink, one yellow, burst in an eye-blink.

AJ bounces up with the small bear dangling. "Good job, My Tail."

"Thanks." He nods at the board. "You want to pick the next colors?"

AJ nods. "Yeah."

"You know your colors?"

Her boy points low on the wall. "Blue." Renee sees him skim the board and point to another balloon up top. "Green."

"Trick shot, huh?" Matteo nods approvingly. "I like it."

He takes aim again, brow pinched in concentration. It's the same look he had doing puzzles at his dining table. The look when he reprogrammed her computer, when Renee mused aloud if multiple orgasms were real or made up by women's magazines to—

Pop! Pop!

Two more balloons, the exact ones AJ picked.

"Wow." She looks at him. "You're good."

Green eyes flash. "Yep."

She shivers and touches her son's shoulder. "Should we move along?"

"No, Mama." AJ tugs Matteo's pant leg. "More!"

Matteo squats down. "More what?"

AJ frowns. "Balloons?"

"What else?" He rolls the darts between his palms. "What's the magic word you say when you want something?"

"Please?" AJ bounces. "Pleeeeeease?"

"Okay." He points at the board. "Can you find a white one?"

Her boy scans the board. "There!" He points at a colorless balloon near the upper left corner. "And there!" A second one, roughly six miles from the first.

"AJ," she chides, as Matteo stands up. "We don't want to make things impossible for—"

Pop! Pop!

Both balloons gone. *Holy shit.*

"My Tail!" AJ hoots, swinging the small bear overhead. "Got 'em!"

"I did." Matteo holds out a hand for a low-five. AJ slaps his palm.

This should *not* turn her on. Neither should the look Matteo shoots her, his gaze steady and steely. How long can they do this? Not darts, though she's wondering what it takes to get the damn bear. She consults the chart again. Reads it three times without processing a word.

"Lellow." AJ tugs Matteo's jeans. "Blue."

Matteo glances at her. "Did you teach him colors, or did Nic?"

"Neither," she admits. "He figured it out when he was barely two. I bought him building blocks in different colors and he asked me each one and then remembered. The doctor says he's gifted."

"Go figure."

She's glad he's gone back to scanning. Glad he can't hear her thoughts or her heart drumming in her ears.

"You still like pink?" He tips his chin at the board. "Or do you have a new favorite color?"

"Pink's good."

He looks at AJ. "Pick two pink ones, buddy."

"That one." Scrunching his face, AJ points. "And that one."

"Good job." He looks at the girl behind the counter. "How close am I to taking home the big prize?"

The girl snickers and jerks a thumb over her shoulder. "Careful talking about who's going home with you. You've got a fan club forming."

Renee looks and—*holy crap*. There must be six, no, *seven* women. And they're watching Matteo with undisguised lust. A redhead whispers to a blonde and pulls a lipstick from her purse. A brunette tugs down the neckline on her halter top.

It shouldn't bug her. It *doesn't* bug her.

That doesn't stop her from touching Teo's arm. "You doing okay?"

One brow lifts. "Me? I'm great."

She licks her lips. "You said stay close, right?"

The faintest flicker lights his eyes. "Right."

"It's part of the act, then."

"What's that?" He glances at AJ, who's back on the ground at their feet. He's singing to the bear, paying no mind to grownups.

Matteo looks back at her. "What's part of the act?"

"You guarding me. We're supposed to be together." Heart knocking at her ribs, she steps closer. "That's what you said, right?"

"Yes." The rasp in his voice wasn't there before.

"So maybe…" Her fingers skim the back of his neck. "Maybe just a small kiss to—"

His lips claim hers. Matteo's mouth feels hot and hungry, softer than she remembers. A delicious contrast to strong hands sliding up her waist, pulling her to a chest so broad she gasps.

It's a chaste kiss—two seconds? Three?—but it could be hours. There's no tongue, no moaning, but, *oh God*, she feels it in the tips of her fingers.

He lets go first. Hand still on her waist, he drops his gaze to AJ. Her son hasn't seen a thing. The boy closes his eyes to belt out the last line of the alphabet song.

Renee looks up to see Matteo watching her.

He doesn't break eye contact as he lifts one arm. "Pink."

"Wh—*oh*."

He hurls the dart, not blinking, not glancing away from her.

Pop!

She licks her lips again. "Nailed it."

A rare, wild grin. "Yep."

AJ hops up and tugs Matteo's leg. "Again, My Tail. Big bear."

Matteo grips the last dart and eyes the board. She watches his gaze slip sideways and his eyes narrow. Frowning, he moves closer. Close enough to kiss. She leans in, wanting his mouth again.

"Ten o'clock." His lips brush her ear. "Same guy. Stay behind me."

She shivers. "Oh."

Her heart bangs on her ribcage as she pulls AJ with her. She's scared and turned on and a little alarmed by the broadness of Teo's back. Was he always this solid?

Clutching her child, she coaches herself to stay calm. *There.* Just behind the women, off to the side. Same guy as before. Broad forehead. He's in khaki shorts and sunglasses with a gray shirt.

Twenty feet away, a bald guy leans on the ticket booth. He's got arms the size of hams. Friend or foe? He looks lethal. He's looking at *her.*

Pop!

"Gah!" She grabs Matteo's arm.

He steps back and takes the big bear from the girl. "Thanks." He holds it for an awestruck AJ. "Want me to hold on to it for you, buddy?"

"My hold." He grabs the bear's leg and hugs. "Soft."

It's three times his size, but Matteo lets him have it. Doesn't let go of her as his eyes track the stranger. The man isn't moving.

She forces herself to breathe. "Now what?"

"Stay calm."

Easy for him to say. He could skewer the guy's eyeball with a dart if he wanted. Does he want? She shivers, recalling the bulge on his hip. Is Matteo armed with more than dull darts?

He draws her close, keeping AJ closer. "I don't like how he's watching you."

She bites her lip. "I just saw him touch his ear."

"Really." One word with an edge and no question mark. He's coiled with tension but somehow calm as he fixes the bow at the bear's ear. When his hand draws back, he's got a—*oh, God.*

"That's not a dart in your hand." Where did he get the knife?

"Let's pretend it is."

But it isn't. It's a weird looking knife with a curvy handle and lethal blade. She's never seen a throwing knife, but this might be one. What kind of man brings weapons to a carnival?

A man she's glad is guarding her back.

She scoots AJ behind her with shaking hands. Not a big shift, not one he'll notice. She needs her child out of range.

"So soft." He's snuggling the bear as the crowd congratulates Teo on his win.

"Nice one, man."

"Helluva throwing arm you've got."

He nods but doesn't look away from the stranger. The man moves, and Renee feels Teo tense.

Get ready to run.

"Let Mommy hold your bear, okay?" Her voice sounds sunshine light as she grabs the plushie and gives him the smaller one. "Big bear for Mama, little bear for AJ. Just until we're in the car."

The boy starts to whimper, but Matteo shakes his head.

"Your mom knows best." It's a gentle reprimand, with no room to argue. "We're heading for the car now, okay?"

AJ shoves a thumb in his mouth. "Mmmhmm."

Matteo's lips touch Renee's ear. "That's definitely an earpiece. You've got a good eye." His breath makes her tremble. "The tactical kind, like the Feds use."

"But—why?"

"Good question."

She's not sure she wants the answer. They're moving now, a brisk but casual beeline to the parking lot. The guy touches his ear and starts to follow.

Oh, God.

Matteo curses under his breath. "Yeah, that's not some device he got on Amazon. Not an amateur." He clears his throat and throws some jolly in his voice. "Hey, bud. You mind if I borrow your big bear from Mommy for a minute?"

"Okay." AJ cuddles his little bear tighter.

"Here." She hands over the stuffed animal. Sees the stranger touch his ear again.

Electricity sizzles her legs as they start to move. She's keeping calm, forcing a bright smile for AJ. Matteo sets the pace, and it's slower than she'd like. Her instincts scream for her to flee, to run as fast as she can.

But she trusts Teo to know where they're going. To move like they're seeking a snow cone and not escape.

"Steady." Matteo's low rumble could be for her or the stranger. "Where'd you park?"

"B-gate. Over there."

"We're taking your car. No car seat in mine."

"Okay." Thank God he thought of it. Her nerves are scrambled eggs.

She starts to reach for his hand, but—*oh, God.* That's why he wanted the bear. He's got the knife behind it, gripped in one lethal fist.

Who is Matteo Bello? She's seen glimpses of danger. Of a guy capable of more than programming her computer. But never *this.* Not the lethal protector he's become in a blink.

He catches her looking and nods at AJ. "How about if Mommy picks you up?" He's a cheerful babysitter, not a guy poised to stab someone's brains out.

AJ snuffles. "I walk."

She stoops to grab him. "Come on, sweetie. We need to move quicker."

"But Mama—"

"Your Mama will keep you safe." A pause as they move past the stranger, Teo's body coiled with tension. "Your mom's good at that, isn't she? Keeping you safe?"

AJ snuggles against her. "Good Mama."

Can he hear her heart pounding? His tiny ear drifts to her breastbone, starfish fingers clutching her shirt. She'd give anything to keep him safe.

Anything.

Teo shifts to keep them shielded. God, she's glad he's here.

"No sign of a weapon." Matteo's soft murmur as they move past the big bald guy she spotted before. Nodding, the man slips something to Matteo. Another weapon?

Someone strides beside her, and she jumps.

"Hey, there." A dark-haired man with smiling blue eyes moves his brick wall body to her other side. "Enjoying the fair?"

"Um." She looks at Matteo, who gives the faintest nod. "Yes?"

"That's great. I love a good fair." The grinning guy keeps walking. "A little too much sugar for my taste, but you've gotta live a little, right?"

"Right." Why does he look familiar?

"Been working all day in the Volunteers in Medicine booth, so it's nice to get out." He stretches and nods at Matteo. "Nothing like supporting the community to give you the warm fuzzies."

"Warm fuzzies." AJ bounces in her arms. "I like 'em."

"I'll bet you do." The guy smiles some more and shifts so his shoulder shields AJ.

It's the smile that tips her off. "The dentist." She studies his profile, same as the one she's seen on billboards. "Your office is next to my daycare."

"Dr. Sebastian LaDouceur, DDS." He touches her arm, urging her to slow. "That's a great smile you've got."

She's not smiling, so he means AJ.

Her boy bounces in her arms. "Got big bear and baby bear."

"Nice work." The dentist chucks the small bear under the chin. "And does your bear brush his teeth every night like a good boy?"

"Uh-huh. With *toot-paste.*"

"Atta kid." He looks at Renee. "So important to teach oral hygiene early. You're doing a great job, Mom."

"Thanks?" She doesn't feel like a great mom. She's a mom who put her son in danger when he should be giggling on the Tilt-a-Whirl.

But Matteo's solid and sure beside her, and his friend—a dentist, for God's sake—is shielding them with his own body.

Who are these people?

They slip through the exit, and she dares a glance behind them. The stranger's ten feet back and gaining on them. A chill rips up her spine.

"Mama?"

She hugs him tighter. "It's okay, baby."

Please, let that be true.

The stranger's almost to the gate when the bald guy reappears. His bulk blocks the other man from view, and Renee sees tension in the broad back. She can't see the bald guy's face but watches as he opens his sweatshirt to show something to the stranger.

Sweatshirt? It's eighty degrees.

The stranger takes off running.

"Renee?" Matteo touches her arm. "Where's your car?"

"Over there." She turns and points.

When she looks back, Baldy's gone. So is her stalker.

"Keys?"

She hands them to Matteo as the dentist kneels to peer under her car. "You're an auto mechanic *and* a dentist?"

"I'm a jack of all trades." Frowning at the space behind her tire, he flicks a small flashlight from his pocket. "Clear. Get AJ loaded."

How does he know her son's name?

She doesn't have time to ask as Teo unlocks the car and waves a black gadget. AJ perks up. "Magic wand?"

"Abracadabra." He runs it over the backseat. Is that a bug sweeper? "All clear here."

"Good." The dentist hops to his feet with a friendly wave. "Great meeting you. Bye!"

TAWNA FENSKE

"Wait." She's still not sure what's happening. "Dr.—"

"Call me Sebastian." He salutes as he turns toward the gate. "Enjoy your evening."

And he's gone.

Matteo touches her arm. "We need to go. Let me take AJ."

She hesitates. "His car seat—"

"I've got it. Please, Renee—get in."

As calm as he's been until now, there's tension in his voice. With a nod, she hands over her child. Keeps one eye on Matteo as he bends into the backseat.

He snaps the buckles like he's done it before. "I'd like to drive, if you don't mind."

She gets in the passenger seat and hooks her seatbelt. "Do I have a choice?"

"You always have a choice." He shuts the backseat door and slides into the front.

Hands trembling, she watches him fix the rearview mirror. "That's the problem."

"The mirror?"

She shakes her head, collecting her thoughts as he starts the car. "My choices."

He shoots her a glance and pulls from the parking lot. "Come again?"

A deep breath as she looks over her shoulder. AJ's asleep. A new record. She turns back and sees Teo's eyes on the road.

"I make poor choices," she says softly. "With jobs. With men. Everything."

He doesn't reply. Probably knows he counts as one of the men.

The silence yawns, and she's obligated to fill it. "It's not personal," she says. "It's always been that way. My decision-making. My *picker*—it's just...broken."

Still, he says nothing. Hits the blinker and changes lanes. He's heading south, now west. She's too tired to ask where they're going.

"You chose to have AJ."

She blinks. "What?"

"You were pregnant and alone. You had a choice."

She swallows hard, fingers curling into her thighs. "Yes."

"You chose AJ."

He lets the words hang there. Waits for her to nod.

"I'm sure it's been hard," he says. "Being a single mom isn't easy."

"I wouldn't change it for the world."

"I can tell." He checks the rearview mirror. Merges right. "So your picker's not completely broken."

She nods and looks down at her hands. "Maybe not completely."

They're quiet a long time. He checks the rearview mirror at least a thousand more times. Watching AJ or checking their tail? Both, she sees when his gaze lingers on the sleeping boy.

"I trust you." She closes her eyes, afraid to look at him when she says it. "Maybe not as a romantic partner, but to help us—protect us—"

"That's a start."

She looks up at him. "It is."

They go quiet again. He steers them to the Center Street bridge, headed west. Hands in her lap, heart in her throat, she swallows the question she can't bear to ask.

The start of what?

CHAPTER 5

"*W*here are we going?"

She's asked the question twice. He should probably answer.

"Matteo." She thumps him in the arm, then looks back to be sure AJ didn't see.

The boy's fast asleep.

"Sorry. I shouldn't hit." Sighing, she slumps in her seat. "That's the last thing I need. My kid thinking it's okay to use violence."

Matteo grunts and switches lanes. "Beats the alternative."

"What, pacifism?"

"Dying." He looks in the rearview mirror. They've gone thirty miles without a tail, but he can't be too careful. Dante slipped him a Beretta at the fairgrounds, and he's got a throwing knife. He'd rather not use either.

Renee has a point. Violence should be a last resort.

Speaking of her, she's gone quiet. Too quiet.

He looks over and sees tears rolling down her cheeks.

"Ah, hell." He hits the brakes and glides to a stop on the shoulder. Yanks the e-brake and faces her. "I didn't mean it, Renee."

"Mean what?" She sniffles and swipes at her eyes.

"No one's dying." He should maybe rephrase that. "You're not going to die. Neither is AJ. Everyone's safe."

She's shaking her head, sniffling some more. "I've dragged you into this mess for no reason. You're supposed to be keeping your nose clean, and here I am—"

"Don't." He shakes his head, needing her to believe this. "I can get myself into as much trouble alone as I would with you."

That earns him a watery laugh. "I believe it."

"Besides, maybe I brought this on us."

She bites her lip. "Even if it's true, I feel safer with you."

"Good." He's aching to pull her into his arms. To make her tears go away however he can.

But they've got a long road ahead. "Can I see your purse?"

"My purse." She blinks down at it. "What for?"

"I need to check for bugs."

Reluctantly, she hands it over. "I'm guessing you don't mean insects."

"No, but this is nice." He pulls out a plush lobster. "Technically a crustacean from the phylum Arthropoda. Same class as beetles and ants and lots of other bugs. Six legs, two antennae—"

"Are you seriously giving me a science lesson on the side of the highway?"

"Is it helping?"

"A little."

He sets the lobster aside and leans down to grab the bug sweeper from under the passenger seat. When he sits up, she looks flushed.

"Warn me the next time you reach between my legs."

"Sorry." He's a dick. He settles for being a thorough dick, sliding the sweeper over her purse. No alerts. Not satisfied, he sticks a hand inside. Something sharp stabs his finger and he yanks back. "Ow. What the hell was that?"

"A farmer."

"A what?" He extracts a plastic man holding a pitchfork. "You have an armed plastic man in your purse."

"It's not a weapon, it's a rake."

"Rake can be a weapon."

"It's part of the Farm and Tractor Lego set." She takes the figure as he paws deeper through the purse. "There's probably a submarine in there somewhere."

His fingers find a foil packet, and he draws back expecting a condom. "Balmex?"

"Diaper cream." She watches him scan a child-sized mitten, an empty sippy cup, a lollypop missing its wrapper. "Is this really necessary?"

"Is this really your purse?" He hands it back. It wasn't that long ago her handbags held lipstick and prophylactics. "Didn't you used to keep a flask of vodka and a change of panties in your bag?"

"Life's different now."

"No kidding."

She bites her lip. "Is someone tracking us?"

"I'm trying to find out." He swept for bugs at the fairgrounds but won't feel safe until he does it all again. Gliding the device over the dashboard, he pauses on the glovebox. Nothing. Unhooking his seatbelt, he moves in back. AJ's sound asleep in his car seat. A perfect place to plant a bug.

Matteo moves carefully, trying not to wake the boy. He scans the buckles, the webbing, even the boy's tiny sneakers.

AJ smacks his lips. "Teddy."

"Right here." He tucks the small bear in the crook of the boy's arm.

The boy smiles in sleep, and a hot blade of fondness slips between Teo's ribs.

Satisfied there's no tracker, he drops back in the driver's seat. Renee's watching him, eyes wide and wet. "Thank you."

"For what?"

"For rescuing us." She bites her lip. "I know I haven't sounded grateful enough, but—"

"You don't owe me gratitude. You don't owe me anything." Doesn't stop him from wanting whatever she might offer. "I'm a capricious sack of snot, remember?"

A shaky laugh slips out. "I'm sorry I called you that. And I'm grateful, whether you like it or not."

This was easier when she hated him. "Got a notepad in there?" Pointing to her purse, he leans over her to tuck the bug sweeper beneath the seat.

"Notepad?" She shrugs and peers inside. "I usually make notes on my phone."

"No phone. I took out your SIM card and powered down."

"You what? When?"

Now's not the time to admit pickpocketing skills. "Borrowed it at the fair."

"Jesus." She's partway between pissed and impressed. "All right, here's a notepad. What am I writing?"

"Everything you need from your house and where to find it." He eases back onto the highway. They're six miles from the turn to his sister's vineyard, but they can't go there. They need a better plan.

"We're not going back to my place?"

"Not until I know who's tailing you and what they want." He changes lanes, easing past a slower car. "I don't like how easy it was for them to get to you."

"Right." Her voice sounds shaky, and he hates how she clutches that purse like a safety blanket.

When he looks in the mirror, AJ's holding his bear the same way. His heart hurts as he forces his focus on the road.

Silence yawns like the highway in front of them. He's careful to go the speed limit. To flick on the headlights as they travel the road darkened by thick towers of trees. He's missed this stretch of Oregon. Shaggy pines, mossy bark, the pale blue slice of sky going liquid gold in the fading light.

He saw nothing like this behind bars.

Gripping the wheel, he tells himself not to talk. Silence is good. It keeps things from getting complicated.

"When did you find out?" Shit. He didn't mean to ask that.

Renee lifts an eyebrow. "Find out what?"

"About AJ." He slides a glance at her. "Alessi. When did you know you were pregnant?"

She bites her lip. He sees from the corner of his eye, though he stays fixed on the road ahead. There's such a long stretch of silence that he's sure she won't answer.

"That November."

He frowns. "But—that's months after I left."

He doesn't know he's holding his breath until she speaks again. "I was on the pill," she says. "I took the active pills straight through with no breaks for periods. My doctor's advice with my history of heavy cycles. The downside was not having that monthly reassurance. I didn't know I was pregnant until I was pretty far along."

"I see." She's being cagey with dates, and Matteo doesn't blame her. He wants to ask what it felt like. Was she scared or angry or pissed at him?

She hasn't even said you're the father.

"I dated a lot after you left."

His chest feels like someone's standing on it. "I understand."

"I wanted to get over you. It was a while before I knew I was pregnant. When I found out—" She laughs, but it's not a happy sound. "Well. It put a damper on my dating life."

His fingers ache. When he looks down, he's white-knuckling the steering wheel. "They couldn't handle the commitment?" A dick thing to say since he's the one who cut and ran.

"I didn't have the energy to date. Besides." Another mirthless laugh. "I got morning sickness on a brunch date. Kinda wrecks the date vibe to have a guy hold back your hair as you're puking."

Jesus. And Matteo left her alone to face that. He'll never forgive himself.

"There's this one guy I dated for a few weeks who—"

"I'm sorry, can we change the subject?" He eases his hold on the steering wheel. "I have no right to be jealous, and you have every right to date whomever you like. I'm the dick who ran off."

He expects her to agree, but she shrugs. "All right. If it makes you feel better, one guy I dated turned out to be a con man. I kicked him to the curb when I saw his photo on the news."

It does make him feel better. Not much, but some. "I'm sorry. You deserve better." Better than him, that's for sure. "You always did."

"Thanks."

They both go quiet. It's silent in the Subaru, save AJ's soft snores and the shush of wet asphalt licking tires.

She peers through the windshield and frowns. "Are we headed for the coast?"

"Yeah." He glances over. "Jen got the vineyard when Nondi passed. Nicole got the bungalow for her daycare."

"You got your grandmother's beach house?"

That startles him. "How'd you know she had one?"

"You mentioned it once." She bites her lip. "I'm sorry again about your grandma."

"Yeah. Well." There's not much to say, so he concentrates on driving. It's hours 'til sunset, but twisty trees cloak the Van Duzer Corridor in damp black cotton. "Her beach house was my favorite. She had lots of other properties, but that one—it was special."

Why is he still talking?

She touches his hand and his heart liquifies. "Tell me about it."

He hesitates. Opening up isn't his thing.

Wasn't his thing. He's supposed to be reformed. "It's the first place she bought when she came to America," he says. "She lived there three years before she moved inland, to wine country. Kept the beach place for all her toys."

"Toys?"

"Motorcycles. Dune buggy. A camper van. That kind of thing."

Renee laughs. "My elderly neighbor thinks she's hip with her electric can opener."

He taps the brake as a deer steps out of the woods. Bambi.

Flicking a glance at AJ in the rearview mirror, his heart goes squishy.

Eyes on the road.

He manages for a while, but Renee's watching him. Tension fills the space, like wax poured from a candle. It's not his job to put her at ease. He's here to protect, not entertain.

"Did you play road trip games as a kid?" He catches the misstep and winces. "Before your dad took off. Maybe with a foster family or something."

"Yeah." Her voice wobbles. "I loved the word association game."

"I don't know that one."

"It's been a long time." Unhitching her seatbelt, she stretches back to set her purse beside AJ. While she's bent over, she straightens Little Bear. Her breast skims Matteo's arm, and he grips the wheel so he doesn't reach for her.

Once she's resettled, she starts again. "Okay, so one person starts with a word. Say, 'taco.'"

"Taco." Seems simple enough.

"That's just an example. But pretend that's your word. As quick as I can, I come up with something tied to that. Taco makes me think guacamole, so that's my word, and you'd say—"

"La Paz."

Renee cocks her head. "Peace?"

That's right, she speaks Spanish. "The city in Mexico." He clears his throat. "It's where I had the best guacamole in my life."

"Yeah?" Again with the head tilt. "When were you in Mexico?"

He's already stepped in it.

"Because that was something we had in common," she continues. "We'd never seen Mexico. So, it must have been after you left?"

Either that, or you were lying.

She doesn't say it, but the words bob between them like leaky balloons.

He gives a tight nod. "It was after I left. I...thought I'd get lost there for a while."

Not untrue, but not the whole truth. A side job for the Duke of Dovlano, he got sent to take down a drug kingpin. A simple tech job. Car bomb with no casualties besides the target.

Too bad a butler borrowed the car. Lucky for that guy, Teo's as quick disarming explosives as he is at building them.

Unlucky for the kingpin, plan B meant messier. Throwing knife to the throat, quick and simple. Matteo's specialty.

If only he'd stayed in Mexico. Kept safe in the land of warm cobblestones and good tequila.

But then he wouldn't be here, right now, with Renee and AJ and—

"Matteo?"

He jolts back to the car. "It was great guacamole."

Renee rolls her eyes. "I asked if the beaches were nice. I always wanted to see the Baja Peninsula."

He tries to remember the beaches. "I'm not sure I saw any."

"Seriously?"

Shrugging, he locks his eyes on the road. It's easier than thinking about how he meant to take Renee there. They'd been together four months—hardly any time at all, so his fantasy seemed silly. That didn't stop him from pausing at the ring shop, admiring the sparkly one in the middle. Picturing himself giving up the life, being a husband and father and—

"Potato."

Renee looks at him. "That's your word?"

"Sure."

"Okay, stamp."

"Stamp?" He glances over. "As in postage?"

She rolls her eyes. "The object of this game is to move fast. The person who pauses is the loser."

"I'm a loser." Nothing new. "Why does potato make you think stamp?"

"There's a craft project your sister did at daycare with the kids." She fiddles with the coil on her notepad. "They picked out shapes, and she carved them into halved potatoes. Then they got paint and—"

"Stamped designs on wrapping paper?" He swerves left, dodging a pothole. "Tell me she got smart and skipped the glitter."

Renee looks at him. "You know potato stamps?"

"My grandma taught me." And he taught his sisters, carefully carving potatoes with the knife Nondi gave him for his birthday. "We'd make big rolls of wrapping paper every Christmas. Grandma did a lot of charity stuff, and we wrapped all the gifts ourselves."

"That's so sweet." She shakes her head. "I'm not sure if you should start with 'stamp' or if I should do a new word."

"New word." He wants to hear what's in her head. Renee's beautiful brain always slayed him. Book smart, though she never went to college. Street smart, because she had to be. God, she's clever. And funny and beautiful and—

"Okay, I'm thinking." She rubs her hands on her thighs. "Cocktail."

"Molotov."

"What?"

Shit. "Gin and tonic."

"That's three words."

"Margarita?"

68

She laughs. "And we're back to Mexico." A pause to check AJ again. "You seriously went with explosives?"

He shrugs and tries again. "Manhattan?"

"The drink or the city?"

"Your pick."

"Then I'm staying with Margarita. I had a good one to follow that."

"By all means."

"Okay, ass."

He's got this. "Tits."

She laughs and shakes her head. "I knew you'd go there. For the record, I meant donkey."

"You didn't." He steers them around a massive puddle. "You wanted to curse, but not around AJ. That was your workaround."

"You think you know me that well?"

He hesitates. It's a trick question. "Not as well as I wish I did."

"You're such a charmer, Matteo." She crosses her legs, seatbelt squishing her breasts. "All right, so it's tits to me?"

"Yep." He fights to keep his eyes on the road.

"Okay, bird."

"Blue tits!" He slaps the wheel. "That documentary we watched about the bird called blue tits. Those European chickadees that follow milkmen around and poke holes in containers to drink the milk?"

"Good memory."

He's grateful they've moved on from breasts, but this feels more intimate. The shared history he tried to forget behind bars. If he pictured their nights together, curled on his couch, he'd go nuts.

"Cuckoo." He waits for her to say *clock*.

"Springfield."

"Springfield?" He needs to know the thought process. "How'd you get to Springfield from cuckoo?"

"It made me think of *One Flew Over the Cuckoo's Nest*."

"Jack Nicholson?"

"Right, but the book was written by Ken Kesey. Oregon author who grew up in Springfield. I lived there nearly a year with a foster family."

His heart hurts picturing that lost little girl. The girl growing up with a jailbird dad and a mom who left a newborn in a criminal's care. If her parents weren't dead already, he'd hunt them down and—

It's his turn, isn't it?

"Um."

But Springfield reminds him of the school shooting in '98, which reminds him of guns and revenge and the reasons he doesn't deserve Renee. That he's not the kind of guy who gets a beautiful woman and a sweet, sleeping son in the backseat.

He lets his gaze drift to AJ, just a glimpse in the rearview mirror. Feels his gut coil like it's clutched in tight fists.

"Bear." Matteo inhales and locks his eyes on the road.

* * *

It's dark by the time they reach the beach house. He's lucky Jen and Dante came last week for a getaway. They aired out rooms and stocked the pantry with essentials like shelf-stable food and firearms. He's grateful for both.

Matteo waits until dinner's done and Renee's in bed with AJ. Checking the locks for the hundredth time, he digs out a burner phone.

"It's me." He peels back the curtains and scans the dark beach. Nothing.

It's been an hour since he sent the packing list to his pals via encrypted system. He's been worried ever since, guilty for dragging his buddies into his private turmoil.

Scratch that. He was worried way before that.

"Hang on." There's rustling on Dante's end as he moves to a

quiet spot. Quiet, meaning Jen's not listening. His sister knows Dante's history, but not details. Not everything.

Not Matteo's role. She's probably guessed, but they don't discuss it. Teo's not big on sharing. Not even with family.

Dante's back on the line. "Okay, go."

"Jen's okay?"

"Of course, Jen's okay. You want to talk to her?"

"No. I want to know where you stashed the...frying pans."

"Frying pans?" Dante snorts. "There's a code I haven't heard."

"I'm evolving."

"Sure." He snickers. "There's a cast-iron skillet in the back of the linen closet. Top shelf. And a...wok?" Another snort. "That's in the garage. Under the dune buggy."

"Thanks." Nice to have friends with suspicious natures. "What happened back at the fair? Did you catch the guy?"

"Ran into the swine barn. Lost him there."

"Damn." He can't fault Dante for not firing in a crowd. He's got a soft spot for women and children and pigs. Pigs in particular.

"Would've been tough to question him even if we'd caught up to him," Dante says. "Can't really interrogate someone between a corndog stand and the bumper cars."

"Did Seb get a tracker on him?"

"No." Dante grunts. "Had to pick between guarding Renee or sticking with the mark."

"He chose right."

"Yeah." There's a long stretch of silence. "Cute kid."

Matteo lets go of the curtain. "Thank you."

"You're sure you get credit?"

He mulls that a minute. "She hasn't said so."

But he's sure. He doesn't blame her for not confirming, but... yeah. AJ's his. He felt it when he held the kid's hand at the fair. When AJ dipped his tots in dill relish at dinner. That's always been Teo's thing.

Even if the boy weren't kin to him, he'd fight to the death to protect him. But knowing that's his child...

"Seb and I stopped by her house."

Matteo kicks his mind back on track. "You got all her stuff?"

"Everything on the list." Another pause. "She have some kind of hang-up for old furniture?"

"Yeah." Closing his eyes, he sees Renee's living room. His first and only night at her place. For months, she refused to have him over. "Your place is nicer," she'd say, and he felt happy to host her like a normal guy.

Then came the invitation. His first time seeing her threadbare armchair. The ancient coffee table. The lumpy sofa where he laid her back against a clean, new slipcover and—

"Lots of old stuff that looks like it came from thrift stores," Dante says. "Weird, since she's not broke. Sebastian checked her bank accounts. Not wealthy, but she's doing okay. The furniture, though—"

"I know." He sighs. "It belonged to her grandmother."

"Granny didn't like her much?"

He laughs because it's easier than missing his own grandma. "Renee never met her grandma. Died before she was born."

"How'd she get her stuff?"

"Her father had it. She kept it when he got locked up." Some kind of strange nostalgia. Common in kids who grew up in the system, or so he's read. "I'm surprised she still has it. Guess it's about family legacy." Lord knows Matteo gets that.

"Their family legacy has some ugly lamps."

He remembers those lamps. The orange one with beads. The pink one she kept because her dad bought it the day he learned Renee's mom was having a girl.

"I don't really know why she kept all that." Except maybe he does. "She got fucked over in the family department."

"How?"

"Teen mom ran off four weeks after having her." Matteo looks outside again. "Dad was in and out of prison until CSD sent her to foster care."

"Jesus."

"Yeah." And he's the asshole who abandoned her again. Matteo sighs. "You searched the place?"

"Top to bottom. Found two hidden cameras in the office. A tracker on the baby stroller. Bugs all over the place. Someone's spent a lot keeping tabs on your girl."

"Fuck." Teo drags a hand over his head.

"We're talking professional-grade equipment. Not amateur stuff off the internet."

So they're dealing with pros. He'd guessed already, but it sucks knowing for sure. "You mind keeping an eye on things?"

"On it." Dante covers the mouthpiece and murmurs something. A promise to take out the trash?

Amazing how things change. Wasn't long ago when "taking out the trash" meant something else in their world. Now Seb's cleaning teeth, Dante raises farm animals, and Matteo...

God knows what he's doing. He's still waiting on a call back from the tech firm where he applied.

He knows what he's *not* doing. "I'm not letting this go until we figure out who's after her. Until I know they're safe."

Dante grunts. "Seb's free tomorrow. He'll come meet you with their stuff."

"Thanks."

"No problem." A pause. "You sure you're not too close to the subject?"

"Positive."

The first time in his life he's lied to his buddy. Closing his eyes, he's safe from staring holes in her bedroom door.

As he hangs up the phone, he doesn't feel safe at all.

CHAPTER 6

"*A*im for the center of the target."

Matteo's voice rips her from sleep. Renee bolts up in bed, fighting through sleep fog to figure out where she is. Where *they* are. She pats the bed beside her and finds cold flannel.

AJ!

She flies from her nest, feet tangling in blue-striped sheets. With a thundering heart, she sprints for the sound of voices.

"If you hit the middle, it's called a bullseye," Teo's saying. "We like bullseyes."

"Bulls-why."

"Close enough. Okay, point toward the middle. Got it?"

"Uh-huh."

"Widen your stance like I showed you."

"Dis?"

"Perfect. Ready? Aim. F—"

"Stop!" She sails through the bathroom door in the oversized shirt Teo loaned her. Hair in her face, eyes blurred with sleep, it doesn't click right away what she's seeing.

AJ?

Her son and Matteo stand by the toilet. AJ's on a stepstool,

74

with Matteo pointing to the bowl. Her ex's eyes do a slow slide up her body, lingering on her legs. "Good morning."

"Morning, Mama!" AJ beams. "I potty like a big boy."

She blinks at Matteo. "You're potty training."

"I hope that's okay." A frown. "He wandered out when I was taking care of business. Asked what I was doing, so I explained."

"I'm a big boy." AJ grins and turns back to his task. "Watch, Mama."

Glad she's five feet away, she steps back. Recalls what she's read in potty-training guides on positive reinforcement. "Good job, sweetheart."

"Aim down, buddy!" Matteo grabs a wad of Kleenex. "You want to hit the red circle next time."

"Red circle." AJ pulls up his pajama pants. "Red circle inside blue circle inside black circle."

"Yep." Matteo taps the sink. "Remember what's next?"

"Wash off germs." The boy drags his step stool and turns on the taps. "With soap, My Tail. See?"

"Good job." Teo lays a hand towel on the counter and winks at Renee. "We'll keep working on the target practice."

"I—" She's not sure what to say, so she puts a hand to her mouth. Checks for morning breath and wishes she kept mouthwash by the bed.

Matteo hands AJ the towel. "You'll be an excellent marksman before you know it."

"Marshman."

"Atta kid." He points to the toilet. "Gotta remember to flush, buddy."

"Hafta?"

"Yep. It's your duty." A quick glance at Renee. "Men take our duties seriously."

"So do women." Renee looks at the toilet. "Matteo?"

"Yeah?"

"Where did you get the floating target?"

"Made it." He washes his own hands while AJ pulls the toilet handle. "Some scissors, some Kleenex, some magic markers—voila. Instant target."

She's not sure what to say. No pleading. No tears. No bribing with snacks. He's just...potty training her son. "We've tried before. Just sitting on the potty, not standing. He wasn't into it, and the pediatrician said not to push."

"I promise, no pushing." Matteo rubs his hands on a towel. "It was his idea."

Guilt nibbles her heart. *Of course* her boy needs a male role model. *Of course* it would help with stuff like this.

"I'm impressed." And jealous. But mostly impressed.

Matteo's watching her. "Are you upset?"

"Not upset." Flabbergasted. Amazed. Confused by the fizz in her stomach. "Thank you. Really."

AJ throws his arms wide. "Hug, Mama. I did good?"

"You did great, baby." She squeezes tight, breathing his sweet scent. "Such a big boy."

"Big boy." He nuzzles her chest, and her heart liquifies.

Matteo moves out the door. "Breakfast is almost ready." He calls from the kitchen. "I've got cornetti coming out in ten minutes. Want to shower before or after?"

Renee follows with AJ on her heels. "We're—showering together?"

Matteo turns. "Wasn't the plan." He grins. "I'm open to new plans."

"No, that's—okay." God, she needs coffee. She darts for the bedroom with her face flaming. "I'll pull on clothes and be right out."

Slamming the door shut, she faces the mess. Yesterday's shorts and T-shirt lie crumpled where she left them. Ugh. The scent of grease clings to the shirt. There's mustard on the butt of her shorts, and she's only got yesterday's underpants.

Matteo yells from the next room. "I set some clean stuff on the dresser. Help yourself."

"Thank you." She leans against the door, struggling to catch her breath. A glance at the dresser reveals three women's shirts, a pair of yoga pants, and some jeans she can see are too small.

It's the thought that counts. She has several thoughts right now.

"I'm trapped in a beach house with a convicted felon." Muttering it aloud doesn't make it less weird. "A felon who potty trains my kid and bakes Italian pastries and saves me from wearing yesterday's gross clothes."

Still weird. And jealousy's tickling her tummy as she surveys the pile. The yoga pants could work, though they look tight in the waist and way too long. Whose are they, and when did Matteo bring her here?

The answer dawns as she shakes out a white shirt.

Bello Vineyards.

His sister, Jen. That makes sense.

As she shrugs off the sleep shirt, she curses herself for caring whom he dates. Since she's already cursing, she hurls more silent swears at the swell of her breasts. Turns to the mirror and frowns. Why did no one tell her how much breastfeeding would change things? She still overflows her old bras.

But she definitely can't go braless, so she wriggles into yesterday's bra. Considers the panties again, but can't bring herself to put them back on.

"Sorry, mystery lady whose clothes are in Matteo's house." She really hopes it's his sister as she puts on the yoga pants. "I'm going commando in your trousers."

When she tugs on the too-tight T-shirt, she looks less like a sagging porn star and more like...um, a clothed porn star?

Well. Nothing to be done for it now.

Padding back to the bathroom, she finds an unopened toothbrush stamped *Dr. Sebastian LaDouceur, DDS.* So he's really a dentist? She wasn't sure with that bodyguard schtick at the State Fair. She considers it as she brushes her teeth, curious about how Matteo met him. Back when they dated, she never knew his friends.

"I like that it's just the two of us." He said it as they snuggled in his big king bed. "I'll meet your friends if you want?"

She didn't want. There were a few casual friends at the diner where she waitressed. None of that long-term gal pal stuff most women had. Too much moving during high school. Too much working afterward, when her friends went off to college.

Besides, she loved being alone with him. Matteo's house felt warm and cozy. He'd cook dinner—some Dovlanese or Italian dish he'd learned from his grandma. They'd eat at the table or curl up on his big, clean couch that looked nothing like her slip-covered mess.

The oven's ding pulls her back to the beach house. Then Matteo's voice. "Stand back, buddy. It's hot."

Rinsing and spitting, she tries not to feel anything. No tug of fondness or longing for what used to be. No admiration for how he is with AJ.

She finger-combs her hair, wishing for a brush. There's one in her purse, plus lipstick and mascara. But she'd have to trudge through the living room, and no way will she admit she cares what she looks like. Squaring her shoulders, she opens the bathroom door.

Her stomach growls as she pads to the dining room. "That smells amazing."

"My grandma's cornetto recipe." He slides one of the croissant-like pastries onto a plate and hands it to her. "Butter and jam on the table."

"Did you go grocery shopping?"

"Didn't have to." He piles more pastries on a plate as she settles at the table beside AJ. "Jen came last week and left stuff for Nic. They trade off tending the place."

"Oh my gosh, Nicole!" How could she forget? "I need to tell her AJ might miss school."

"Already did." He takes a seat at the head of the table. "Stop looking worried."

"I'm not worried." *Fretful*, maybe...

"Nic's good at keeping secrets," he says. "I didn't tell her much, anyway. Just that you're safe with me, and AJ's out for a little bit."

"I—thank you." She wants to be annoyed he's taking over her life. He might run it better than she does.

Turning to AJ, she smiles at his jam-sticky face. "Is that good?"

"Yummy!" He licks his fingers. "More?"

"More what?"

His little brow furrows. "More corn-lettle?

Stifling a smile, she shakes her head. "Nice try."

Matteo reaches past her for the jelly. "Come on, bud. What's the magic word you say when you want something?"

"Please?" AJ bounces. "Pleeeeeease?"

Handing him a cornetto, she notices his chair. "You've got a booster seat?"

"My Tail gave." He grins and bites a hunk of pastry. "It gots Army guys."

"Oh." She scans the faded vinyl. It's printed with gun-toting green figures like the plastic toys a foster brother played with.

"Sorry about the guns." Matteo's sheepish as he grabs a cornetto. "It's all we had."

"I'm impressed you had a booster seat at all." Her first bite of pastry has her stifling a groan. She'd forgotten he bakes like a god. "Did you borrow it from somewhere?"

"Nondi had it made for us." He doesn't look at her as he slathers jam on his pastry. "Nicole went through an Army guy phase. She was so tiny she used it 'til she was probably seven, and then Jen got it."

"God, this is good." She takes another bite and sighs. "I always wished I'd gotten this recipe from you."

He lifts one eyebrow as he picks up his pastry. "Then you wouldn't need me."

Belly fluttering, she looks at her plate. "The jelly's delicious. Boysenberry?"

"Close. Loganberry. Jen grew them herself."

"I love how you've stayed close with your sisters." She watches him wince and reminds herself not to say *prison*. "Some adult siblings grow apart, but the three of you—"

"Have a lot in common." A small smile. "Nothing like a weird upbringing to keep you close."

"I'm glad." She tries to recall what Nicole shared about their youngest sister. "Didn't Jen get married recently?"

"Engaged." His eyes warm a little. "Good guy, the fiancé. A buddy of mine. Bald guy from the fair."

"*Him?*"

Matteo laughs. "He looks scarier than he is." A pause. "Scratch that. He's plenty scary. But only if you're a bad guy. If you're not, he's a marshmallow."

"Schmallow." AJ tries to grab another pastry. "No schmallows for bad guys."

"That's right." Matteo looks at her. "Okay if he has more?"

"Sure." She splits one in two and sets half on his plate. "Sooo… what are you doing for work these days?"

Is that a bad thing to ask a guy who just got out of prison? He's focused on his pastry, covering it with jam, so she can't read his expression.

"There's this tech firm in Seattle." He's not meeting her eyes. "Recruited me pretty hard before…*before*." He clears his throat. "Not sure if they'll still have me, but I'm hopeful. There's a remote job that'd be perfect."

"Good for you." She takes a bite of her own pastry. Delicious. "I'm sorry if this is pulling you away from that."

"Nah, it's the weekend." He looks at her. "You're an executive recruiter now?"

God only knows how he learned that. "I left the diner in a hurry. My boss didn't want to lose me. Put me in touch with headquarters and they trained me as a headhunter."

"Headhunter?" He frowns. "Something's lost in translation here."

She laughs and sips her coffee. Tons of cream and sugar, just how she likes it. Maybe they didn't meet each other's friends, but he knows her taste.

"Headhunters recruit people for certain jobs," she says. "In my case, I find chefs and waitstaff and restaurant managers. That sort of thing. I can do it from anywhere, and they're careful about protecting my privacy."

"Sounds like something you'd be good at. You always had a way with people."

A tap at the door snaps his gaze to the front hall. Matteo frowns and slips a hand in his sweatshirt pocket.

Renee gulps. "You've got a g—"

"—text from Seb saying he's almost here." He holds the phone as he stands. "I'll get the door."

"Right." She pulls a cloth napkin from a basket at the center of the table and wipes AJ's face. "How are you doing, buddy?"

"Good!" Another bite of pastry sends a shower of crumbs down his shirt. "More yelly?"

"You've got enough jelly." More jelly than cornetto. Her baby has a sweet tooth. "Drink your milk."

"Okay, Mama."

Milk. He poured *milk* for her son. It's even in a sippy cup. She takes another swig from her coffee. For a man who never let her in, he's got plenty of intel on her.

"Miss Nicole!" AJ bounces on his booster as the teacher strides in.

"Hey, little man!" Nicole's blond hair twists up in a ponytail. Faded jeans hug her legs. "Good to see you, Renee."

She's using her real name. What else did Matteo share? "This is a nice surprise."

"Just checking up on my favorite family." She winks, but there's worry in her eyes. "Everything okay?"

She recalls a line in the school handbook. The phrase she's meant to say if she needs help.

I have a headache, but I'm great otherwise!

"Everything's fine." She smiles so AJ knows it's true. "Just felt like getting away to the beach."

The dentist walks in looking vaguely befuddled. "She insisted on coming," he's muttering to Matteo. "Climbed in my car and wouldn't get out."

"Sounds like Nic." Matteo pours coffee in two white mugs.

Nicole ignores them and sits on AJ's other side. "I brought some of your schoolwork." She sets a tote bag on the table. "I wanted to make sure you don't miss any of the good art projects."

"Yay!" Her boy squeals as she hands him Crayolas. "I color."

"Oh, Nicole." Renee blinks back tears. "Thank you."

"My pleasure." She squeezes Renee's hand with a knowing look. "Maintaining normalcy is so important when things go sideways."

"Of course."

Nic knows better than most. It's why Renee picked Miss Gigglewink's.

Dr. LaDouceur leans on the kitchen bar as Matteo pours more coffee. "I put your stuff in the big bedroom off the hall," he tells Renee. "Looked like that's where you're staying?"

"Thank you." She rises, wiping crumbs from her hands. "I'd have showered if I'd known we had company coming."

"Please." Nicole plucks a pastry from the basket. "You look great, as always."

Matteo shoves the jam jar at his sister. "Help yourself."

"Already am." She's grinning as she smears jelly on a pastry. "You know I can't resist Nondi's cornetti."

"At what point are they *my* cornetti?" he mutters. "I've been baking them more than two decades."

It's not a question that needs answers, so no one gives him one. Dr. LaDouceur's still leaning on the kitchen counter, and Matteo joins him. "Any news on our friend?"

Renee straightens. The head tilt in her direction tells her there's no friend in this equation. They mean her stalker.

"Nothing new." Dr. LaDouceur frowns. "Still chasing down a few angles."

She looks at AJ, who's happily flipping through a book Nicole's holding for him. The teacher hands it over.

"You loved *Duck and Goose* last week." Nicole's a pro at distracting kids. "Since you're here at the coast," she continues, "I thought you'd like *Duck and Goose Go to the Beach*."

"Yeah!" AJ flips to the first page and touches a drawing of seashells. "Beach."

Renee carts her plate to the sink. Dr. LaDouceur is murmuring to Matteo. "...drove around a lot to make sure we weren't followed," he says. "This place has security cameras?"

Matteo frowns. "I'll take care of it."

Renee bumps his arm as she moves to the dishwasher. "How long are we staying here?"

Matteo's frown deepens. "Until we figure out what the fu—nky town is going on." He glances at AJ. "For now, we're safe here."

Dr. LaDouceur looks at her. "Need extra toothbrushes?"

"We're good." She bites her lip. "Would you all mind if I grabbed a shower quickly?"

"Take your time." Nicole turns in her chair. "Does our main man need a diaper change?"

"Thanks, but I'm good." Dr. LaDouceur's wink earns an eye roll from Nic.

"Come on, AJ." Nicole stands and holds out a hand. "Should we take a look?"

"I go in the potty." AJ looks at her. "Right, Mama?"

"You did." She smiles at Nic's wide-eyed response. "Your brother's been potty training."

"Good job, buddy." Dr. La Douceur elbows Matteo. "Now that we've got you out of diapers, we should teach you to tie your shoes."

Matteo ignores him. "AJ did great."

Nicole helps AJ from his booster seat and smiles at Renee. "Figures. He potty-trained Jen and me."

Renee gapes. "Seriously?"

"My brother's a dork, but he's got the magic kid touch." She sets AJ on the floor. "I've got some big-boy pullups in my bag. Want to try one, just in case?"

"Big boy." He scampers to where Nicole set a sand pail and shovel. "Beach?"

Nicole looks back at Renee. "I wasn't sure about the rules."

Renee's not, either.

Matteo points his sister to the sliding door. "Remember that little alcove below the rocks?"

"Oh, that's perfect." She offers Renee a reassuring smile. "Very hidden. No exposure walking down there."

Matteo watches her face. "You okay with that?"

"Are you?"

"Yeah." His eyes scan AJ and warm. "As long as they stay close. Away from any open areas."

Dr. LaDouceur pushes off the counter. "I'll go with."

"Because we need a big, burly man to protect us." Nicole rolls her eyes. "It's fine. Strength in numbers and all that."

The dentist's grin gets bigger. "I'm liking the part where you called me big and burly."

Nic ignores him to look at Renee. "You sure you're okay with the plan?"

"Mama, please?" AJ's got the sand pail in hand. "Magic word *pleeeease?*"

"All right." A glance at Matteo. "He's been begging to go down there since we got in last night. As long as you think it's okay—"

"Seb and Nic know what they're doing." Interesting word choice. "Go enjoy your shower."

"Okay." How long since she showered alone? Years, maybe. As a single mom with no family, she's always had a baby monitor or an open door. Sometimes a fussy toddler sharing the bath with her. Imagining herself solo, sudsy in the spray, warms her to the core.

Picturing herself with a partner...well. She can't go there.

"Thank you." She starts to clear the table as Matteo steps in.

"Leave it." His fingers brush hers as he takes the plate. "I've got this."

God. It's getting harder to hate him for ditching her.

"I owe you one." She starts for the bathroom. "I'll be quick."

"Girl, take your time." Nic's loading a mesh bag for the beach. "Take hours. Take a bubble bath if you want. My idiot brother could whip you up a mimosa."

"No champagne." Matteo, ever the realist. "We've gotta stay clearheaded. And it's a small water heater, so hours in the bath might be pushing it."

"Just a quick shower sounds good." Even two minutes alone sounds like heaven.

"Towels are in the hall closet." His eyes follow her. "I'll stand guard out here."

"Need to use the bathroom before Mommy goes in?" Nicole has AJ by the hand.

"Nuh-uh."

"Let's try a pullup then." Nic starts to steer him toward the bathroom, but he pulls back.

"Big boy." He squirms away. "No diaper."

"It's a pullup, not a diaper." Renee gives an encouraging smile. "Even big boys have accidents sometimes."

His little brow furrows. "My Tail have ass-idents?"

Renee struggles not to laugh. "There are all kinds of accidents." She stoops to zip his hoodie, kissing his soft cheek. "Big boys have bigger accidents."

"No ass-idents, Mama." Pressing his palms to her cheeks, he lands a sticky kiss on her chin. "Big boy."

"I love you, big boy." She squeezes him tight, then lets go. "Be good for Miss Nicole. Do whatever she tells you, okay?"

"Okay."

As he toddles off, Renee collects her things. A fluffy green towel from the cupboard. Her toiletries packed in a cloth bag on the dresser. She paws through the duffel they brought her, grateful for her own clothes. Grabbing denim capris and her favorite pink shirt, she piles them together with panties and a bra.

Her cheeks warm as she pictures the bald guy from the fair packing her things. Or Dr. LaDouceur, God forbid. At least they grabbed her curly girl shampoo, which she tucks under her arm and heads to the bathroom.

A door creaks at the other end of the house. "We'll text you beach pics," Nicole's saying. "So you know we're okay."

Matteo's low rumble. "You've got the burner phone?"

"It's not my first rodeo, big brother."

Renee slips through the bathroom door as they troop past with Dr. LaDouceur trailing Nic like a bemused puppy. A big, burly, bemused puppy who's admiring Nicole's ass.

Pulling the bathroom door shut, Renee sighs out gratitude. For Nic's ease with worried moms. For the two strapping men and a daycare owner giving her these blessed, blissful moments alone.

Assessing the shower, she finds the faucet. It's one of those fancy kinds with several levers and a detachable, handheld spray head. Must be a new addition, since the house seems older. She twists a knob but nothing happens.

Turns another dial, trying the other direction. Still nothing. "Huh."

She tries for the showerhead, but she's too short to reach it from this angle. "For crying out loud…"

Stripping off her socks, she stops at the edge. There's water puddled in the tub and these pants are too long. No sense soggying someone else's hem.

She takes off the pants and steps in. T-shirt tugging up over her bare butt, she stretches for the showerhead. That lever on top that might do something. If she could just reach it—

"Renee?" Matteo's voice sounds far away.

Not far enough. Did she lock the door?

"I'm in the bathroom." Like that wasn't obvious.

Footsteps draw close. "The shower's kinda tricky. Need help?"

"I'll figure it out."

"You sure?" More shuffling of feet. "It'll take two seconds for me to show you."

"It's fine, I'll get it." Nope, the lever on the showerhead just adjusts the angle. How to turn the water on? Stooping, she tries the tap handles again. Still nothing. Wait. Maybe if she pulls this lever on the side of the—

"Aaaaaargh!" She shrieks as icy water blasts her to the shower wall. It's cold and fast, and how the hell is there this much water pressure? "Ack, make it stop!"

The door bursts open and there's Matteo, wild-eyed with a knife. "Renee? What's wrong, are you hurt?"

Sputtering, she struggles to peel herself off the wall. "Get out! I've got this."

"You yelled 'make it stop.'"

"I was talking to *myself*." She sputters and tries to grab the handle.

"You scared me." He sets the knife on the counter and twists the taps. "It's the opposite of what you'd think. Left instead of right and then this one pulls down." Another twist and the water gets warm. "I installed it when I was sixteen and got it back-wards. Always meant to fix it, but—"

"Matteo! Jesus." With one hand over her breasts, she tugs the shirt hem down with the other. "Can you not see I'm nearly naked here?"

He straightens. Takes his time looking. From that slow, lazy smile, she knows he saw all along. "Thanks for the invite."

"What?" Water drips in her eyes, and she lets go of the shirt to swipe it away. "What invitation?"

"To look at you. I was trying not to, but since you suggested it—"

"You're such a jerk." It's fury bubbling inside her. Definitely not lust. Definitely not desire stoked by heat in his eyes.

The water's still running. Hot and steamy and not helping at all. Spitting hair from her mouth, she glares. "Why are you staring?"

A pause. "Because you're so fucking beautiful, I can't breathe."

The air leaves her lungs, and now they're both breathless. She should tell him to go. Just point to the door, order him out, and lock it behind him.

She lifts her hand, but her fingers won't comply. Her palm snares the back of his neck, and she drags him down to her. Blinking through steam, she looks deep in those green eyes.

"I hate you."

He nods. "You should."

"Leaving like you did—"

"I know," he breathes. "I'm a jerk, like you said."

This is a bad idea on so many levels. "Kiss me, jerk."

"Gladly." His mouth claims hers, hot and wet and hungry.

Water pours over her, rinsing off the anger. Wet cotton hugs her skin as his hands cup her bare butt. She squeezes her eyes shut to pretend this isn't happening. To savor the sensations.

She needs more. Needs *him*.

"Matteo." His name slips out on a gasp. "Please." She's not sure what she's asking, but her body knows. Gripping his shoulders, she draws him close so they're plastered together.

"Fuck, Renee." He's in jeans and a shirt—barefoot, thank God —and stumbles as she drags him into the tub. Recovering his footing, he boosts her up, pressing her back to the slick tile wall. Water drips off his face as he breaks the kiss. "You feel so fucking good."

"Don't stop." She pants it against the hot slick of his throat. "Don't you dare stop."

He doesn't stop. Doesn't hesitate to glide his hands over her bare ass, under her shirt, up her belly, over her ribs and...*oh God.* Why did she put on a bra?

It's no match for Teo. He flicks the clasp one-handed, spilling her breasts into his hands. She groans and presses into his palms.

"You're killing me." It's a growl in her ear. "I can't believe how good you feel."

"Yes. *Yes.*"

It's been years since anyone touched her like this. Scratch that. No one's *ever* touched her like him, his hands hot and huge and possessive. Groaning, she grips his shoulders and hops to twine her legs around his waist. He catches her easy, hands holding her ass as he pins her to the wall.

His kisses grow urgent as she grinds against him. The hot, hard bulge in his jeans is definitely not a knife.

"Off." She spits it between kisses, tugging the wet tee that clings to his back. How does she get this damn shirt off him?

"Sure." He grabs her hem and strips off her shirt, somehow keeping her pinned to the wall. How does he do that?

And how is she naked when he's...not?

"Not what I meant." She claws his shirt, ready to slice it off with her pink Daisy razor. "Need. Your. Skin." She's panting as she grinds on him, aware of how slippery she is.

It's been so long.

She somehow drags the shirt halfway up his back, and he

takes it from there. One hand on her ass, he peels off his tee. Bare skin meets hers, flesh licking flesh. With a moan, she spears her nails in his back. The wet heat between her legs isn't from the shower. She could come just like this.

He knows it, too. Breaking the kiss, he wipes a wet curl from her face. "I want to be inside you when you come."

"Do it." What is she saying?

He cups her breast in one huge hand. "I've waited this long. We need to savor."

Spoken like a man who doesn't live with a toddler. "Please, Matteo. I need you to f—"

His kiss cuts off the curse she shouldn't say anyway. *"Fuck"* hasn't graced her lips since AJ arrived. She's a responsible adult, a mother, for God's sake.

But here she is grinding naked on the man she swore to spend her life hating. "Please." She's *begging*. This is what it's come to.

If anything, he slows down. His thumb swirls agonizing circles around her nipple, and she shivers. Pushing her higher up the wall, he covers her with his mouth. "Perfect." He breathes it like a prayer. "You're so perfect."

"Please, Matteo." She's going to die. Just collapse like a corpse on the tile floor. "I need you inside me."

It's a bad idea, but she's been good for so long. Once won't count. Not when they've slept together hundreds of times. There's a condom in her makeup bag. Will one time really matter?

She drags her hands down his chest. "So much muscle." She's never been into big chests, but he's an exception. "You got ripped while you were—"

"Don't say it." His kiss stops her words.

Away. That's what she meant, not *in prison.* But she'll take more kissing. More touching to wipe out the questions buzzing her brain.

Why am I doing this?

Why does it feel so good?

What is that banging?

She comes up for air. "Matteo?"

"Mmmph." His mouth's at her breast, tongue teasing her nipple.

"Matteo, someone's here."

He jerks like she kicked him. Reeling, he sets her on the ground. Voices in the living room, three at least.

"Gotta go potty in the potty." That's AJ, and *oh God*—there goes her libido.

"Little man, wait." Nicole, of course. "Your mommy needs privacy."

"Gotta go, gotta go, *gottagogottago!*"

A dazed Matteo swipes a hand over his mouth. "Stay put." He leaps from the tub and jerks the curtain closed. It's navy blue and too dark for her to see through, which means no one can see in.

And she can't see AJ as he crashes through the door. "My Tail." Sneakers squeak to a stop. "You wet."

"I—uh—"

"You going potty?"

Never mind the shower's running. Her son seems laser-focused on his new skill. Denim crinkles as he shucks his pants, and there's a clang as someone lifts the toilet seat.

"Whoa, Matteo." Nic's voice ripples with laughter. "Did you have an accident?"

He clears his throat. "Problems with the shower."

"Sure." Nic knows he's full of it.

Renee shuts her eyes and slides down the shower wall. Maybe they won't guess she's here, except why is the water running? And cooling quickly. She crawls from the spray as a tepid puddle pools beneath her butt.

So much for romance.

"I'm...uh...fixing the shower." A clink tells her Matteo's

picked up the knife and stashed it somewhere. "It needs to run a few minutes to clear out the sediment."

"Whatever you say, big brother."

If Renee shuts her eyes, she can pretend this isn't happening. But that didn't work when she took the pregnancy test and tried to tune out those two blue lines. Wrenching her eyes open, she spots her soaked shirt on the shower floor.

"Shirt off."

AJ's voice makes her jump, but he's not talking to her. "Miss Nicole. Need shirt off."

"Your shirt?" Nic sounds perplexed.

"No shirt. Like My Tail." A swoosh of fabric says it's already happening.

"Wait, buddy." Matteo's voice now. "Why are you taking off your clothes?"

"Big boy." He tosses it so it hits the shower curtain, and Renee scoots back. There's a swath of orange showing through the part in the curtain, and she prays he doesn't come for it.

God, it's getting cold. But she can't switch off the water without someone noticing. Inching back, she seals the shower curtain shut with her foot.

"Big boys potty with no shirt." Her son's determination is absolute. "Need target."

How the hell is he holding it? There's no way he hasn't soiled his pullup. Her son's always been an exception, though. Leave it to AJ to have a bladder of steel.

"Oh. Uh, sure." A squeak as Matteo opens the medicine cabinet. Good Lord, how long can this take?

"Hurry, My Tail."

"I'm hurrying, I'm hurrying."

Renee slaps a hand on her mouth to keep from laughing, from crying, from throwing back the curtain and confessing to her son's teacher why she's sitting nude on the shower floor. She glares at the showerhead and its cursed cold water. Could a hookup get any worse?

"What's everyone doing in here?" *Oh, God*—Dr. LaDouceur.

Screw cold. Renee yanks on the wet shirt and wishes for a towel. Maybe the drain to suck her down.

"*We* are going potty." Nicole sounds haughty, so she's addressing the dentist. "Did you need a lesson?"

"I mean, if you want me to take out the trouser snake—"

"Ew, no. Hands off the zipper, Minty Fresh. I definitely *don't* want."

"Suit yourself."

The water's icy now. How long will this last? Maybe Renee could turn the showerhead to blast the wall instead of the shower floor.

"Almost done, buddy?" Matteo sounds strained.

"Uh-huh."

"Shy bladder," Nicole murmurs. "Common with potty training."

Renee closes her eyes and prays for this to end.

Dr. LaDouceur again. "Look, it's probably nothing. But do you know anyone with a red Toyota Prius?"

"A Prius?" Matteo's hand slips through the curtain. As Renee stares, he makes a swirly motion with his fingers.

He wants to fool around *now*?

"Sediment's cleared." Matteo clears his throat. "Just gonna go ahead and turn the taps."

Right, okay. He's letting her know he's turning off the water. He twists the handles, and she sighs with relief.

But relief's short-lived.

Crash.

A blast from the living room. Is that glass shattering?

"Get down!" That's Matteo, sounding frantic. "AJ, stay right here! You understand?"

"Where's Mommy?"

Oh, God. She wants to reach for him. To pull him into her arms and hold him against her breast. But her breasts are plastered with wet cotton, and she'll scare him if she leaps out like a crazed and dripping stripper.

Someone takes off running. "Stay here!" It's Dr. LaDouceur. Something tells her he's armed.

"The hell I will." Nic's voice, Nic's footsteps. Renee recalls daycare orientation.

"I don't allow weapons in the classroom," Nic assured her as they filled out confidentiality forms. "But if anything threatens your child—threatens any of our children—you have my word I will defend them."

Scared as she is, *naked* as she is, Renee's grateful for friends with those instincts.

"You're doing great, buddy." Matteo's voice sounds close to the door. She knows without looking he's blocking it with his body. "Anyone ever tell you, you've got remarkable focus?"

"Fuckus?"

"Close enough." A pause. "You'd be a great sniper."

"Whassa sniper?"

Renee squeezes her eyes shut and reminds herself to kill her ex-lover.

"It's, uh…" He may not have meant to say that out loud. "A baker. Someone who bakes cakes."

"I like cake." A flush. "All done, My Tail."

"Nice work." Matteo's voice sounds cool and calm. "Wash your hands. And let's get you a fresh T-shirt."

"This one." Her son's small hand snakes out to grab the one by the shower curtain. "I like."

"I know you do, bud. But it's wet from sitting in a puddle."

There's fussing and flushing and a sound of arguing from the living room. Renee shivers, wondering what's happening. If they're in danger. If her son's in danger.

"Let's head in here." Matteo's voice moves to the bedroom next door. "Here's shirts to pick from. How many?"

"Five."

"Good job." The creak of a door pulled shut. "I need you to stay right here and study these five shirts, okay? Really look 'em over, decide which one's best."

AJ loves tasks like this. "One red, two blue, one stripes, one brown."

"Exactly. You stay right here and decide which one to wear. Really think about it."

"Uh-huh."

"Don't come out of this room until I say to. Promise?"

"Promish."

Renee bites her knuckles.

"I'll just be gone a minute."

"Okay, My Tail."

"I'll close the door for privacy."

"Pricey?"

"Yep." A thud as the door shuts. Then footsteps as three adults clomp into the bathroom.

"Renee?" Nic drapes a blue terrycloth robe over the top of the curtain. "You okay in there?"

She pulls on the robe, shuddering from more than cold. "I'm fine." Grateful to be upright, she throws back the curtain. "What happened?"

Nic looks at Matteo. Something passes between them. Something dark and dangerous and chilling.

Dr. LaDouceur meets her eyes. "I'm sorry, Renee." His jaw clenches. "You've been found."

CHAPTER 7

*M*atteo curses and scans the trunk of Renee's car. "I'm so fucking stupid."

"Says the guy with the genius IQ." A seagull squawks as Sebastian punches him in the shoulder. "Don't be so hard on yourself. You had to haul ass leaving the fairgrounds."

"Not an excuse." He grabs the tracker from Renee's trunk and shoves it in his pocket. He wants to smash it in a million bits but needs to study it first. Find out who planted it. "How'd you get rid of him?"

"The shit who shot out your living room window?"

"Yeah."

"I didn't." There's a smile in Seb's voice. "Your sister did."

"Nic?" Figures.

Matteo sucks in some salt air. His favorite smell when Nondi brought them here as kids. She'd throw sticks down the beach for Jen's dog to fetch. After, they'd eat clam chowder in paper bowls as sea mist kissed their faces. The shush of waves always soothed him.

He's not soothed now. He's edgy and angry and needs to get back inside to make sure Renee and AJ are safe.

Seb's still dissecting the shootout. "Your sister whipped out a pop gun and returned fire." He sounds delighted. "Clipped the guy in the shoulder with a nine-millimeter from over a hundred yards. I didn't even know she was carrying."

"Nic's a good shot." They learned together, Nondi supervising as they lined cans on the fence and fired until their arms ached. "She hit him, huh?"

"Just a graze, but yeah." Seb scuffs a toe through the gravel. "Got the sense she'd have hit him square in the head if she wanted to."

"Nic's smart. Knows we'd need him alive for questions." Questions like *"who the fuck are you and why are you stalking the woman I love?"*

Not *love*; that's dumb. He's not capable of love. He shakes his head to clear it. "Which way did he go?"

"North down the beach. Tried to go after him, but your sister thought it might be a trap."

"Could be."

"You should have seen her." Seb's like an awestruck kid. "Aimed like a pro. Very hot."

Matteo glares. "That's my little sister."

"Technically," he points out, "your little sister sleeps with Dante." He grins and leans against the car. "Your middle sister's fair game."

He glares some more. "Are you egging me on as a distraction?"

"Is it working?"

"No." Matteo kicks the gravel. "Nic wouldn't give you the time of day."

"I like a good challenge." He's entirely too cheerful for a guy giving up his Saturday to dodge gunfire and a woman who hates his guts.

"Come on, focus." Matteo slams the trunk and stares at the ocean. No answers there. Just a bunch of drunk seagulls flapping at foamy gray waves. "What's Dante finding back in town?"

"Nothing yet." That wipes the smile off Seb's voice. "We set up surveillance at her place. Dante's got an eye on things. If the bastard's watching, he knows she's not home."

"Because he knows we're *here*." Goddammit. This was meant to be a safe space. He took precautions, got them here without incident. Prison made him rusty. "I can't keep them safe here."

"True." A pause. "You thinking what I'm thinking?"

He scowls. "If it involves my sister, no."

"Sick fuck." Seb jerks a thumb toward the garage. "Granny's camper is a pretty slick ride."

"You've been casing my garage?"

Seb shrugs. "Dante mentioned it. He plans to take it camping next month."

"It still runs?"

"Apparently. He and Jen had it tuned up." Seb scrubs a hand over his chin. "Seems like a sweet mobile setup for someone on the run."

He hates the thought of running. He's done it too much to have any pride left.

Screw pride. There's Renee and AJ to consider. "We need to sweep for trackers. *Thoroughly*."

"On it." Seb pushes off the car, then pauses. "It's great, what you're doing. I'm impressed."

"What am I doing?"

"Keeping her safe. Keeping the kid safe." Seb shoves his hands in his pockets and looks like a goddamn movie star. "Not sure I could do it. I'd worry all the time that having me around does more harm than good."

Crushed ice churns in his stomach. "That's a concern."

"Nah, you're doing great." Seb slaps him on the shoulder. "Guys like us don't get a shot at happy endings much. But look at Dante."

Matteo grits his teeth. Tries to focus on his friend's good fortune. "He makes Jen happy."

"Sure does."

But now he can't stop seeing Jen in jeopardy. Jen kidnapped and afraid with a gun to her head like she was months ago. He wasn't there when she needed him. He was stuck behind bars like a useless piece of—

"Get out of your head." Seb kicks gravel at his shoe. "Has she admitted yet that the kid is yours?"

Matteo's still stuck on his sister, so it takes him a second to catch up. "AJ? Renee won't say." Yet. "Doesn't trust me."

"Yet." Seb grins. "Keep 'em safe, and maybe she'll change her tune."

And if he doesn't keep her safe?

"Just don't ditch her again." Seb starts backing toward the garage. "Prove you're sticking around this time."

"What if sticking around is the last thing she needs?" Seb's right that he could do more harm than good. Renee's a mom now. "What if—"

"One thing at a time, Teo." Seb waves him off. "Go. Get packed while I scan your camper van."

"We can't just leave Renee's car." Hell, Jen's truck is still at the fairgrounds.

"We already got Jen's truck." The man's a mind reader. "And I'll drive Renee's car back. Nicole can drive my car."

He scowls at Seb's BMW. "You sure she's safe in that? If someone followed you here—"

"*We* weren't followed. *You* were." He points to the pocket where Matteo stashed the tracker. "And yes, Nic's safe in my car. It's got bulletproof glass, remember?"

Right. The asshole thinks of everything. "I need you guys on this one. You and Dante. If you've got time—"

"We've always got time for a friend." He grins. "Gotta keep the skills sharp."

"I need to know who's after her." Seb brought Matteo his laptop, but being on the road limits him. "Ex-boyfriends, old bosses, former foster homes, her fucked-up family." Hell, his own associates or even shady cops. Could one of them have a reason to threaten her? "Anything's fair game," he says. "Someone's trying to get to her. We need to know who."

"On it." Seb shifts toward the garage again but doesn't go. "Sorry we busted up the shower shag."

"Nothing's going on."

Seb doesn't pretend to believe that. "She seems smart. Pretty and funny, with a good head on her shoulders."

"Don't."

"I'm not." He backs away. "But don't think I don't see you looking at her like you've spent two years starving and she's a side of prime rib."

Matteo growls. "You did not just compare the mother of my child to a slab of beef."

"Maybe your fish don't even swim."

"Fuck you."

"And this is why we don't have heart-to-hearts about our love lives." Seb's still chuckling as he walks away.

"Goddammit." Matteo drags a hand down his face and sighs. He needs a plan. Scans the sea for inspiration. It's gray and choppy with wicked whitecaps. Wet sand spreads like glittery peanut butter dotted with driftwood. A family strolls the shore, jeans cuffed at their knees. Two pigtailed girls run barefoot while their parents hold hands, stopping to pick up agates.

Teo's chest aches. He'll never have that.

Focus.

Where to hide? He needs to buy them time to identify the enemy.

The Oregon Outback.

An isolated part of the state not known by many tourists. Desolate desert sprawls for endless miles with a few lonely ranches dotting the fringe. There's surprisingly strong Wi-Fi out there. He can hack systems from the road, doing his part to find her stalker.

Fingering the tracker in his pocket, he shoves off the car. He'll do what it takes to keep them safe.

Even if it means leaving when this is over.

* * *

"Your camper van is...interesting."

Matteo looks up from tinkering with a security camera. "My grandmother sewed those curtains years ago." He watches Renee stroke the floral fabric, twisting a stem around one finger. "Jen loved the squirrels holding daisies. Nondi made extras for when they faded."

"They're nice, but I didn't mean the curtains." She points to the berth where AJ's napping. "Call me nuts, but I don't think most RVs have bulletproof safe rooms."

"Nondi was big on security." Seems normal enough to him. "Don't worry—our berth's bulletproof, too."

"Our berth, huh?" She's smiling as she sits on the queen-sized mattress. "How quickly you talk your way back into bed with me."

"Uh—" How does he gauge that? She could be flirting, could be accusing. Best to play it safe. "I'm being practical. The kids' berth is too short for adults." Nondi had it built for the three Bello children.

Renee's staring like he missed the point, and maybe he has.

"We can keep all our clothes on," he continues. "We could even put a pillow between us if you—"

"I'm not worried you'll grope me in your sleep, Matteo." She's definitely smiling, so that's...good? Or not. "I trust you to be a gentleman."

That makes one of them. Awake or asleep, he's not sure how he'll keep his hands off her. She changed into yoga pants for the six-hour road trip. They hug her lower half like he'd love to do, and that T-shirt—how does plain pink cotton look that good? And she's on the bed, for God's sake. The bed where he'd like to lay her back and—

"We're safe here." Teo clears his throat. "I'll make sure."

"I know you will." She scans the space and shakes her head. "This thing is crazy. An actual gun turret mounted on top?"

"Nondi bought it like that." He never questioned it as a kid. "It's well hidden. AJ won't spot it behind the solar panels." He wouldn't have pointed it out if Renee hadn't seen it.

A deep sigh swells her breasts. "This is all so *strange.*"

"Being on the run from stalking weirdos?"

"That, sure." She sweeps a hand at the cabinet storing night-vision goggles. "I meant the camper. It never seemed like overkill to you?"

"Not really." He considers it as he slips the security camera in its housing. "We were kids when Nondi took us touring. By the time we were old enough to ask questions, we'd mostly outgrown it."

Renee leans back on her elbows, then sits up quick and looks behind her. "Wait, where's that button you showed me?"

"The one for the escape hatch?" He points his screwdriver to the opposite wall. "Over there. You're good on that side of the bed."

"Right." She sinks back down and gives him a look. "What did you say your grandma did for work?"

"I didn't." His family ties to the Dovlanese mob aren't something he broadcasts. "Nondi came to America with some savings. Multiplied it in stocks and real estate. She was always good with money."

Renee scans the panel over the gun safe. The cupboard where he showed her Nondi's stash of bulletproof vests. *A survivalist.* He didn't know the term as a kid, but that's what she was. He's pretty sure, anyway.

"It's just...interesting."

He looks at Renee. "What's interesting?"

"All this. The camper." She shifts, and he tries not to watch her breasts move. "I had foster families with strange homes and habits and rituals, but this doomsday camper is next-level."

He sets down the screwdriver and looks around. Tries to see it through her eyes. There's a panel by the door for the alarm system. A glass case filled with knickknacks built to hide a set of throwing knives. Under the dinette, the gas masks he glossed over when he gave the tour and...okay, yeah. Some of this is strange.

He clears his throat. "Give me an example."

Renee cocks her head. "An example of what?"

"Of strange family rituals. From your father, maybe?"

She gives him a dry look. "Robbing banks isn't something Ward Cleaver did a whole lot."

Bad example. "How about ones you saw in foster homes?"

"Okay, let me think." She leans back on her elbows to get comfortable.

It's making him *uncomfortable* because Jesus—did her breasts get more perfect? He turns so she can't see it's affecting him. Fiddling with screws on this housing should shrink what's swelling in his jeans if he just—

"One family had this big bone."

He looks up. "What?"

"A femur, I think. That's the big leg bone, right?"

"You mean a real human femur?"

"I'm not sure, honestly." She sits up fast and there's a whole lot of movement in that shirt. "I was twelve, maybe thirteen. At the time I thought it was plastic, but it did feel awfully real. And the father was a funeral director, so..."

"Jesus. Okay, that's weird."

"That's not the weird part." She grins and tucks her legs under her. "They had this game called hide-the-bone."

"I'm familiar."

"Perv." She swats at him and misses. "They'd take turns hiding the femur around the house. Like, someone would stick it in the dishwasher, and the person who found it became 'it.'"

"It? Like Stephen King?"

"No, like hide-and-seek. Then it's the new person's turn to hide the bone and they might stick it under the bathroom sink or in someone's bed or maybe in the garage. They thought it was funny."

He stares at her. "And you think Nondi's rolling safe house is weird?"

She laughs. "Point taken."

Now she's got him curious. "How did someone win hide-the-bone?"

The light dims in her eyes. "You know, I'm not sure." She looks down at her lap. "The family moved to Idaho, and it was too much trouble to take me. The paperwork or whatever. I went back into the system."

His fist clamps the screwdriver. He hates them all. Her father. Her mother. Her endless line of foster families. Hates anyone who'd treat a child as expendable. "If your dad were alive, I'd punch him in the face."

"Don't say that." She sighs. "He wasn't a horrible guy."

"Apart from the criminal activity?"

Renee lifts an eyebrow. "Did you really just say that?"

She's got him there. "Not all criminals are terrible people. But most criminals are terrible fathers." He needs to remember that.

"Your turn." Renee rolls over and fluffs a pillow. "Tell me something else weird about your family."

"I doubt I can top treating a human femur as a fun family game." He thinks about it for a minute. "My grandma won a martial arts tournament at sixty-two."

"Did she live in Dovlano in 1962?"

"No—*at* sixty-two. She set out to do it before she turned

seventy." Teo smiles fondly. "She was always an overachiever."

"No kidding? That's awesome."

"You should have seen the guy she beat in the finals. Big dude —Army Ranger off his third tour in Iraq."

"Wait." She's frowning now. "I thought you meant some sort of senior tournament."

"Nope, a regular one."

Now she looks perplexed. "How old was her opponent?"

Matteo rubs his chin and tries to recall. "Thirty, thirty-five maybe?"

"Holy cannoli, Matteo!" She darts a glance to the berth where AJ's napping. "That's soundproof, right?"

"Yep."

She's bouncing on the bed, making everything else bounce with it. *Goddamn.*

"That's nuts!" She laughs and stops moving. "I can't believe your grandma kicked ass on a guy half her age."

"She was quite the woman." Sorrow hugs his heart with icy arms. "She retired when Nic beat her in the championships. Nondi was so proud. Took us all out for ice cream after—"

"Wait." She lifts a hand. "Back up the truck. Your sister fought her grandmother in a martial arts tournament?"

She says it like it's not normal, but he's pretty sure it is. There were tons of other families at the tournament. Maybe not fighting each other, but—

"Nondi trained Nic herself." Surely *that* makes it normal. "Jen wasn't interested. Said she didn't have the heart for it." Familial affection pokes an edge of his mouth. "I've got one sister heavily into humane farming practices and another who shot a guy in a daycare parking lot."

"*What?*" She's off the bed in a flash. "AJ's teacher *shot* someone? At the school?"

Crap. He assumed she knew. It was in the news, but that's been a while and...okay, maybe it wasn't common knowledge.

"She didn't kill him." Maybe he can fix this. "The guy she shot was an escaped child abuser who took a kid at gunpoint. Nic called the cops and let him reach his car, so no one got caught in the crossfire. But the guy tried to leave, so…yeah. She took him out."

This all sounded better in his head. Judging by her expression, it's not the fuzzy family story he thought it was.

"She wasn't charged with anything." He should wrap this up fast. "Self-defense, since the guy fired first, and the kid was totally okay. Got a lollipop afterward." Matteo clears his throat. "Your turn."

Renee blinks. "What?"

"To tell a story about weird family dynamics."

"There's no way I can top that."

"Try." Anything to ebb this self-consciousness.

She shakes her head. "I've got nothing even close." Her brow furrows as she gives it some thought. "Maybe the family that summoned each other in stores by meowing."

"Meowing?"

"Yeah." Uncrossing her legs, she lets one dangle off the bed. "The mom would take us all grocery shopping, and we'd scatter in a thousand different directions. When she wanted us back, she'd just…meow."

"Like a cat?"

"You know another animal that meows?"

"Squirrels." He read it in a science text. "It's a biological defense against predators that wouldn't fear squirrels but might fear cats."

She stares at him for a very long time. "You are a strange man, Matteo."

Brown eyes hold his, and his chest caves in on itself. *That look.* The way she smiles with her eyes. The way she calls him strange like it's a plus and not a minus. "You've always had a taste for strange."

"No kidding, huh?" Rolling her eyes, she flops back on the bed. "I guess that's how I ended up nude in the shower climbing you like a jungle gym."

Oh. "We're going there?"

She turns to face him. "You'd rather we just avoid uncomfortable conversations like we did when we were dating?"

"Kinda." That's not helping. "Okay. We can talk about it."

She sighs and props her head on her hand. "I have a son now, Matteo. I can't go making rash decisions to quench my libido."

"Understood." Mostly. He kinda likes her rash decisions.

"I'm no longer the party girl who keeps a flask and spare panties in her purse."

He nods and drags his eyes off the curve of her hip. "And I have a prison record. *Expunged*," he adds quickly. "But no one does hard time without coming out changed."

She bites her lip. "You're right." A pause. "I'm sorry that happened to you. In case I haven't said that."

"It's okay."

"It's *not* okay. Did they at least punish the cop who set you up?"

Teo's temper flares. "No." He'd like to change the subject. "Anyway, it's behind me."

Renee's shaking her head. "I still can't believe they locked up a man who wasn't guilty."

One edge of his mouth tugs up. "Not of that particular crime."

She laughs and shakes her head. "Jesus. Considering my dad, you'd think I'd swear off bad boys forever."

"I'm not *that* bad." Sometimes he thinks he could even be good. "I *have* changed, Renee. The stuff I was doing before—"

"Which you never actually told me about."

"Right." He sighs. "The less you know—"

"If you finish that sentence with 'the better,' so help me God, I'll strangle you with your shoelace."

He'd kinda like to see that.

He'd also like to be better about opening up. Setting down the screwdriver, he locks his eyes with hers. "Look, I really can't tell you everything."

"Have I ever asked you to?"

Not once. Not ever. Renee's never pushed. "I would if I could." He spins in his seat, needing to face her head-on. "I want to make you a promise, okay?"

"Okay." She's wary, and he doesn't blame her.

This feels weird not touching her. He hesitates. Gets up and eases to the bed beside her. Lies on his side so they're facing each other. "Is this okay?"

"Yeah." She sounds a bit breathless.

They're two feet apart but not touching. The way her eyes hold his, they may as well be. He aches to reach for her, but something holds him back. "I may not be able to tell you everything about my life. Who I am, what I've done." He draws a breath and sees his hand shaking. He starts to shove it under the pillow but stops. Lays it on the bed between them like an offering.

She's looking at it when he speaks again. "I can promise you one thing."

"What?" Her gaze drifts to his face. Back to his hand again. Fingertips move to stroke his knuckles. It's almost too much, and he closes his eyes to say the rest.

"I can't promise to tell you everything," he says. "But I can promise when I tell you something, it'll be the truth."

"Okay." Her voice is a whisper. "That's something."

It's more than something. It's everything. Everything he's never been able to give. If he doesn't open his eyes, he's going to miss it.

When he looks up, she's staring at his throat. Not his throat —*the scar.*

As she lifts her fingers to touch it, he holds very, very still. "How did you get this?" She's asked a hundred times. A running joke between them. Her lips twitch at the memory. "You used to make up stories. Remember?"

His nod is hardly a nod. "Tragic spatula mishap?"

"A fight with an angry turtle?" She laughs. "My favorite was the hula hoop accident."

"Mine's the one where I called it an allergic reaction to your bra."

Another laugh. "Bonus points for creativity." She's still touching him, skimming her thumb up and down the line. "Will you tell me now?"

He hesitates. It's a basket of larvae he shouldn't open.

Larva? That's not right. "Worms," he says. "A can of worms."

Renee blinks. "You cut yourself on a can of worms?"

The moment's gone.

Or maybe not. She's not disappointed. And she's still touching him, fingers gliding slow and sure against his skin. "You have the warmest skin. You're like a human heater."

"Renee." He breathes her name and feels his heart squeeze. "Can I kiss you?"

"Yes." Perfect lips part. "Yes, please."

He moves slowly, needing this to be different. The hot, steamy hunger in the shower—was that only this morning?

That's not what this is.

His lips touch hers, and she breathes him in. Soft, so soft, as he lifts a hand to her hip. She touches his face, fingers drawing over his cheekbone, his jaw, his ear. He squeezes his eyes shut and then opens them again, needing to see her. To tell her he loves her, he's always loved her. That he wants to kiss her again and again and—

"Mama?" AJ's voice calls from his berth.

Renee draws back and smiles. "To be continued."

His heart sucks into his throat, and now he can't swallow. "Right."

She gets off the bed, splatting his heart on the floor beside it.

CHAPTER 8

*I*t's dark when she wakes. She lies blinking in the blackness, flannel sheets bunched at her breasts. She's in a tank top and sleep shorts, fist gripped around the hard, solid length of...

"Oh, God." She yanks her hand back as her face goes hot.

"That's a first." Matteo's voice, close to her ear.

She squeezes her eyes shut in the dark. Maybe he'll think she's asleep.

"I know you're awake, Renee." There's laughter in the sleepy growl. "Your throat moves when you swallow."

Rolling to face him, she opens her eyes. "What kind of creeper stares at a woman's throat while she sleeps?"

"The kind who wakes up to said woman squeezing his cock." He tucks a curl behind her ear. "I've heard of sleepwalking and sleep talking, but never a sleep hand job. That's a first."

"It was an accident." She flops her head back on the pillow and prays he doesn't press.

"Whatever you say."

"I was dreaming." Why is she still talking?

Matteo's quiet. "What were you dreaming about?"

She shouldn't say. She absolutely shouldn't— "About our last night together. Do you remember?"

He's quiet for so long, she's sure he's forgotten. "We were at your place," he says softly. "On your Grandma's old couch."

It sounds weird when he puts it that way. "Your first time coming over." She can't believe she's saying this. "I'd bought the new slipcovers. I wanted to impress you."

"You didn't need slipcovers to impress me."

She keeps going, needing to get the words out. "You thought they looked too crisp and pristine, so you thought we should—"

"Dirty them up." He laughs. "Defile the davenport. Sully the slipcovers. Besmirch the—"

"Right." They certainly did. It wasn't slow, gentle lovemaking. It was rough and frantic and hungry. Teeth, claws, the bite of twill against her knees.

She'd been so hungry for him, bent over the arm of the sofa with his hand in her hair, tugging her head to bare her throat.

He was seeing her, really seeing her for the first time in her natural habitat. Her gray sweatpants on the floor. The mushy homemade brownies she baked that morning. Her battered hand-me-down furniture. He saw it all and stripped her bare, tossing the beige bra on the floor.

"I want you so much," he growled against her pulse.

He must've known it was their last time. Did he already have his bags in the car? When he drove away, did he even look back?

Matteo shifts beneath the covers. She starts to move, but he grabs her hand. "I'd take it back if I could."

"What's that?" She's holding her breath.

"Leaving like I did." A long, slow sigh in the dark. "If I traveled back in time, I'd do it differently."

"How?" Her voice sounds needy and breathless. She hopes he can't hear it.

"I don't know." He squeezes her hand. "I thought I was

protecting you, but now…" He trails off, shaking his head. "Maybe I was wrong. No. I *know* I was wrong, and I'm sorry."

"It's okay."

"It's not."

She hesitates. "Why didn't you tell me? At least say goodbye or something?"

Part of her doesn't expect an answer. Or maybe he'll make a joke out of—

"I was scared." His voice growls low in the dark. "I told myself it was easier. That if I said goodbye or tried to explain, you'd ask questions. You'd learn things to put you in danger." A pause as he swallows. "Or maybe I worried you'd make me stay."

She squeezes her eyes shut. Had she really held that power? Doubtful. But—

"I'm sorry, Renee. So fucking sorry. I know that doesn't fix anything, but I want you to know how deeply I regret it."

"Thank you." She bites her lip. "I forgive you."

There's rustling in AJ's berth, and Renee goes still. Waits for her son's sleepy murmur, wanting juice or a song or a snuggle.

But there's just a soft snuffle behind the bulletproof hatch. "He's asleep." She looks at her watch. "He wakes up between ten and eleven every night and then falls right back to sleep."

"Always?"

"Since he was a baby." She rolls to face him, eyes adjusting to the darkness. "I sometimes think it's because that's when I fed him. He'd start moving around ten, and I'd get him out of his crib, and we'd sit in Grandma's rocking chair, just gliding back and forth." She smiles at the memory, heart squeezing hard. "He'd barely wake up, and then he'd drop into this deep, trancelike sleep."

Matteo shuts his eyes, the furrows in his forehead gouged by sharp knives. "I wish I'd been there."

"When he was a baby?"

"All of it." He doesn't let go of her hand. "When you learned you were pregnant. The day he was born. Those first months of his life. I wish—"

"You're so sure he's yours." She presses her lips together. "Would it change things if he's not?"

Silence. Eyes still shut, he rolls to his back.

Five seconds. Ten. At twenty, she's sure he's gone back to sleep. "Matteo?"

"I'm thinking." He rolls back to face her. "I promised honesty. I need a second to process."

"Fair enough." More silence. She shouldn't have put him in this position. "Matteo, you don't have to—"

"No." He squeezes her hand. "It wouldn't change anything."

"Oh." That leaves her more questions than answers. "What were you thinking through?"

"About us together." His thumb skims her knuckle, circling the base of her ring finger. "A month or a year or ten years from now. I pictured you and me, together again." He swallows, and his throat crackles. "And I pictured AJ. I didn't think about DNA. I thought about us, together, as a family. Biology doesn't matter. He's part of you. Part of the big picture." He lets out a long sigh. "And I love that fucking picture."

Tears sting her eyes. She blinks hard, hoping he can't see. Some discussions belong cloaked in darkness.

She owes him information. He deserves to know how AJ came to be. "Matteo—"

"Wait." He lifts a hand to cup her cheek. A sliver of moonlight falls on his face as he shifts closer. "Before you say it, can I kiss you?"

She laughs. "What do you think I'm about to tell you?"

"I don't know." He takes a shaky breath. "But I know kissing you can only make it better."

No argument there. "Okay. Kiss me."

Palm skimming her face, he slides his fingers through her hair. "You're so beautiful."

"It's dark. You can't see me."

"Yes," he whispers. "I can." There's that tiny ghost smile. "I got good at it when I was...gone. Every hour of every day, I saw you."

God. Why is he saying these things? He can't mean it. There must be a motive.

"I saw you, too." A shaky laugh slips out. "Sometimes I'd yell at you in my head. We'd argue, or I'd call you a selfish jerk for leaving like you did. But I always saw you clearly in my mind."

"Renee." His hand slides to her back as he pulls her close. Lips brush hers in the darkness. "I missed this so much."

She closes her eyes to hold back tears. It's too much, but also not enough. "Same," she breathes. "Same."

His palm skims her shoulder and curves up her bent arm. Bicep, elbow, the edge of her breast. She groans and throws a leg over his hip. Too soon, she knows this. Knows, but can't stop.

He deepens the kiss, tongue brushing hers, breath quickening. When he shifts, she feels steel behind his fly. Can he tell how needy she is? How her sleep shorts dampen between her legs?

She moves so her breast fills his palm. "Don't stop. Matteo, please—"

"I won't." Another kiss, this one on her collarbone. "And I'm not going anywhere."

Renee runs her hands down his back, claiming thick ropes of muscle. Is the condom still in her makeup bag? Might be expired, but he must have something. A man who camps with night vision goggles is a man who comes prepared.

"I want—" She breaks off, breathless, as his mouth finds her nipple. "I want—"

"Damn."

She pulls back. He's frowning out the window, eyes reflecting headlights. "Someone's coming."

"Where?"

"Sounds like they turned off the main road."

She holds her breath to listen. "I don't—*oh.*" Yeah, that's a car.

Or a truck, bumping down gravel. Pressing her lips together, she watches twin beams slash the black.

It's getting closer. She scans the rock they've parked behind. Two stories tall, a perfect shield from the highway. But not if someone drives around.

Matteo's on his feet. Pants and boots and shirt lie folded by the bed like he planned for this. She watches him dress as her heart starts to gallop.

"Stay here." His growl is back. A flash of steel as he slides something into a sheath on his hip.

Oh, God.

Turning to the panel for the hidden safe, he keys in the code. She watches in shock, not sure what to do.

When he turns to face her, there's something in his hand. "Here." He lays it on the pillow like a gift.

She gasps and covers it with her hand. "A *gun?*"

"Remember our date at the firing range?"

"I don't—"

"Remember?" His need makes her nod.

"Yes. I do." She doesn't want to touch it but feels herself pick it up. "It's loaded."

"It is." Of course, it is. "Safety's on." He steps into a shadow, and there's the snick of a zipper. The bulletproof vest? Must be. "I know you hate guns, but sometimes it's necessary."

Exactly what he said before that silly gun date. She never knew she'd need it.

She licks her lips and darts a glance at AJ's berth. To the window where the truck glides into sight. White Ford, dual cab with a black grille on the front. It's parked on the other side of the boulder, but close. Too close. Have they been found?

The hum in her chest says *yes.*

Matteo grabs the doorknob, and she gasps. "You're going out there?" She assumed he'd guard from inside.

"Assessing the threat. Lock the door behind me."

He can't just leave her alone. "What if they're here to hurt us?"

Steel sparks his eyes. "I hurt them first."

Renee shivers. "How will I know you're okay? It's pitch black out there. If someone knocks—"

"When I come back—" He stoops to touch her face. "*When* I come back—I'll knock the first few notes of our song. Got it?"

She nods and forces herself to swallow. "Okay."

Her hand falls to the gun. She covers it with her palm.

Please, God. Don't let AJ wake up.

Matteo's thumb skims her earlobe as he drops his hand. "You've got this."

Forcing a nod, she swallows. "So do you."

And then he's gone, slipping out the door in silence. A whiff of sage and desert dust as he shuts the door and slips into the night.

Gripping the gun, she goes to the window. Dammit, she can't see anything. Night vision goggles. Where did she spot those?

She finds them in a cupboard and puts them on. There's a bulletproof window in the door, and she cracks the blinds to peer at the green-gray darkness. Where is he?

There!

He flows around the boulder, cloaked in inky night. He's a hundred feet from the truck, then fifty. Thirty. The white rig gleams in moonlight.

"AJ?" She whispers his name, hoping he won't wake. That he sleeps through whatever happens.

Please, please, don't let anything happen to him.

Matteo or AJ, either one.

She sinks to the dinette bench. Resting the gun beside her, she peels back an edge of the daisy-print curtain. Panic swells when she can't spot him. Scanning the sagebrush, the craggy basalt columns, she tells herself not to panic. *There!*

He's ten feet from the truck now. What is he planning? She's helpless and scared and captivated by the shape of him. He glides catlike toward the truck, one with the shadows.

Shouting erupts, and Renee draws a breath. She can't make out words, but Matteo freezes. What's happening?

The intercom.

He showed her earlier, a system rigged to communicate with the outside. Seemed weird at the time, but relief floods her as she recalls his instructions.

"The camper's nearly soundproof," he explained earlier. "But hook this headset to the audio jack and sounds outside get crystal clear."

She's never been gladder for Nondi's rolling safe house as she shoves the plug home. A crackle of static and then—

"Because I know where I'm going, goddammit." A man's voice, not Teo's. A lumpy white guy in a red T-shirt stomps around the truck, a physique honed by French fries and manual labor.

He glares at someone on the passenger side. "We're not fucking lost, okay?"

A coyote howls in answer. Then, a female voice. "Dillon, please."

Renee recalls another Dillon, a daycare kid AJ called *Dilldum*. Mean little bastard...

"Dillon." The woman's voice is pleading. "Let's just get back in the truck and—"

"No, listen to me, Bex." Dilldum hocks a loogie. "I know where I'm going. Last thing I need is some bitch breathing down my neck."

"Honey, I'm just trying to help." Bex's voice, so small. So like her figure slinking around the truck to touch his arm. "The map says—"

Smack!

Renee gasps and claps a hand to her mouth. Bex crumples, a greenish lump through night-vision goggles. At the corner of her eye, Matteo moves.

Oh, God.

"Dillon, don't." A child—a boy no more than ten—leaps from the truck and runs for Bex's fallen form. "You *hurt* her."

Renee darts a glance at Matteo. He's rounding the rock, still cloaked in shadows. Moving slow but drawing closer. Of course he'd move *toward* danger, not away. That's Matteo for you.

The boy throws his body between Dilldum and the woman. Skinny shoulders shake. "Don't hurt her again."

Dilldum's fists clench. "I told you to stay in the fucking truck."

"But my mom needs—"

Dilldum lunges. Matteo springs, quick as a cat.

It happens so fast she doesn't blink. Down they go, Matteo like a lion on the man's back. He's got one knee shoved in Dilldum's spine and a hand locked on his neck.

"Stay down." The words snap like iced lightning in Matteo's cold snarl. He shoves the man's face in the dirt. "Stay down, or I will hurt you."

Renee hugs herself. It's not an idle threat.

"Who the fuck are you?" Dilldum spits dirt. "This is none of your fucking business."

"I'm making it my business." Hand on Dilldum's neck, he calls to the woman. "Ma'am? Are you okay?"

She sits up and tries to nod, wincing as she touches her face. "I just slipped and fell."

Oh, God.

"Mama, he hit y—"

"Hush, Hunter." She strokes her boy's hair. Baby fine swirls, just like AJ's. "I'm all right. I—" Her voice trembles as she studies Matteo warily. "You should probably go. We don't want any trouble."

Matteo's not leaving. He whips something from his coat. A knife? A gun?

The woman cowers as Matteo grips a length of rope. "Please." She holds up a hand. "Whoever you are, please don't hurt us."

"I'm helping, not hurting." Matteo's eyes glint in moonlight. "Helping *you*, not him." His eyes narrow as they slide to Dilldum. "You're safe, ma'am."

The boy looks uneasy as Matteo cinches Dilldum's hands behind his back and gets to his feet. Teo scans his surroundings as he walks to Bex and Hunter. "How bad are you hurt?"

Hunter moves to shield his mother. Even now, the boy's not sure who to trust. "My stepdad—"

"Needs a timeout now." Matteo draws a handkerchief from his pocket. "You have my word I won't hurt you. I've got a son of my own. Swear to God, I'd never lay a hand on him or his mother."

Something in his eyes, in his voice, must signal he's a man to trust. A man unlike the one lying in the dirt, spitting curses.

Renee watches the boy's shoulders ease. Watches Matteo kneel and hold out the handkerchief. "Ma'am, you're bleeding. Right there, by your ear."

She flinches, then blinks at his hand. "Thank you." She takes the hankie and dabs her cheek.

Dilldum growls behind him. Matteo straightens, and the man falls silent.

"I don't know what happened." Bex staggers to her feet, blotting her temple with the hankie. "I must have tripped. I'm so clumsy sometimes."

"Ma'am." Matteo gets up and clears his throat. "He hit you. Your husband?"

Bex looks away. "He didn't mean anything by it."

"Intent doesn't matter." He scowls at Dilldum. "Actions do. Learned that from my parole officer."

He seldom brings up prison, so there's a reason. Scare tactic? Renee touches the gun.

"I—" Bex falters. "He's having a bad day."

Matteo looks at her for a long time. "Ma'am, I won't tell you what to do. I'm sure you get that plenty already."

Bex looks at her hands. "I guess."

The boy rests a hand on his mom's back. "We could go. Just leave and—"

"Shhh." Bex darts a look at Dilldum. "Don't talk like that."

Matteo's a statue, rigid with rage. "Bex." His voice gentles. "Is this how you want to live? How you want your boy brought up?"

Her gaze darts to Dilldum. "He's a good provider. I make him mad sometimes, but he's a good man."

The good man spews a stream of curse words. "Stupid bitch. I knew I shoulda left you at home."

Matteo stalks over and plants a foot on his back. "You will shut your mouth right now." The calm in his voice sounds scarier than fury. "Or I will shut it for you."

Renee gulps. She's only seen glimpses of this Teo. This fierce and fiery protector.

Is it wrong that she likes it?

His hand goes to his pocket, and she shuts her eyes. Matteo could kill him. She can't watch a man die. Not even if he deserves it.

"Take this."

She opens her eyes to see him handing Bex a wad of bills.

"Be your own provider."

Bex stares at the money and shakes her head. "I—shouldn't."

"What's stopping you?"

"I—" Her voice shakes again. "I don't even know you."

"Mom, he's like Batman." Hunter lifts his eyes to Matteo. "Right, Mister?"

"Sure."

Bex's eyes dart to Dilldum, and Renee holds her breath. She's seen this before. A foster mom too scared to leave the man who had her cowering in corners.

He doesn't mean it. He's a good man, a kind man—

"He'll come for us." Bex's voice, so quiet. "If I leave, he's right behind."

Matteo doesn't drop the money. "You've tried?"

Bex nods. "A long time ago, when Hunter was little." She touches her throat. "It's not his fault. It's hard for a man raising a boy who's not his own—"

"Don't." Matteo's voice is velvet steel. "Please don't make excuses. A man marries a mother, he makes a pact. To respect you and protect you—both of you—no matter what. You deserve that, Bex."

"Bitch." Dilldum snarls. "Don't you dare even think about—"

"You're not part of this discussion." Matteo's eyes harden. "I'll deal with *you* in a minute."

Bex swipes her eyes. "You're right." She sniffles. "I know you're right."

"Here." Matteo finds more bills in his pocket. Hands them to the boy, who pockets the cash.

Matteo moves to the truck. "You have a driver's license, Bex?"

"I—yes." She glances at Dilldum. "I'm not allowed to drive his truck."

"I hereby grant permission." He opens the cab and grabs the keys.

Bex shakes her head. "I really shouldn't. It's registered to him. He'll call the police if he knows I'm driving it and—"

"The Department of Motor Vehicles will have an updated record within ten minutes." Matteo holds out the keys. "Trust me."

Renee can't speak for Bex, but she trusts him with her life. Now more than ever.

Bex blinks. "But—how?"

"I have it handled."

Renee holds her breath. Sees Bex hesitate.

Do it. Please. Take him at his word.

Memory moves through Renee's mind. Matteo, years ago. Laptop light bathing his face as he tapped the keys. "It's not even fun when they make systems this easy to hack." He looked up like he hadn't meant to say it out loud. "I'm using my powers for good and not evil," he added. "In case you're worried."

Then, she was worried.

She isn't now.

Bex takes the keys. "Where do we go?"

"Away." Matteo stands over Dilldum. "Far from him. You deserve better. You and your son. You hear me?"

She nods but looks unsure. Hunter slips a hand in hers. "Mama? I—think we should go." He looks at Matteo. "He's right. You know he's right."

Bex chews her lip. "You won't—kill him. Will you?"

Renee sees his jaw clench.

"No." Matteo's fist curls. "Not if you don't want me to."

"I—" Bex pauses. "I don't want you to."

A flash of disappointment. A nod. "All right." Matteo steps back as the boy runs to the passenger side. "I'll stay and have a word with your husband."

Bex moves to the truck. Hesitates again. "And you swear you won't kill him?"

"Yeah." His fingers touch the scar at his own throat. "I swear."

Renee holds her breath as Bex gets behind the wheel. There's a roar as the engine starts, a flicker of headlights. The truck lurches with grinding gears. Dilldum curses. Stops when Matteo says something. Eyes on the truck, Renee watches it back out. Scans the headlights as it heads toward the highway, pausing at the road's edge.

"*Go,*" she whispers. "*Be free.*"

The truck turns west. Renee releases a breath she doesn't recall holding.

Sixty-five miles from here to Highway 97. From there, south to California, north to Central Oregon. A couple hours west of that would get them to Portland, Salem, Eugene, Seattle. They could be anywhere by daybreak.

Matteo turns back to Dilldum. All warmth has left his eyes. "Get up."

Dilldum snorts. "How the fuck do I do that with my hands tied?"

"Figure it out." No room for argument.

The process is slow. There's swearing and sweating as Dilldum climbs to his feet. The moon ignites eyes filled with rage. He'd kill Matteo if he could.

Matteo isn't worried. "Wait here." He turns and heads back to the camper.

"Where the fuck would I go?" Dilldum's shout echoes off the rock.

Teo taps the camper door. Six raps. The rhythm of "Hey, Jude."

Renee's on her feet before the last knock. "Are you okay?" She's whispering, praying AJ stays asleep.

"Never better." He smells like desert and dominance. Opens the box of survival gear. "Could you grab the protein bars, please?"

"Sure." Of course, he's hungry. Spinning around, she grabs the box. "Do you want peanut butter, chocolate chip, fudge mint—"

"Doesn't matter." He fills a canteen at the tiny camper sink and takes two bars. "I'll be back."

He strides out and doesn't lock the door behind him. Renee waits on the first step, shivering in shadows. She doesn't need the headset from here.

Matteo loops the canteen over Dilldum's neck. Pats his pockets, then shoves one full of protein bars. Keeps going as he pats the man's legs. When he gets to his ankle, Dilldum kicks out. "Don't touch my—"

Wham!

He's on his back before the words leave his throat. Matteo bends over him, flinty eyes flashing. "I promised not to kill you." His voice is a low growl. "Didn't make any promises about pain."

Dilldum gulps and nods. "Yeah, fine." He spits. "All right, all right."

Matteo bends and grabs the other man's ankle. Comes up with a switchblade. "I'll keep this."

"Oh, come on—"

"Get the fuck up." Matteo jerks him up. "Now."

"Jesus." Hands bound, he shakes dirt from his hair. "What are you going to do with that?"

"What I *should* do is make sure you'll never hurt another woman or child." He pockets the knife. "I've got two dozen ideas for how to do that. Want to hear some?"

A grunt, but no response.

"Answer me!" Matteo shoves him against the rock.

Dilldum's eyes bug. "Come on, man! I've had a rough week."

"I don't care if your week starts with getting gang raped by clowns and ends with a rat gnawing off your balls. You. Do. Not. Hit. Women. Or. Children." Each word gets punctuated by a finger-jab to the throat. "Understood?"

"Yeah, man." His voice has gotten smaller. "Fine."

Renee darts a look at the clock. Fifteen minutes since Bex drove away. Is she far enough?

Dilldum's still grumbling. "What are you going to do?"

"I'm going to cut you—"

"No! God, please, no!" He falls to his knees. "Please, man. I've learned my lesson, okay?"

Matteo sighs. "I'm going to cut you *loose*." He holds up a knife, blade lit by the moon. "You have snacks. You have water. You have shoes and a jacket and a space blanket I put in your pocket. In other words, you've got good odds of survival."

"Survival?" He pales. "What do you mean?"

"The town of Paisley's twelve miles east. Summer Lake's that way, maybe twenty miles." He holds up the knife, letting Dilldum get a good look. "Turn around."

"What? Wh—"

"Turn the fuck around." He jerks his shoulder to make it happen. Cuts the rope at his wrists. "Go."

"Where?"

"You think I give a shit?" Matteo shoves the knife in a sheath. Stalks back toward the camper, then turns around. "I know people. And I have eyes everywhere. *Everywhere.*"

"Jesus, man—"

"If I ever learn you've laid a hand on your wife or stepson, I will not be this merciful."

Renee shudders. This is Matteo's brand of mercy.

She should hate it. She should fear him. She should run like hell from this wrath, this temper, this malice in his eyes.

But as he strides back to the camper, what she feels isn't fear.

It's the closest thing she's known to love.

CHAPTER 9

*H*e should have killed the guy.

Or not. He gave his word, and his word is his bond.

His bond is dumb sometimes.

"Matteo?" Renee shifts in the passenger seat. "You sure you don't want to talk about it?"

"Yep." They've been on the road for an hour. Once he set Dillhole free, they had to get gone. No sense sticking around so some dipshit could bash rocks through their windows. It's shatterproof glass, but still. He can't risk Dillhole identifying them.

She's watching, so he tries to stop clenching his jaw. He owes her an explanation. Words or feelings or something besides stony silence. "That shit makes my blood boil."

As sharing goes, it's not great.

But it's a start. Her face softens in the corner of his eye.

"Men who hit women?" She pauses, picking her words with care. "That's true." She's not sure how to ask this. "I couldn't help noticing you seemed particularly…passionate."

She lets that hang between them. An opening for him to fill. He's not sure what to say. "It's not my story to tell." That's good.

Keeps his promise of not lying. It's honest, but not the whole truth. "It's personal though. Yeah."

"Matteo. I *know*." She touches his arm across the console. "Nicole told me her history the day we toured her daycare."

He nearly drives off the road. "She talked about the asshole who hit her?"

"Yes." She clears her throat. "Your sister's a little more open than you."

"Shit." He never thought she'd talk about it. If it were him, he'd take that to the grave.

"She explained how she started her daycare to help people escaping bad situations. Your sister got out, but it's harder for some victims." Another pause as she draws her hand back. "For what it's worth, I'm glad you stood up to him. Dilldum, I mean."

"Dilldum?"

She makes a face. "Sorry, *Dillon*."

"No, I like Dilldum. It's better than what I've been calling him."

"Which is?"

"*Dillhole*." That makes him smile. "That's actually what Jen called Nic's ex."

"Was his name Dillon?"

"Nah, Clint." He taps the steering wheel. "I looked *dillhole* up on Urban Dictionary." He clears his throat and quotes from memory. "'A dumbass. See also dumbfuck, fuckhead, asswipe.'"

"Goodness." She laughs. "Fitting."

They're getting off track here. He glances over to gauge her mood. God, she's beautiful. She's back in yoga pants, gray ones this time. They hug her perfect legs, while her white tank makes him wonder what's underneath. That pink bra he saw earlier?

And now he's hard. He drags his eyes away, so he doesn't steer off the road.

"It was a brave thing to do." She crosses her legs, and he's distracted again. "Maybe not the right approach for everyone, but for a guy like you—"

"A guy like me?"

She smiles. "A guy who's big and burly and terrifying and not afraid of anything."

He likes the "big" and "burly," so it takes a sec to catch the other stuff. "You think I'm terrifying?" He'd die before making her afraid.

"I'm not scared of you, no." A pause. "I'm scared for anyone who'd double-cross you."

Fair enough. He rolls that round in his mind. "I'm afraid of plenty."

"Yeah?" She laughs and adjusts her seatbelt. "Like what?"

"Spiders." He shudders. "Not a fan of snakes, either."

"That's right, I remember." She laughs and shakes her head. "So much for my romantic picnic in the park."

"I liked it." Especially once she chased off the harmless garter snake. Scooted the spider off the picnic table. God, he loved those picnics.

She shifts in her seat. "Anything else you're afraid of?"

I'm afraid of losing you again.

"Claustrophobia." He grips the wheel tighter. "I was a model fucking prisoner so I wouldn't get sent to solitary."

"I'm so sorry." She watches as he hits the signal to turn east. No one's in sight, but he checks the mirror anyway. "Truly, Matteo—I feel awful you got sent to—"

"Could we change the subject?"

Pressing her lips together, she nods. "Fine." A few beats of silence. "Can you tell me where we're going?"

"East." He shoots her a wry glance. "That's not me being cagey. It's me admitting I don't know southeast Oregon that well. Not this far out."

"Same."

Which hopefully means her stalker doesn't either. "As far as I know, it's mostly sagebrush and sunstone mines out here."

"A good place to get lost."

"Exactly." They fueled up back in Lakeview. They've gone an hour since then. It's one in the morning, and they'll need to rest soon. "You can sleep if you want to."

"I don't." She crosses her legs again. "I can drive if you need a break."

"I'm good." He glances over. "I'm not some macho dick who doesn't want you driving my rig. I meant we're stopping soon."

"Here?" She scans the moonlit landscape. Round hills roll through a horizon spiked with bitterbrush and sage. "I've never seen so much open space."

He steers them down a deserted road he marked on the map. "I'll bet the stars out here are incredible."

"Isn't there a meteor shower?" She pulls out the burner phone he gave her back at the beach house. "There is. All week long, but the peak should be tonight."

"I'd like to see that." He parks and gets out, checking to see they're stable. "This okay with you?"

"Perfect." She steps outside, shrugging one of his shirts over her tank. She leaves it open in front, and he looks away so he can't see her nipples through white cotton. His brain's fuzzy enough.

"Could you shove the wheel chock under that rear tire?"

"Here?"

"Good." *Not* good. As she bends over, the blood leaves his brain.

When she stands, it's not much better. She stretches and yawns, breasts pressing through the thin cotton tank. "Oh my God, look!"

"I am."

"What?" She points at the sky. "Shooting star!"

He looks up too late to see it, but another streaks past. Sparks of silver twinkle in its tail as he watches it fade to nothing. "Did you make a wish?"

She's smiling when he looks at her. "I thought you weren't superstitious."

"A guy can change, can't he?" He gets back to work, cranking the stabilizers so they're level. "I wished good luck to Bex and her kid."

"That's sweet."

"What did you wish?" He sounds like a silly teen girl.

Renee just smiles. "If I tell you, it won't come true."

"Touché." He finishes setting up camp. They filled water tanks at the coast, but this one's low. Hoisting a jug, he slowly fills the freshwater from one of three spares he brought.

Renee's gone quiet. When he looks up, she's watching him.

"How much does that weigh?" She licks her lips. "Just curious."

"Dunno." It's maybe 30 kilograms. About 65 pounds. Enough to have his arms flexing.

Only a loser would get off on the hunger in her eyes. He's definitely a loser.

"I should check AJ." She's reluctant as she backs away. "I'm sure he's fine, but I'll worry if I don't see for myself."

"Go ahead." He hesitates. Flicks a glance at the sky. "I know we both need to sleep, but—"

"Yes." She smiles. "Were you going to ask if I wanted to sit outside a minute?"

"I know you love shooting stars. Used to."

"Still do." She turns back to the camper. "Give me a second to be sure he's okay."

He watches her go, reminding himself to get that shirt back. It'll smell like her, and he'll never wash it again.

Shaking himself, he unlocks a storage box. Finds a pile of blankets to spread on the ground. They smell like fabric softener, so Jen must've washed them. Or Dante. The man's a domestic god, always cooking or sweeping or polishing guns.

Blanket nest finished, he looks at his watch. Five minutes pass. Fifteen. From inside the rig, he hears Renee reading *Blue Truck*. AJ's awake.

With time to kill, he pulls out his laptop and the little red notebook where he jots ideas. It's been hours since he hacked the DMV site, listing Bex on the registration. It all looks good and… yep. He scrolls to be sure, watching the blip on his screen. The tracker he stuck to the driver's side door is working. California, huh? Good for them.

So. That's that.

Renee's still not back, so he taps out a message to Dante. It's too late to call, and farm life means he must be fast asleep.

But harvest season makes for weird hours, so he gives it a shot.

Any word on our stalker?

A few seconds pass. Then three dots indicating a response.

Some. I've got a cop friend running checks on guys she dated.

Jealousy flares in his chest. Jealousy and…confusion?

You have a cop friend?

The thought makes his skin crawl. Blame Reggie Fucking Dowling for Matteo's lifetime aversion to law enforcement.

Austin's a good guy.

Matteo frowns.

Austin?

The bubbles hover awhile.

Austin Dugan. Police chief from Ponderosa Resort. Poker buddy.

Dante plays poker with cops? And feeds chickens and makes chili and snuggles at night with Jen?

That's fucking weird.

Another pause. Then Dante again.

I'm a new man.

He is. Maybe Matteo's changed, too.

Thanks for the news. Keep me posted.

Will do.

So. That's that. Should he check with Seb? Might as well. A few more taps on the burner phone.

Any updates?

It's two in the morning. No way a guy with a nine-to-five job is up at this hour. Or maybe dentists stay up late on Sundays.

Might've found something. Call at noon. Will know more then.

Interesting. He's about to reply when Renee walks out. She's still in his shirt with the receiver for the baby monitor tucked in the breast pocket. There's an odd look in her eye and two fizzing glasses in her hands.

"Sparkling cider." She hands one to him. "Do you know what Lacinto is?"

"A type of kale." He frowns. "Also a mythical Dovlanese creature. Sort of a cross between a unicorn and a parrot."

"I'm guessing my toddler wasn't asking for a 2 a.m. kale snack." She sets the baby monitor on the blanket and settles beside him. "Did you tell AJ about Lacinto?"

He sips his cider, glad it's the booze-free kind. He needs to keep his wits. "He woke up in the night at the beach house. Asked for a story, but all we had was a romance novel and one of Nondi's *Guns and Ammo* magazines."

"Thank you for not introducing a three-year-old to bodice rippers and Uzis."

"Hey, now. Don't diss the romance genre."

"What?"

"I read a lot of it in pr—" He clears his throat. "In my spare time."

"No kidding?" She smiles and lifts the glass to her lips. "I guess that explains it."

"Explains what?"

"Why you seem so much more..." She trails off, rolling her wrist like she can't find the word.

132

"Sensitive?" he suggests. "In touch with my feminine side? Attuned to the importance of female orgasm?"

She laughs. "I was going to say 'sentimental,' but yes to the rest of that." A flush rolls up her neck, and she sips her cider some more. "The first part. I can't speak to the other stuff."

"Orgasms?"

Her cheeks go pinker. "You had that part nailed already."

Why is he doing this to himself? Like he wasn't already blue-balled. Time for damage control. "AJ's awake?"

"I got him back to sleep." She sounds bemused as she drains her glass. "But only when I promised you'll tell him more about Lacinto tomorrow."

"Tomorrow or today?" A glance at his watch tells him he should be asleep. "Doesn't matter. I can tell Lacinto stories anytime."

"Thanks." She leans against him, tilting her face to the sky. "Thank you for what you did today."

"At the risk of sounding cocky, can you be specific?"

Another laugh as she looks at him. "Getting us safely from the coast to this exquisite hidey-hole. Saving Bex from that bully. Feeding us, driving us, telling stories to my kid. Want me to keep going?"

"Kinda." What he really wants is to kiss her. "I'm sorry you've been running these past few years."

"Me, too."

"And I'm sorry you're scared." A pause as he gathers his thoughts. "But I'm not sorry you're back in my life."

She laughs and sets her cider on the ground. Looks at him for a long time. "I've read romance novels, too."

"Okay." Odd segue, but intriguing.

"There's always a hero's journey." She spins her glass on the ground. "A growth-arc, if you will."

"There's lots of sex, too." Damn, he's doing it again.

Renee ignores him. "I was thinking about your scar. About

how many times I've asked about it. And I know it's personal, and you're entitled to your privacy, and—"

"Ask me again."

She blinks. "What?"

"Ask me again how I got my scar." His heart thuds in his ears. It's a bad idea, but it doesn't feel that way now.

Renee licks her lips. "How did you get your scar?"

He hesitates. Takes a deep breath. "Knife wound." Matteo looks at the blanket. He can't meet her eyes and say the rest. It's a blue and red afghan, one Nondi knitted the fall before MIT. God, it's so long ago.

So is this. "I was eleven. Still living in Dovlano at the time. My parents—they were into some…stuff. Illegal stuff. People were after them and—" God, he can't believe he's sharing this. "They came for me. Held a knife to my throat and asked where my mom and dad were. I—I told them."

He shuts his eyes, squeezing back the pain.

"God, Matteo."

"It's my fault. My fault they found them and killed them and—"

"No, Teo." She puts her arms around him and squeezes hard. "You were a kid. There's no way any of that's your fault."

When he opens his eyes, she's watching with such sympathy he can't breathe. "They tortured me for an hour. Maybe two—I passed out a couple times. But in the end…"

He trails off. There's no need to tell the rest. He's already said so much.

"I'm so sorry." She wipes a tear, then strokes his cheek. "I can't even imagine what you've lived through."

"Took us a while to get to America after that." God, he's still talking. It's like a goddamn dam burst. "I brought both my sisters. Had a helluva time getting us out of the country, but I did it. With Nondi's help, I did it."

"You were brave."

"I was terrified."

A pause. "I'm not sure it's possible to be brave if you're not scared."

Maybe that's true. He lifts his eyes to look at her. "Losing my parents was the worst thing that ever happened to me." He draws a breath. "Until I lost you."

"Oh, Matteo."

Tears flood her eyes. Tears and sympathy and admiration.

There's more, though. Kindness. Respect. Maybe even...*heat?*

No. That can't be right.

He licks his lips. "Okay if we change the subject?"

"Of course." She picks up her cider and takes a long drink. "It's beautiful here."

"It is." He takes a breath and gulps the rest of his drink. Wishes it was whiskey.

They stare at the sky in silence. A star streaks through darkness, drifting to sparkly dust behind a high cliff. A coyote calls in the distance. The breeze brings a whisper of sage and shampoo, and now he's remembering the shower. Picturing Renee, naked and wet and wrapped around him.

"Thank you for telling me that."

He looks at her. "About the scar?"

"Yes." She hesitates. "You have changed, haven't you?"

"I like to think so."

Silence stretches, but it's different now. Peaceful, not pocked with nervous energy. He's getting used to this.

"What are you thinking?"

Drawing a breath, he turns to look at her. "I'd really like to kiss you."

She laughs. "What's stopping you?"

A pause while he gathers his thoughts. "Once I start, I'm not sure I can stop." He looks back at the sky. "Not even if we're shot at or interrupted by AJ or attacked by wolves or the blanket bursts into flames or—"

"Okay."

He looks at her. "Okay?"

Nodding, she holds his gaze. "I want you."

The words zing from his ears to his dick. They're too good to be true. "Yeah?"

"Jesus, Matteo." She laughs and slugs him in the arm. "Do you want me to beg or something? Say the magic word like you coached AJ?"

"Uh—"

"Pleeeeeeeease?" She goes up on her knees and cups a hand behind his neck. "Matteo. Please make love to me."

He swallows hard. Searching her eyes, he sees it's no joke. How did he get this lucky?

He spends way too long sitting like a dumbass, but it doesn't matter. She pulls him down with her, easing back on the blanket. As his brain catches up with his cock, he slips between her thighs. It's like coming home.

Kissing her slow and deep takes all his self-control. He wants to ravage her, rip her clothes off, cover every inch of her with kisses.

Kissing's great, too. Better than great. She tastes like apples and sunshine and all the sweetness he doesn't deserve. Against his chest, her breasts shift lush and round.

He draws back breathless. "You okay on the ground like this?"

"It's well-padded." She pats the blankets. "I admire a man who builds a nice nest."

"Here, let's pull this one over us." Not that they need privacy in the middle of nowhere, but AJ could walk out. "Nondi sewed it."

Nice, dumbass. Talking about your grandma gets women hot.

Renee just smiles. "This is a bucket list fantasy here."

"Defiling a family quilt?"

She rolls her eyes. "Sex in the desert under shooting stars."

He looks at the sky. Another gold dust ball streaks the horizon. Does he get one more wish? He hopes so. This one's already coming true.

More kissing her under a velvet cape of sky. Her tongue brushes his as he holds his weight on his forearms. What else does her desert star fantasy entail? Not a felon slipping his hand up her shirt, but she moans anyway. Drags her nails down his back as she arches against him. Bitterbrush breeze swirls as his tongue sweeps hers. She's fire in his arms, hot and bright and beautiful.

"Matteo." She nuzzles his neck, groaning as he kisses his way down her throat. She's still wearing his shirt, so he peels it off her shoulders and finds the hem of her tank.

Pink bra. Another wish come true.

"Why are you looking at me like that?" She laughs and touches his cheek.

"Like what?"

"Like you haven't seen me topless a hundred times."

"Not like this." It's not the desert or the stars or the blankets, either. There's something raw and new and naked between them. He's fully clothed but never felt this bared.

Renee grabs the hem of his shirt and yanks it over his head. "Magic word pleeeeeeease?" Her laughter turns to moans as he unhooks her bra and drops his mouth to her nipple.

"Oh, God." She's tugging his belt, wild and hungry. "Hurry. Please hurry. I've waited this long, and I don't want something to interrupt again."

Not much would stop him this time. Her resistance, sure. But she's not resisting as he strips off her pants and pulls the blanket over them. She's got his pants down past his hips as he kicks off his shoes.

Gratitude melts, warm and gooey in his chest, as he strokes her body. Worships her with his hands, his mouth, his heart. When he kisses her belly, she bows up off the blanket. "Please say you brought condoms."

He grins against her navel. "Please tell me you won't be pissed I presumed I might need them."

"Thank God."

He fumbles in his jeans and finds a foil packet.

"Hurry." She lets go of his cock and looks at him with liquid eyes. "I need you inside me."

He needs that, too. He's shaking as he rolls on top of her, arms trembling as he holds himself up. It's not the strain, because he's shaking everywhere.

Don't screw up this time.

Notching himself at her entrance, he hesitates. Slides in slowly, so slowly, and he's never felt anything like this. Not all the times he's been with her before. It's magic, bright and blazing and so powerful it steals his breath. Squeezing his eyes shut, he breathes her in.

"Yes, right there." She moans and arches up. "I forgot how good you feel."

He grits his teeth and fights the explosion. Wishes he'd thought to jerk off six or twelve times so he'd have some damn endurance. Not much time for spanking it these days.

Finding his rhythm, he starts to move. God, she's soft. Breasts, hips, her sweet, slick center. Soft thighs clutch his hips as he moves faster. He can't stop kissing her, sliding her hair between his fingers. When she arches again, he knows she's close.

"Oh, God!"

He fights to hold on, but it's too much. The tight clench, her muffled cry as she bites his shoulder. It pulls him like an undertow, swallowing him in waves. He gasps as the rush hits.

"Renee, *Jesus*."

"Don't stop, don't stop, *don't stop!*" It's a chant, a mantra, a hymn he hears in his soul.

The sting of her nails in his back, the hot gasp in his ear—they're what he dreamt of. For years, he thought he'd never have this again.

They float up together. Break the surface and bob in rippling warmth. He kisses the spot behind her ear that makes her shiver. Curling against him, she closes her eyes and puts a palm on his chest.

He rolls so they lie face to face. When he pushes a curl off her face, she opens her eyes. "Do you want to know?"

Matteo blinks. "Know what?"

"About AJ." Her fingers curl on his chest. "Who his father is."

He hesitates. "You know for sure?"

She nods and bites her lip. "I'll tell you if you want. But once I say it, there's no un-knowing it."

He starts to answer, then stops. It should be simple. Of course he'd want to know he fathered a child. Or if he didn't, that's vital, too.

You started this by not thinking things through.

He promised honesty, so he owes this some thought. Does he want to know? Would it change things if he did?

Holding her gaze, he nods once. "Yes. I want to know."

"Okay." Her fingers curl over his heart. She takes a breath.

A blast shatters the silence.

CHAPTER 10

"*A*re you okay? Renee, are you okay?"

She sputters and rolls out from under him. They're naked, and her hair feels full of grit. Not how she pictured the pillow talk.

"It's the generator." She spits hair from her mouth and touches an arm tight with tension. "Matteo? I think it's just the generator coming on."

"Jesus." He flops on his back. Throws an arm over his eyes. "I'm an idiot."

"You're not an idiot." She tunnels through blanket to get to him. Palm on his chest, she finds his heart hammering wildly. "You're just a little high-strung."

Shaking his head, he drops the arm to his side. "I sure killed that moment."

"You didn't." She kisses his cheek, then the edge of his jaw. "It's actually kind of charming."

"Mama?" AJ's voice, small and tinny on the baby monitor.

Sighing, she gives Matteo a tight smile. "*That's* more a ruin-the-moment kinda thing."

"No." He sits up and finds her clothes. "That's charming."

"It's parenthood." She pulls on her pants and tank, skipping the bra to run barefoot to the camper.

AJ sits sleep-tousled on the edge of his bunk. *"Loud*, Mama. Whatsa sound?"

"Just the power coming on." She settles beside him, smoothing rumpled hair from his face. "Nothing to worry about."

He yawns and snuggles close. "You sing?"

"Of course." She tucks the covers around him, stopping to stroke a finger down one soft cheek. "What should I sing?"

"Not words." He sighs as his eyes drift shut.

Not words? "Oh. Humming?"

"Mmmmmmm." He's already half asleep.

Stroking his hair, she hums the first bars of a song she can't place. A tune she knows but doesn't know. A few lilting notes. A couple more. AJ drifts quickly, fingers curled around the pillowcase.

"Everything okay?" Matteo slips in with a whisper. "I can tell a story if you want."

"No need." She eases off the bunk and draws the door behind her. "He's easy to get back to sleep."

"My sisters were the same." He strips off his shirt and pulls a pair of sleep shorts from a drawer. "Jen would wake up in the night, but it only took a few lines of that song to get her back down."

"What song?"

"The one you were humming." He hums a few bars, then cocks his head. "It's a Dovlanese lullaby."

"It is?" That makes no sense. "How would I know it?"

"I used to sing it to you." He peels back the covers. "When you got restless in your sleep, I'd sing it 'til you'd settle."

The layers of her heart peel back. He somehow keeps surprising her. "You sang to me? Besides the Beatles song?"

A flicker of unease in his eyes. "Sorry. Was that creepy?"

141

"Matteo, no. It's amazing." She should change out of gritty yoga pants, but she's too tired. "Thank you."

"Sure." He's not facing her, so maybe he's embarrassed.

Tapping the light, he gets into bed. She snuggles beside him, and he curls himself around her. Releasing a breath, she eases against him. Spooning's nice.

Nice, but not what she needs. To have this conversation, she should face him. To look him in the eye, even in darkness.

She's lost all hesitation for sharing her son's biology. The lullaby shushed it away. Reaching out, she touches his cheek. "You still want to know?"

A nod. No asking what she means. "Yes."

Soap bubbles fizz in her chest. She didn't expect to feel like this.

He must feel her trembling because he kisses her fingertips. "Whatever you tell me," he says, "it won't change how I feel. About you. About AJ. About *us*."

Does he have to be so decent?

She swallows hard. Forces herself to take a breath.

"He's yours." She says it fast, the rip of a Band-aid. "I know we didn't talk about monogamy, and maybe you were just in it for fun, but I didn't date anyone else while we were together. There were a few guys after, and one I went out with more than once, but we didn't have sex. If you'd feel better having a paternity test, I can prove—"

"I don't need a test." He kisses her palm again. "I already knew."

There's a pinch between her eyebrows. "You hacked birth records or something?"

"Wouldn't have told me anything, would it?" He squeezes her hand beneath the covers. "My name's not on the birth certificate."

It's not. Which he'd know only if he hacked the records. She wants to be angry, but she's really just...relieved?

Relieved it's out there. Relieved he's not running. Relieved *she's* not running, at least now. They're warm and cozy in this weird little camper with their son sleeping soundly nearby.

Our son.

She takes a breath. "I guess it's kind of anticlimactic then, isn't it?"

"What's that?"

"If you already knew, I didn't need to make a big deal of it."

"You're wrong." He tucks a curl behind her ear. "I knew you'd never tell me unless you trusted me. And I wasn't sure you'd ever trust me."

Tears sting her eyelids, but she blinks them back. "I do." She squeezes her eyes shut, afraid to believe it. "It's silly, and it's scary and probably unwise, but—I trust you. Not just with my life, but with everything."

"Thank you." Emotion strains his voice.

When she opens her eyes, there's glitter in his. She's never seen him cry. He's not crying, not really. But there's no masking the emotion in his face.

It's hard to swallow with her throat squeezing tight, but she makes it happen, makes herself take a breath. "So, now you know."

"Thank you," he says. "For telling me. For having him."

"You're welcome." A nervous giggle slips out. "I guess that's it, then."

It's not, though. She doesn't want to wreck the moment, but she needs to know the truth. AJ's future rests on it. So does hers.

Another calming breath gets the words out. "Now what?"

He frowns. "I'll pay child support, of cour—"

"That's not what I meant." She has to be brave. She has to just say it. "When this is over, when we're safe—what then?"

Smiling, he dots a kiss on her cheekbone. "We've already crossed a big hurdle."

"What's that?"

"You said when. Not if. *When.*"

She hadn't even noticed. "You're right." A yawn sneaks up on her, swelling up from her chest. "I'm so sorry."

"Don't be." His lips brush her chin, then move to kiss her earlobe. "It's been a long day."

"Still, that's so rude."

"Not rude." One more kiss, on her lips this time. "Human. You're comfortable with me. That's the best gift of all."

Struggling to stay conscious, she knows he's right. Against her better judgment, she feels safe with him. "Mmm...maybe so."

His smile is the last thing she sees before her eyes drift closed. She's dimly aware he didn't answer the question. The one about the future, about what comes next.

But right now, it's enough.

"Good night, Renee." His lips brush her forehead. "Sweet dreams."

* * *

THEY MOVE camp the next morning. Well, the same morning. Neither of them got much sleep.

It reminds her of the untethered years, drifting through foster homes. The ambiguity, the packing, the blur of gray highway.

This time, though, there's hope.

"Mama? We swim now?"

"Not yet." She flips a page in the *Blue Truck* book Nicole brought. They're belted at the dinette while Matteo drives with an earpiece. His voice commands urgency, but his hands stay steady on the wheel. "What do you mean, *missing*?"

Glancing out the window, she sees they're gaining elevation. "Soon, okay?"

"Okay." He snuggles against her, the warm, sleepy scent of him filling her with calm.

A false sense of calm. Matteo's still talking. "How many greenbacks are we talking here?"

AJ turns a page in the book. "What's a greenback, Mama?"

"Alligators." It's the first thing she thinks of.

"I like aggilators." He turns another page. "They gots big teefs."

"And hopefully they brush them." That seems like something Dr. LaDouceur would say. Is that who Matteo's talking to?

"I still can't believe you have a cop pal." Matteo hits his turn signal to pass a slow-moving semi. "Thank Chief Dugan for me. I'll buy him a beer next time I'm near Ponderosa Resort."

Ah, so it's Dante. He mentioned the cop friend when they packed up this morning. Said Dante's pal was chasing angles they hadn't tried yet. Maybe she should mention her own police acquaintance. She hasn't seen him in years, but if it could help—

"Mama." AJ pats her hand. "Last page."

"Right." She clears her throat and reads. "*Now I see a lot depends on a helping hand from a few good friends.*"

He smiles and closes the book. "My Tail read another?"

"My Tail—*Matteo* is driving." She should really start correcting him. "We'll be there soon, okay? And when we get there, you can play in the water."

They're bound for Boxer Lake, a resort Nic knows in Central Oregon. "The owner's a friend," she said this morning on the phone. "I let her know you're coming. That discretion is important."

It means backtracking a bit, but that's okay. The happy camper family façade lets them pretend there's not a threat bearing down. That they're a regular family and not a family running for their lives.

Family.

She told him. She actually told Matteo, when she swore she never would.

If she'd known she'd feel such relief, she'd have done it sooner. Now that it's out there, it's like a weight's been lifted off her shoulders. She's picturing a future, one with Matteo in it.

Maybe figure out who's after you first...

"We're almost there." Matteo's voice from the front of the rig. "Hey, honey?"

Honey?

Unhooking her seatbelt, she gives AJ a kiss as she moves to the front of the rig. "Yes, sweetie?"

A muscle twitches in Matteo's jaw. Is he blushing?

"Sorry about that," he mumbles. "I was trying it out in my mind, and it sorta slipped."

"I like it." She settles in the passenger seat and hooks her safety belt. "What's all that talk about greenbacks?"

He flicks her a glance. "Why'd your dad go to prison?"

That's a surprise. "Which time?"

"The last time."

She's not even sure. "Theft, probably. Or embezzlement. The time before that was a counterfeiting charge, and before *that*—"

"Always financial crimes?"

She shrugs. "Not always. They got him on assault and battery once." Someone stole money he'd filched from someone else, so maybe it's the same thing. "He watched a lot of heist movies. Fancied himself a modern Butch Cassidy."

"What happened to all the money?"

"I assume they took it back when they arrested him." She scans the road and thinks. "We didn't talk much once I went into foster care. Sometimes, he'd get out and make big promises about going straight."

The words still ring in her ears.

"We'll get a big, beautiful house on the water." His pledge the day she turned twenty-one. "I know you want to go to college, and it's not too late. The house will be so big you'll have your own space. Lots of room for Grandma's furniture. Big yard for a dog. And one day you'll have kids, and I'll be the best damn grandpa who ev—"

"He ever talk to you about the Hamdorf job?"

"Hamdorf job?" Renee scrolls through her brain, then shakes her head. "Doesn't ring a bell. Why?"

"Big bank robbery in '09. Rumor has it your old man was involved."

That sounds like her father. "Could be."

"Lots of guys involved. Lots of finger pointing over where the cash ended up. Cops never did find it."

"Huh." Wheels roll in her head. "You think this has something to do with who's following me?"

"It's a lead we're chasing down. Thought it might ring some bells."

"Not really." She bites her lip. "At a certain point, I stopped taking his calls. It was just too painful, you know?"

"Yeah." He reaches over. Puts a hand over hers. "Sorry. Didn't mean to upset you."

"You didn't. I'm glad you're chasing down all the leads. Anything else you need to know?"

"Actually, that's not why I called you up here." They pass a green sign with *Boxer Lake* in white script. Matteo hits the blinker. "Could you check that notebook on the table? Red cover, silver spiral on the spine. I wrote the campsite number in it."

"Sure thing, babycakes."

Matteo groans. "I'm not going to live down the *honey* thing, am I?"

"Not sure what you mean, snookums." She heads to the back, swaying as he rounds a bend. There's the notebook on the table. Red cover, silver spiral. She flips it open and scans a few pages of handwriting.

R. Dowling.

She blinks. Looks at the name again. That couldn't be—

"You find it?" The rig swerves as he grumbles something about chipmunks with a death wish.

"Got it." She flips to the back page and yep—there's the campsite information. "Site 27, campground B." She grins. "Snick-erdoodle."

"Christ." The look he gives her falls somewhere between grimace and grin as she drops into the passenger seat. "Never had a relationship with pet names before."

"We're in a relationship?"

His eyes flick to the rearview mirror. AJ's humming, lost in the Dovlanese lullaby. God, that's sweet.

"This is awkward," he mutters. "I'm kinda not ready for rela-tionship talk."

Understandable, since they're running for their lives. "Look, you don't have to say anything, okay?" She draws a breath and waits for a nod. "If there's one thing I've learned, it's to ask for what I want. And what I want—once this is all over, I mean—I want the real deal."

"Real deal?" His brow furrows, and she knows he'll ask for a translation.

"A relationship," she says. "The whole enchilada. You and me and AJ together as a family."

Holy crap, she said it. There's no going back now. "Like I said, I don't want you to say anything. Just think about it, okay? And if we're on the same page, we'll talk when this is over."

He doesn't respond. That makes her nervous. Speaking of nerves and *pages*, she pictures his scrawl in the notebook.

R. Dowling.

She should say something. "Um, I know I brought it up last night. That I dated a little after you left?"

He darts a quick glance in her direction. "I don't need the test, Renee."

Test? Oh, right. Paternity.

She should really address this. "I just want to be clear that I didn't—you know—sleep with anyone else."

"Renee." It's gentle, but firm. "Look, I won't pretend I'm not jealous of any man you dated. I won't even pretend I didn't run

148

background checks on old boyfriends. But I'm willing to leave the past in the past if you are."

Right. She licks her lips. *Message received.* "I am."

"Good." He grins as they arc around a corner and the lake sparkles into view. "Look at that. I hear there's good fishing out here."

"There is. Caught a tiger trout on Boxer Lake when I was nine."

"You've fished here?"

"With a foster family. One of my shortest placements—just a month—but I got to go camping."

He grabs her hand and squeezes. "Let's make some better camping memories."

Contentment courses through her. "Deal."

As he navigates to their campsite, she heads back to check on AJ. He's flipping through the book again, reading to big bear. "*Honk! Cried the Dump, and he sounded scared, but nobody heard (or nobody cared).*"

"We're just about there, sweetie. Need to go potty?"

"Nuh-uh." He flips a page in the book.

"Are you sure?" Maybe he went. She tries to check his pullup, and he wiggles away.

"No, Mama. I go after."

"After what?"

"*After.* With My Tail."

And people think only women hit the restroom in packs. "Just be sure you let one of us know when it's time."

"I swim now?"

She peers out the window as Matteo backs into the site. They're closer to other campers than she'd like. A ring of other campsites curves around them, with scant trees for privacy.

No naked stargazing here.

She changes AJ into swim trunks and slathers him with sunscreen while Matteo sets up camp. He pops his head in as

Renee's buckling their son's sandal. "Want me to take him to the water while you get changed?"

"That'd be great."

"Come on, little man." Matteo holds out a hand. "How about we learn to skip rocks?"

"Sip rocks?"

"Throw," he amends, smiling at Renee. "Skipping means you throw the rock so it moves across the water."

"Yeah!" AJ shoots like lightning to the door. "I throw like My Tail."

"Be safe," Renee calls after them. "AJ, you stay with Matteo, and don't run off."

"Okay, Mama!" He scampers for the water's edge with Matteo behind him.

Pushing back a ripple of unease, she reminds herself she trusts him. Matteo has his faults, but he'll guard AJ with his life. She's sure of it.

Ducking into the tiny camper bathroom, she pulls on shorts and a tank. Checks herself in the mirror and swipes on some lip balm. Straightens her ponytail.

Because looking good is super-important when your life's in danger.

Stepping out, she peers through the window. Doesn't see AJ, and panic wraps a fist around her heart. *There.* They're on the other side of a tree, her baby standing ankle deep in water. Matteo's wrestling him into a child-sized life vest, a blue and red one Nic brought. Her heart sighs as she shoves open the door.

"Howdy, neighbor! I'm Susie."

She turns to see a sixty-something woman waving from the site next door. Behind her sits an airstream trailer strung with Christmas lights and an area rug in the dirt. Flamingo statues dot the campsite's corners, and there's a hand-painted sign that reads "The Burkes."

"Hi, Susie." There's nothing threatening about the smiling

lady with Bermuda shorts and a salt-and-pepper perm. Still, Renee's on guard. "Looks like you're set up to stay awhile."

"Oh, about three weeks, give or take. Stanley—" She gestures to a grizzled guy with a paunch who's chopping wood. "Stanley and I are traveling around hitting every national park in the country."

"Good for you." Renee wipes her hands on her shorts and shakes the woman's hand. "Sounds like an amazing adventure."

"Almost as amazing as your husband's abs!" She says it so brightly, Renee's stuck for a response.

"My husb—oh, M—Matt?" She shouldn't use his full name. "Right. Yes, well. He works out a lot."

"Nice, very nice." Susie shoots a look of longing at Matteo's arms, which flex as he flings a rock at the lake. "What time does your son go to bed?"

Alarm prickles her arms. "Pardon?"

Susie steps close, chipper as hell. "Having alone time is so important, isn't it? When they're little like that?"

Renee swallows hard. "Right. So important."

"Stanley and me, we're swingers." Susie offers this like they're scuba divers or Elk's Club members. "If that's something you're into, you could bring your baby monitor and your camp lingerie, and we could—"

"Um, thank you, but I'll pass." What the hell is camp lingerie? "I appreciate the offer, though."

"Suit yourself. Lotsa folks swing on the camp scene, so I'm sure we'll see you around." Still smiling, Susie ambles back to camp. Consults with Stanley, who stops chopping to wave.

Renee waves back as AJ runs over and grabs her by the leg. "Mama, they have swing?"

Oh, God. Her son and his bionic hearing.

"It's just for grownups, sweetie." She steers him back toward the lake. "Did I see you skipping rocks like a big boy?"

"Uh-huh." He grabs one shaped like a potato. "My Tail said go away while he hits the tree."

"Hits the tree?" She looks at Matteo, who—okay, yes. Definitely looks great without a shirt. "Why would you hit a tree?"

"Not me, *him*." Matteo nods to the next campsite where a bearded guy bickers with a pine tree.

"I *said*, would you like a beer?" The man's slurring his words, so that's not his first can of Budweiser. "What, you think you're too good for the king of beers? You want some crappy craft shit? Maybe Heineken?"

Heineken comes out on a hiccup as the man circles the tree and swears again. "Fuckin' pretentious prick. I warned you, didn't I? Okay, it's go-time."

Renee scoops up AJ and turns him away as the man takes a swing at the trunk. He misses—thank God—but punches again. Another miss. Staggering, the guy drops to the picnic table bench. "Oh, hey." He brightens and opens his cooler. "Beer."

She looks back at Matteo. "Are all campers weird?"

He grins and hands AJ a flat skipping rock. "Try this one."

"Okay, My Tail." As Renee sets him down, he bounces away and chucks it out over the water. Matteo skims her ear with his lips. "Don't look now, but there's a guy in his underwear at the campsite behind us."

"What?" She cranes her neck and cringes. A man in red boxer briefs paces by a pup tent with a phone to his ear. "Sorry, you said don't look."

"It's fine." Matteo hands AJ another flat rock. "Just trying to keep little man from noticing. Far as I can tell, his buddies played a prank."

"A prank?"

"Took his stuff while he slept. He's calling someone but can't get a signal."

Renee snorts as AJ scans the shore for more rocks. "So, back to the question of campers being weird."

"Yep." Matteo bends and finds another flat rock for her son. *His* son.

Wow, that's weird. Weird, but...nice?

"Speaking of signals," he says. "I'm thinking I'll walk over to the lodge. Buy stuff for s'mores and check in with Seb."

"There's Wi-Fi over there?"

"According to the lady who stopped by selling firewood." Matteo winks. "Word of advice—don't ask about aliens."

"Why would I ask her about aliens?"

"You wouldn't, but she'll volunteer it. There's a government conspiracy to cover up the spaceship crash last summer."

"Lay-liens!" AJ grabs a rock beside her foot. "Mama, I go with My Tail?"

"No, sweetie." She bends to wipe a streak of sunscreen off his nose. "You need to stay here and keep Mama company."

"But My Tail gets some oars."

"Oars?" They're going boating? "Oh, *s'mores.*" She smiles at Matteo, a private, parent glance she never guessed she'd share with her son's father. "I haven't had s'mores in forever."

Matteo grabs his T-shirt off a tree branch and tugs it on. "You know what s'mores are, buddy?"

"To eat?"

"Exactly."

"They're a special camping treat for good boys who stay close to Mama." She smiles as Matteo leans close, bracing for his kiss.

His lips brush her ear again. "Beretta's in the safe, unlocked." The whisper spurs a shiver. "He can't reach, so it's there if you need it. Camper keys are on the hook by the door."

"Okay, I—" She pauses as panic pushes its way up her throat. "You're going now?"

"Yeah. I promised Seb I'd be in touch." They watch as AJ chucks another rock. "I guess he has more info for us."

"Good. That's...good." What's with the rocks in her gut? "Why would I need the keys?"

"Just in case." This time when he leans in, he skims a kiss down her throat. "I'll be right back."

"Okay." She sounds shaky but forces a smile. "Need cash so we don't leave a paper trail?"

"I've got it." He kisses her again. "I won't be gone long. See you soon."

She watches him go, words echoing in her ears.

I won't be gone long.

See you soon.

The same thing he said three years ago. Matteo's last words before he walked out the door and never came back.

Drawing a breath, she squeezes her eyes shut.

Opens them to watch him walk away.

CHAPTER 11

Sebastian answers on the first ring. "Was starting to think you wouldn't call."

"It's three minutes past noon." Matteo steps around a sign for boat rentals to reach a quiet spot near the campground's general store. Sliding on sunglasses, he tucks himself behind a row of paddleboards. "Tough to stay on schedule when fleeing armed thugs." Besides, he had to buy s'mores stuff first. Convenient cover and all that.

"You're getting soft, Teo." It's good-natured ribbing, but with an edge. "Got a couple things for you."

His eyes follow a family stacking fishing gear in a gray wooden boat. Tackle box, ice chest, colorful floaties for the kids. The dad tickles the youngest, a boy about AJ's age. With the kids settled in the boat, Dad offers a hand to Mom. She laughs and laces fingers through his, smiling as the husband sneaks a butt pat.

"...dated a cop," Sebastian's saying, and Matteo knows he's missed something.

"What about a cop?" He drags his gaze off the family and tries to focus.

"You asked me to look into Renee's ex-boyfriends." Seb says it with exaggerated patience. "In case one of them had a grudge."

"Renee dated a cop?" Seems like something she'd mention. "Why?"

"I don't know—maybe he's hot?" Sebastian snorts. "This isn't a deep dive into your girlfriend's emotional motives. It's a freakin' background check."

Matteo drags a hand through his hair. "What do we know about the cop?"

"Not much. Doesn't sound serious. Some guy she went out with a few times after you ditched her. Pissed off her criminal ex pretty good."

As another criminal ex, Matteo relates. "I'm surprised she didn't mention it."

"Because you'd be so supportive if she had?" He's laying it on thick with the cynical shit. "I assume she knows your love of law enforcement."

"Some." Maybe he should have shared more. Given details of his story. "She's not a fan, either."

"Of cops?" Seb chuckles. "We should form a club."

"So it wasn't serious?"

"Doesn't sound like it. Probably an unbidden quest for safety and security. A way to stick it to her old man if you want my best guess."

"I don't." Renee dating a cop gets him growly. "One of your contacts told you about it?"

"A dude she dated after you. I guess there was some overlap with the cop. Nothing serious with either."

That's comforting. Not that he doubted the story she told him. He sits on a bench behind the paddleboards. "What else? You said you had a couple things."

"Right, yeah." There's tapping in the background. Building a bomb or writing patient charts? Hard to know with Seb. "You know someone named Rebecca Payne?"

"Rebecca Payne?" He scrolls through his mental archives. "Not that I can think of."

"Her husband filed a missing person report. Name's Dillon Payne, and he's a piece of work."

"*Dillhole?*" His bark draws a look from a couple strolling the lake shore. Matteo lowers his voice. "Abusive prick. I helped his wife and kid get away."

"Well, he's raising a stink. Dante's cop friend, Austin—he says there's a BOLO out for you. Well, not *you*. 'Burly asshole with a scar on his neck and a tricked-out spaceship camper-van.' I guess that's you."

Fuck. He knew Nondi's ride was recognizable. "Is Bex safe?"

"Who's Bex?"

"The wife. She was trying to get away."

"Oh. Yeah, I think so." More tapping. "He's trying to find her but can't."

"Good."

"Not good, Teo. You've got a target on your back. Don't go riling up law enforcement."

Seb's right, which sucks. If he could go back and *not* help Bex, Matteo would...do exactly what he did.

So would Sebastian. Dante, too. They might be criminals, but there's a code.

"I'll be careful." He watches a man in uniform. Green pants, badge on his chest. Park ranger? He's clean shaven and smiling as he greets two teens playing frisbee in the grass. The ranger tips his hat and ambles past.

Matteo's arms prickle.

"Teo?"

"Yeah?"

"We're close, okay? Just keep them safe a while longer. We've almost got it figured out. Then you can all come home and live happily ever after."

"Sure." As if.

Only...*what if?*

The ache in his chest tells him it's not so silly. He wants that happy ending. Wants it more than he realized. "Thanks, Seb. Take care."

"You, too. Stay safe out there."

He hangs up and stuffs the phone in his pocket. The ranger's getting closer. Spots Matteo with the paddleboards and gives a good-natured wave.

A rush of adrenaline shoves him off the bench. He's on his feet, watching the man in green. Something in the guy's posture, in the cardboard cut of his smile, sets Matteo's skin itching.

"Evening, buddy." The ranger laughs and looks at his watch. "Guess it's barely afternoon."

"Right." His fingers twitch. There's a knife at his hip, but no reason to need it.

No reason but the buzz in his chest. It's getting louder, adrenaline whooshing in his ears.

The ranger laughs and rubs his paunch. "I don't know about you, but I've had a long day already."

Matteo forces a smile. "I'm good." He's *not* good, but good at faking it. "Camping, you know. So relaxing." He twists his grocery bag of marshmallows and wonders what a normal guy would say. "Nothing soothes the soul like being outside."

He sounds like a damn Patagonia ad. The ranger looks bemused. "Can't say I hear that much from folks camping with small kids. I remember that with my own. Talk about a tough time!"

The itch in his skin flares to flame. Teo edges back a foot. "How'd you know I'm camping with small kids?" He leaves it plural, just in case. Maybe he's paranoid.

The ranger rocks back on his heels. "You bought stuff for s'mores. Not that grownups don't eat 'em." He hoots at his own joke. "Hoo boy, I tell ya. If the wife didn't keep tabs on sugar, I'd eat marshmallows with every meal."

Matteo's not buying it. Maybe he's crazy. Maybe he's got issues with guys in uniform. Something to unpack in therapy. "Right, well." Swinging his bag, he takes another step back. "Good talking with you. I need to get back to—"

"Now hold on a minute, son." Something shifts in the ranger's eyes. "Got a BOLO out for a guy driving a silver camper-van. Oregon plates, solar panels on the roof. You wouldn't know anything about that, would you?"

"BOLO?" He knows damn well what it means. BOLO, *be on the lookout*. Cops used to say APB, and he knows that one, too. Knows more cop lingo than he'd like.

Knows they can't be trusted, even when they're rangers.

Especially when they have broad foreheads and eyes that look...memorable. He's not the guy from the Fair. Not Renee's stalker, but still. Something's familiar—

"Folks are looking pretty hard for you." The ranger puts his palms up with a smile. "I know, I know. Probably a misunderstanding, right?"

"Right." He needs to get out of here. Renee's alone with AJ, and Ranger Rick's not giving him warm fuzzy vibes. "If the cops want me, you know where I'll be."

"Campsite 27. Loop B."

"Yep." Not good. Not fucking good. "I'll be there if they need me."

He absolutely won't. Seven minutes, five if he runs. Enough time to pull the wheel chocks and drive like hell out of here. Matteo clears his throat. "I'll get going now."

Turning away, he takes two steps. A zing blasts his spine, shooting pain to his fingertips. He roars as lightning arcs through him. Each muscle constricts—hamstrings, hip flexors, that weird one in the arch of his foot. Tibialis posterior?

He's delirious and dizzy as his head hits the ground. He should be running, crawling, clawing his way back to AJ and Renee.

159

But he can't move a goddamn inch.

The ranger squats beside him. "Sorry about that, son. Can't have you running off. Local police asked me to bring you in. Nothing personal."

He tries to speak, but his tongue won't work. That's a muscle, too. One of six hundred in the human body. What the hell is happening?

"Taser." The ranger jerks something from Matteo's back.

"Fuck." It's barely a croak, but the shocks subside.

"You might be weak for a bit." The ranger stuffs the taser in a holster and grabs his elbow. "Let's get you in the car so we can swing by the station and get this cleared up."

Matteo tries to stand, but his legs won't work. There's fire in his palms and gravel in his knees. His head feels like he used it to pound fence posts. Did his forehead hit the ground when he fell?

Dragging him up, the ranger fires a cheerful smile at a couple pedaling past on bikes. "Afternoon folks. Nothing to worry about." He slings Matteo's arm over his shoulder and starts for a mint green truck. "Fella's had a little too much to drink."

Matteo tries to argue, to scream, to fight.

But nothing in his body works.

Not even the balls to get back to Renee.

* * *

HIS CAR RIDE to the cop house is a blur. Maybe he did hit his head because he's sure tasers don't leave someone this dazed.

He's hauled to a small room in an ugly cinderblock building. A small-town cop shop if he's ever seen one. A spotted dog dozes by the door on a homemade rag rug. Posters display America's Most Wanted, plus some guys who stole a goat. Small-town America at its finest.

He's sitting in an empty room, rubbing his arms, when a cop

comes through the door. Young guy with baby fat in his cheeks. Can't be more than twenty-three, and Matteo feels old.

Baby Cop holds out a paper cup of water. "Sorry about that, sir. Park Ranger Harris said you bonked your head pretty good. Those tasers are nothing to mess with. Had to get hit with one for new recruit training, so I know how it feels to—"

"Why am I here?" Matteo takes the water but doesn't drink. No way he's trusting this. "What the hell happened back at the campground?" He knows he's not asking the right questions, but the blow to the head must've dropped his IQ. "I was just minding my own business, talking to the park ranger when—"

"I sure apologize for Ranger Harris." The young cop's cheer dims just a little. "He's a good man. Gets excited sometimes, but he doesn't mean any harm."

Matteo shakes his head, fighting to clear it. Is this small-town cop crap, or something else? He should lawyer up. Maybe ask for a phone to call Renee.

But unease holds him back. The risk of leading them to her, or maybe just the fuzz in his head. "Seems like excessive use of force to me."

"Well, now." Baby Cop frowns. "You running off like you did when he was trying to talk to you—that set off alarm bells. We get some shady folks out here hiding from the law, and you do match the profile of a guy we've been after. You understand."

He doesn't understand a damn thing. His head hurts like a bitch and he needs to get out of here. "Why am I arrested?"

"Oh, you're not under arrest." Baby Cop's smiling again, and Lord, the kid has dimples. "Nah, the chief just wants to talk to you. Ranger Harris, he's the chief's cousin. Heard 'em talking this morning about a stolen truck near Summer Lake. You wouldn't know anything about that, would you?"

Jesus. He looks at the water and sighs. Lifts the cup and dumps it on his head.

"Whoa there!" Baby Cop grabs a paper towel. "Are you okay, sir?"

He needs to shake out of this. To be clearheaded for what's coming. Maybe it's all a misunderstanding. If he can talk his way out of this, he'll get back to Renee and AJ before they know he's gone.

"I'm good." He takes the towel from Junior and wipes his face. Nods to the sink in the corner. "Mind if I get my own water?"

"Uh...I think that's okay." The cop steps back as Matteo gets to his feet.

He stumbles and grabs the counter. Dammit, he's weak. *Focus.*

"Let me help with that." Baby Cop takes the cup and fills it at the tap. Holds it with a hopeful smile. "Chief Dowling should be here any minute."

All the blood leaves his head. Reeling, he grips the counter. "Chief—Dowling?"

"That's right. Just started a few weeks ago."

Matteo grabs the cup and gulps. Fills it again and drinks until his head starts to clear.

This can't be happening.

He crushes the cup and looks at Baby Cop. "How much money do you have?"

The kid blanches. "Sir?"

Christ, he's not thinking clearly. "I'll pay you ten thousand dollars to let me walk out of here right now."

Baby Cop takes a step back. "I'm not that kind of man, sir. Bribing a police officer is—"

"I know, I know." Damage control time. "I was kidding. Just... uh...testing your morals."

A grin splits the young cop's face. "I hope I passed. Wasn't sure what to think when I saw your rap sheet. There's some sealed stuff in your record and...well. You know." He shrugs as color warms his cheeks. "Sometimes it's hard to know who's the good guy and who's the bad guy."

"No shit." Those words wedge in his gut like a sideways brick. *AJ*.

And Renee.

Christ, they're alone.

Are they still on the lake shore waiting? He looks at his watch and nearly throws up. "I've been gone over an hour."

"Shouldn't be much longer." The cop backs toward the door. "Chief'll be here soon, and then we'll give you your stuff back. Cool throwing knife, by the way."

Matteo slides a hand to his hip. The sheath's still there, but the knife's gone.

This is bad. So bad.

He squeezes his eyes shut and wills this to be a dream. Pleads with God or anyone else to let him walk out of here alive. He doesn't need long. Just ten minutes to get Renee and AJ safely on the road. This mess, whatever it is, it's his fault.

He'll be damned if he drags them into it.

There's a rush of air as a door swings wide, and Matteo opens his eyes. At the threshold stands the one man he hoped he'd never see again.

"Matteo Bello." Reggie Dowling saunters in, kicking the door shut behind him. "Fancy seeing you here."

CHAPTER 12

There's no way it takes two hours to buy graham crackers and cheap chocolate. Renee checks her watch and swallows a surge of frustration. She's not even sure who she's mad at.

Matteo for leaving? *Again.*

Herself for trusting him. *Again.*

She's texted six times and called four. No response, and the line goes straight to voicemail. The connection's bad up here, but not *that* bad.

The camper keys dangle on their hook by the door. That should have been her first clue. At least he gave her wheels before ditching her in the woods with a toddler.

She looks at the untouched sandwich on her plate. Listens for the whoosh of the toilet. Forces her face into a happy mommy smile as AJ steps shirtless from the tiny camper bathroom.

"You washed your hands?"

"Uh-huh." He wipes them on his balled-up shirt.

"Put your shirt back on and come have your snack."

"Okay." He pulls it on inside out and she's too tired to fix it. Too fretful to brace for his questions.

"Mama?" He hops on the bench across from her. "Where My Tail?"

She squeezes the back of her neck. "He should be back soon, sweetie."

Maybe not a lie. Could be he went for a hike to clear his head. Maybe he's hurt. Maybe unconscious or busy explaining quantum physics to fellow campers.

Or maybe he realized commitment and fatherhood aren't in his cards. Why did she throw that on him about wanting a relationship? She should have left it alone, just enjoyed the sex and called it good. This is her fault.

"Stop it."

"Mama?" AJ's got a grape halfway to his mouth.

"Sorry, sweetie." She pats his free hand. "Just talking to myself."

"Stop it." He grins and shoves the fruit in his mouth. "No sad, Mama."

"Good idea." This fatalistic thinking gets her nowhere. "You're right."

Maybe he didn't leave this time. He could be wandering around reeling with bad news from Dr. LaDouceur. Maybe someone showed up looking for them, and he's leading them away from camp. Or Nicole came to see them and he's having lunch with his sister.

Nicole.

She'll know something. Renee slips her phone out and frowns. No bars. She starts to put it away, then remembers a trick. Matteo taught her to reset a phone's signal search by switching to airplane mode, then back again. She taps the button. Waits a few seconds. Lays it flat and waits.

AJ pats her hand. "Mama. We go look for My Tail?"

"Finish your snack first." It's not the worst idea to search for him. "Maybe after we eat and get changed."

"Okay." He grabs a cube of cheese. There's a tidy row of apple slices ringing the rim of the plate, plus goldfish crackers and grapes.

It's the sort of snack she envied in friends' childhood lunch boxes. Normal childhood nourishment served by a normal mom on a normal, wholesome day.

Nothing about this feels normal. "Maybe he got news about his job."

AJ looks up. "Job?"

"He's been applying for something." Maybe that's it. He got a phone interview and took it someplace quiet.

Even AJ looks skeptical. His forehead scrunches. "Bad sammitch?"

"What? Oh, no." She picks it up to prove it's fine. "Mmm, yummy." Biting the bread, she makes herself swallow. "So good."

AJ goes back to eating. She sets down the sandwich and picks up her phone. Taps it out of airplane mode, then sets it down to cycle. Stares at the screen. Two bars. She picks it up.

"Drink all your milk, sweetie." She nudges the sippy cup in front of him. "This is just a snack, okay? We'll have real lunch soon."

"When My Tail comes?"

When. Not *if.* There's a lump in her throat. "Yes."

"Want goldfish?" He holds out a sticky cracker, and her heart liquifies.

"No, thank you, sweetie." She stands up and tousles his hair. "I need to make some phone calls now, okay?"

He nods and shoves a grape in his mouth. "My Tail?"

"Yes, for sure."

He chews and swallows. "Miss Nicole?"

"Maybe." Definitely. But she can't have him asking to talk to his teacher. "You stay in your seat, okay? Don't get down. I'll just be right over here."

"Okay, Mama."

She moves to the back of the camper, where she still has eyes on him. It's not ideal, and she'll need to choose words carefully.

Matteo's line goes straight to voicemail. No surprise. She swallows disappointment and hangs up. AJ's happily crunching goldfish crackers. Time to try Nicole.

Her hands shake as she dials. It's a risk, calling from the road. Anyone could be monitoring. The burner phone gives some protection, but if there's a trace on Miss Gigglewink's—

"Hello, this is Nicole."

"Nicole, it's me." She breathes relief and sinks to the bed. "*Raina*," she adds, because the teacher hasn't said anything. "I know it's a risk calling, but—"

"Are you okay? Don't tell me where you are, but—are you safe?"

She nods and licks her lips. "We're fine. We're—we're where you suggested, and it's great, but—we've lost my son's father."

If she's surprised by the word "father," Nic doesn't let on. Or maybe she thinks they're talking in code. "Lost?"

"He went to get supplies. To make a phone call, I think. That was over two hours ago."

"Don't panic." Nicole must know she's past panic and moving to terrified. "Who did he need to call?"

"One of his friends." She shouldn't name names. "Um, the one who makes a living doing something to people. Something some folks are scared of."

Nicole bursts out laughing. "Wow. Okay, that's one way to put it. I've got you, all right? Just hang on."

There's shuffling on the other end and Renee steals a glance at her son. He's got a goldfish in each hand, making them talk to each other. Her heart hiccups as she blinks back tears.

Hold it together. You're a mom, dammit.

"Raina? I'm going to give you that person's number, okay? I'd call for you, but that might land us in a messy game of phone tag where I'm in the middle and time's wasting and—anyway. Are you ready?"

She grabs the red notepad Matteo left on the dinette. "Yes."

"Okay, the first digit is the number of monkeys. Got it?"

"Monkeys?" Is she high? A light blinks in her brain. "Oh! Yes, I've got it."

She scribbles five on the notepad, heart pounding in her head. *Five Little Monkeys* is one of AJ's favorite books.

"The next number is how many times your son has been absent this year before our current situation. Understand?"

Zero. She writes it on the notepad and darts another glance at AJ. "Got it."

"All right. What number is the caterpillar?"

Caterpillar, caterpillar, caterpillar...

"Oh." The numbers on the daycare wall. *Three!* That's the number formed by the fuzzy green bug. "Yes, got it."

"Next is how many stitches that little sweetie needed when he fell and hit his chin on the jungle gym."

Six stitches. Her throat squeezes shut as she sneaks another look. AJ's sipping his milk, palms wrapped around the cup.

As Nicole recites more numbers, Renee writes them down. Her palms feel clammy, and she can't shake the spikes in her gut.

"You got all that?"

"Yes." Renee licks her lips. "I have the number."

"Good. I'm going to hang up so you can make that call. That's a personal cell, not a work number. If there's no answer right away, hang up and call back exactly one minute later. No more, no less. That's the code."

"The code." If she were less stressed, she'd wonder how Nic knows this. "Nicole, thank you. I can't thank you enough."

"I'll help however I can. You know that."

"I know." She squeezes the phone, not wanting to break her connection to Matteo's sister. "I'll keep you posted."

"Good luck."

She hangs up and dials Dr. LaDouceur. The phone rings once. Twice. She checks her watch in case she needs to hang up and call one minute later.

"Dr. LaDouceur speaking."

"Dr. LaDouceur, it's—"

"Hello there! Could you hold on just a second?"

"Yes, of course."

The line goes silent, and she wonders if he's scrambling the signal somehow. Or maybe he's with a patient, elbow deep in a root canal. She waits and prays he comes back on.

"Renee, hi. We're on a secure line, all right? Go ahead and speak freely."

"Thank you." She squeezes her eyes shut and says it. "I've lost Matteo. Or maybe he left me or got kidnapped or arrested or—"

"Renee, breathe. Deep inhale, hold at the top. Let it go." Spoken like a man accustomed to treating nervous patients. "Tell me what happened."

"I don't know what happened!" She looks at AJ. He's watching with wide, nervous eyes. "Can you hang on a second?"

"Sure."

She stands and moves to the front of the camper. "Finish your snack, sweetie. Mommy's going outside for a second. I'll be right on the other side of this door, okay?"

AJ shoves aside the curtain. "I see you?"

"Yes, you'll be able to see me."

She steps out the door as Dr. LaDouceur's voice rings in her ear. "AJ's okay?"

"He's fine. He's…confused." That makes two of them.

"Right, so walk me through it." The dentist sounds calm and soothing. "Tell me what led to Matteo disappearing."

She sinks to the top step and hugs her knees to her chest. "He went to get marshmallows and to call you."

"Right, we spoke." A pause. "That was over two hours ago. You're saying you haven't seen him since then?"

169

"That's right." Her voice sounds scared, so she orders herself to breathe. "He walked over to the lodge to get a signal." Which is weird, come to think about it. If she's got coverage, wouldn't he? "I guess he wanted privacy." Or a chance to escape...

"Renee, don't think that."

She gulps. "Think what?"

"That he ran off and left you."

"You're a psychic dentist?"

He ignores that. "I know he cares about you and AJ. He wouldn't leave, all right? Something happened."

She wants that to be true. Or does she? If something happened, she'll never forgive herself. She's sitting here thinking the worst of him, while he's somewhere hurt or injured or—

"It wouldn't be unprecedented for him to just leave," she says.

"No way." He sounds sure. "He's changed, Renee. If you could have seen him after he left you last time—the man was a wreck. I swear on my life, he wouldn't leave you again. I'm positive."

Squeezing her eyes shut, she wills herself not to cry. "Okay, so what happened?"

"I don't know. Can you hang on a second?"

"Sure."

There's murmuring on the line, and she wonders if he's at work. She should probably let him go.

A gravelly crunch tugs her gaze to the road. A police rig, a white SUV. Her heart pounds as it slows. The rig angles to a stop in front of the camper. Sun blinks off darkened windows, and she can't see inside. That's definitely a cop car. There's a light bar on top and *County Sheriff* painted on the side.

"Dr. LaDouceur?" She's not even sure he's there. "The police just pulled up. Oh, God—something happened to him. He's hurt or in trouble or—"

"Breathe, Renee." His voice is calm and steady. "Stay with me, okay?"

"Okay." The driver's side door opens and out comes a leg

swathed in navy blue. Then another. "A male cop. He's getting out."

"Stay on the line no matter what happens." He's on alert. "Pretend you're on hold with the bank or something. That you can't hang up."

She looks around. The swingers aren't in their campsite. The drunk guy who fought the tree left in his fishing boat an hour ago, and there's no sign of the man in red boxer briefs.

Which means she's alone. "Speak with an agent." It's the first thing she says when stuck in her bank's automated loop. "English."

"Good," Sebastian says. "It'll be okay, Renee."

She wants that more than anything. The cop's legs aren't moving beneath the car door, and the tinted window hides his face. Her hands shake as he stands and turns and slams the door. She stares at his back, at the crisp blue shirt, and reminds herself to breathe.

"Renee?" Sebastian's still on the line. "Are you okay?"

"Mobile banking." The cop turns and she gasps. "Oh."

Why is Reggie Dowling here?

She stares as he slides on sunglasses. Stretches and checks his watch. He's twenty feet away, and she risks whispering in the phone. "I actually know this guy."

"Renee." There's an edge to the dentist's voice. "This cop. He's not someone you dated, is he?"

Her heart skids to a stop. How does he—

"Yes." She holds the phone tighter and whispers again. "Yes."

Reggie strides toward her. "Hey, Renee. Long time, no see."

Sebastian's breath draws out in a hiss. "This is bad, Renee. Real bad. Stay with me, you hear?"

"Hello." She waves at Reggie, then points at the phone. "Can you wait a sec? I'm on hold with the bank. Automated system black hole, you know?"

Sebastian's breathing faster. "Renee, I need you to listen to me. Matteo got screwed by a dirty cop. I need to know this guy's name. Can you—"

"Great to see you." Reggie doffs his cap. "It's been a long time."

She licks her lips and speaks clearly for the phone. "Reggie, what brings you all the way out here?"

"Oh, fuck." Sebastian's not calm anymore. "Reggie Fucking Dowling. I knew it. I fucking *knew* it."

"What?" Her heart's racing now. "Um, talk to a representative." Crap, she has to keep this going. Her eyes go to Reggie. "Is there a problem?"

She's asking Sebastian, but Reggie steps closer. "There is a problem, actually. I'm hoping you can help me."

"Renee, don't trust him." The dentist is downright panicked. "And whatever you do, don't hang up."

She clears her throat and smiles. "We can talk while I'm on hold."

"We don't have much time." Reggie puts his hat back on. "There's a problem with a friend of yours. I need you to—"

"Problem?" She stops herself from saying Matteo's name. "What kind of problem? And how come you're here, anyway? I thought you were still in Seattle."

"Good," Sebastian coaches. "You get information from him, not the other way around."

Her palms are so sweaty she can hardly hold the phone.

Reggie leans calmly on the camper. "Got tired of the big city. I've got family out here, and small-town life is much quieter." He laughs. "Mostly. We do have our moments."

She shoves her free hand under her butt so he can't see it shaking. "You said there was a problem?"

The cop frowns. "Can't you hang up and call later?"

"Renee." The dentist's voice is urgent. "Do not trust him, whatever he says. Reggie Dowling is a crooked cop. He's the reason Matteo went to prison."

Oh, God.

A chill swoops up her arms. "I just need a minute." She sounds calmer than she is. "I've been waiting on hold forever and finally got a signal. Shouldn't be long."

"Good, that's good." Sebastian's tapping a keyboard. "You're a three-hour drive from here. I'll cancel my appointments and call Dante—he's closer."

Reggie's frowning. "Renee, I need you to come with me."

"Oh?" *Three hours.* She can't wait for someone to save her. And if Matteo's in trouble… "Where are we going?"

"Just a short drive." Reggie shoves off the camper. "I'll have you back here in no time."

"How about I drive myself?" Thank God Teo left the keys.

"Sorry. No dice." Reggie shakes his head sadly. "Sorry Renee, this is serious. If you don't come willingly, I'll have to take you into custody."

"You're arresting me?" She gulps. "What for?"

Sebastian's gone silent. Is he still there?

"Aiding and abetting a criminal." Reggie hooks his thumbs on his belt. "Look, we can do this nice and easy. Just hang up the phone, grab your son, and let's go see Matteo."

AJ. He knows she's not alone. And that's the first time he's said Matteo's name. Any doubts she had go up in flames.

Sebastian's talking again. "I'll send someone. There's gotta be a ranger nearby, or—"

"Okay, I'm hanging up now." She's not, but Reggie can't know. With trembling hands, she taps a spot half an inch from the power button. "There."

Call still connected, she shoves the phone in her pocket. Stands and wipes her hands on her shorts. "You can't arrest me, Reggie. I haven't done anything."

The man who held her hair back while she threw up brunch gives a charming smile. "And we can sort that out down at the station. If you'll just come with me—"

"Why should I trust you?"

His eyes narrow. Just a flicker, but she sees it. "Because if you don't, I'll cuff you and take you in." He pulls out a sheet of paper. "A warrant for your arrest."

She scans the paper, heart thudding in her ears. It looks real, but what does she know?

"It'd be a real shame, wouldn't it?" Reggie's eyes sweep hers.

"What's that?"

"Me dragging you off to jail like a common criminal while your son's stuck here." He shakes his head and looks at the lake. "A lot can happen when a little kid's left alone."

Her blood runs cold. She prays Sebastian's hearing this. That he sends help.

Seconds tick as she weighs her options. If she refuses to go, he'll take her anyway and leave AJ. He mentioned family. Maybe he's got more thugs waiting nearby. Better to keep AJ with her. It's the best way to protect him.

Swallowing hard, she stands and grabs the camper door. "Let me grab shoes and lock up. My son might need the bathroom first."

"Fine." Reggie stares from the bottom of the steps. "Bring the kid. I've got a cop hat he can wear. I'll let him run the siren."

"Great." She wants him dead. It's the first time in her life she's thought herself capable of killing someone. She'd do it in a heartbeat to save her child.

The cop smiles. "Don't forget his booster seat."

"Of course." A ruse, or a sign he won't hurt them? "I'll be right back."

He's got her blocked in, so he knows she can't go anywhere. Sweaty palms twist the knob as she slips through the door. Slams it shut and draws the curtains.

AJ sets down his sippy cup. "All done, Mama."

"Good boy." Please let this work. "Go wash up, sweetie. We're taking a ride."

"No ride." He frowns. "No more driving. *Swim*. Swim with My Tail."

This is not the time for meltdowns. "We're looking for Matteo. There's a police officer who's going to help find him. Hurry and wash your hands."

That gets him moving. The instant he shuts the bathroom door, she's got her phone out.

Dead.

No signal, and no time to redial. Reggie's pacing on the gravel outside.

Heart pounding, she shoves a hand in the gun safe. Her fingers close around the Beretta, and she pulls it back to check. Still loaded.

She makes sure the safety's on and shoves it in the back of her shorts. Her T-shirt hides it, but she ties a sweatshirt at her waist anyway. In the cupboard to the left, she spots the knives tucked behind knickknacks. Slipping a hand inside, she grabs three of them. They're heavy on the end with a weird looking blade.

Snatching a dishrag, she wraps up the medium-sized one. Shoves it in the back pocket of her shorts and prays she doesn't stab her butt. The other two blades get dropped in her purse. She's officially armed to the teeth.

"Ready, sweetie?" She slings the purse over her shoulder. "We need to go."

AJ comes out with his shirt off. "Went pee pee."

"Good boy. Put your shirt back on, okay?"

He complies without complaint.

"Hold Mama's hand, sweetie."

"Okay." He fits his palm in hers. "S'mores?"

"I promise we'll have s'mores later." She shuts her eyes and prays she keeps her word. Checks her phone and sees it's still dead.

The door bangs open and Reggie's at the threshold glaring.

"I'll take that." He snatches the phone and smiles. "You'll get it back when we're done."

"But—"

"Hey, partner!" He drops a small felt police hat on AJ's head. "Want to go for a ride in a police car?"

Her son looks at her. "We go?"

"We go." She hopes she's doing the right thing. Of a dozen bad choices, there's no good one.

Drawing a breath, she puts a hand on his back. "Stay with Mama."

"Okay."

Gun at her back, purse at her hip, she meets Reggie's eyes. "Let's go."

* * *

THE CINDERBLOCK BUILDING LOOKS DARK. As they park in a spot behind a dumpster, a cheerful young officer strolls out.

"Chief Dowling." He touches the brim of his cap. "I'm heading out."

"You got the paperwork done?"

"Yes, sir."

"Nice work." Reggie gets out and meets the guy on the other side of the dumpster. In the backseat of the cop car, Renee squeezes AJ's hand and tries to listen. "I accompanied Mr. Bello back to his campsite," Reggie lies.

"Everything's okay?"

"No worries. Probably eating s'mores with his family right now."

Renee grits her teeth. Not good. She could step from the car, make sure she's seen. Maybe the young cop could help.

But something stops her. What if this guy's crooked? He could be worse than Reggie. At least he let her ride back here with AJ. Her son's squeezing her hand now, watching with wide eyes.

"We see My Tail?"

"I hope so, honey." Her eyes trail the young cop to his car.

"Almost forgot." The officer turns back to Reggie. "Marlene said thanks for letting her go early. She's taking the grandkids to the lake."

"That's great!" Reggie's got his back to them. "It's all about the work-life balance."

"Ain't that the truth." Junior opens his car door. "See you tomorrow."

She watches him drive out of sight. The second he's gone, Reggie opens her door. "Sorry I couldn't introduce you to my colleague." The wink says he's not sorry. "Busy kid, Officer Nobbs."

"Sure." She clamps her teeth shut so she doesn't scare AJ. Unhooking his car seat, she scoops her baby into her arms. The toy cop hat tips sideways as he snuggles her chest. "Siren?"

"Maybe later." Reggie rests a hand on her back, and she freezes. An inch lower and he'll touch the butt of the gun.

"Which way?" She steps out of reach. "The front door?"

"Side door, actually." He gives her an odd look. "I'll show you the toys I told you about."

"Toys." AJ squirms. "And My Tail."

Reggie leads her to the door. "Our secretary, Marlene—we set up a playroom for her grandkids. It's a family-friendly workplace."

"Great." She says it through gritted teeth, which makes him smile.

"I'm a great guy, Renee. You remember."

She doesn't respond. He leads them through a metal door and down a dark hall. The building's small, so she peers through each doorway, hoping to see Matteo. To see anyone who might help.

"Everyone's gone home for the day." Another weird wink from Reggie. "The perks of running a small staff."

It's not a perk for her. "Where is he?" She won't say Teo's

177

name. It's hard enough keeping AJ settled. "Whatever you're doing, let's get this over with."

"Patience, Renee." He leads them past an office. There's a photo on the wall of Reggie holding a fish. The building smells like stale coffee, and there's no sign of Matteo. Is that good or bad?

"Here's our playroom." Reggie pivots and aims his smile at AJ. "How about you hang out in here while your mommy and I talk?"

"My Tail?" AJ curls a fist at her breast. "My Tail here?"

Reggie scowls. "Why does he keep talking about his tail?"

"It's a kids' game. An imaginary friend." She sets him on his feet and looks around. There's a shelf lined with bright board books. A sagging blue sofa looks older than hers, but it's lined with stuffed animals. "Look, sweetie. You want to pick a friend and read to him?"

"*Blue Truck*!" He runs for the battered paperback. Hoists himself onto the sofa and grabs a gray teddy bear. "Hi, Bear."

A lump burns her throat as Reggie grabs her arm. "Let's talk."

She yanks her arm back. "I'm not leaving him alone."

Reggie stares. "You'd rather he join the conversation?" The look he slides her son chills her blood. "We can do that. Gotta say, it's a bad idea. Impressionable minds and all that."

His voice makes her shiver. "No." God, there's no good choice. "We're not going far?"

"Right next door." The smile doesn't reach his eyes. "Come on."

She gulps and bends to hug her boy. "Be good, okay? Stay here and read until Mommy comes back."

"Okay." He flips a page and holds it for the bear. "Be good, Mama."

"I will." She won't. Being good won't get them out of this.

Being smart will.

"Let's go." Reggie shuts the door and grabs her arm. She doesn't shake him off this time as he guides her to the next room.

Pausing at the door, he shakes his head. "We've been looking for you a long time, Renee."

"Me?" This makes no sense. "Who's *we*? And what do you want with—*Oh, God.*"

The door swings open, and there's Matteo. He's lying on the floor, blood oozing from a gash at his hairline. Both eyes puffed shut, and there's an ugly bruise on his forehead.

"Matteo!" She flies through the door and drops beside him. Hands trembling, she probes his throat with cold fingers. She can't feel a pulse. Just her own pulse pounding in her ears. She keeps probing, not even sure where the artery's supposed to be. She's shaking so hard, and his skin seems cold and papery. Is he breathing? He might not be breathing and, *oh God*, this is her fault.

Footsteps drum behind her. "I'll take that."

Reggie grabs the back of her shirt. Whips the hem up, tearing it as he jerks the gun free. "Naughty, naughty, Renee." He laughs and pockets the pistol, then grabs her purse. "I'll take that, too."

"No!"

He snaps the strap from her shoulder. Unzips the flap and sticks a hand in. When he pulls it back, he's got both knives. "So that's what took you so long."

"Reggie, please." She spins so she's shielding Matteo. "Just let us go, and I'll pretend we never saw you."

He chucks the purse on a chair in the corner. It's sturdy wood with ropes on its legs and arms. Ropes?

As she swivels her gaze back to Reggie, she's staring down the barrel of the Beretta.

The cop laughs. "This is working out great."

179

CHAPTER 13

*I*t's hard to keep his breath shallow. Matteo's arms ache, and not from Reggie's beating. He wants to hold Renee close. Promise her he's fine. Not great, but alive. Alive and enraged.

A useful combination.

What asshole binds a man before beating the shit out of him? Hardly a fair fight. Matteo's done lots of bad things. Same with Seb and Dante.

Not one of them would tie a guy to attack him. There's a code for things like that.

"Matteo." Renee strokes his cheek, and his heart curls in a ball. "Oh, God—I'm so sorry."

She's sorry? This is on him. He should have protected her. Should have put the pieces together quicker. Peeking through puffed eyelids, he's rocked by guilt. He wants to kiss her, hold her, warn her why she's here. What Reggie wants from them.

How did he not see this coming?

"Renee?" Reggie taps her with his toe. Barely a bump, but Matteo sees red. "Are you listening to me?"

"What did you do?" Tears streak her cheeks as she touches Teo's hairline. "Sweetheart? Can you hear me?"

Sweetheart. He likes that. Likes the surge of power it sends him.

He makes himself play possum. It's how he'll buy them time and information and the element of surprise. Not the best weapon, but it's all he's got.

Watching through cracked eyelids, he prays Reggie can't tell. The swelling looks worse than it is. If he can feign unconsciousness a bit longer, he'll get some strength back.

"Why?" Renee whips around to face the asshole. "Why did you do this?"

Reggie's pacing the wall, inspecting the Beretta that belonged to Teo's grandma. "I can't believe you brought a gun. You were such a damn pacifist that I never thought to frisk you."

"Fuck you!" She jumps up and pokes Reggie's chest. Matteo admires both the speed and the swearing. "Why are we here?"

"Come on, Renee. Don't play dumb." He leans against the wall and stuffs the Beretta in his jacket. He's got a service revolver holstered at his hip, plus the knives in Renee's purse. Four weapons in play, and all out of Matteo's reach. He clocks the distance to each one. Calculates his odds.

Reggie toys with the cord on a set of mini blinds.

Mini blinds? That's an interior wall. One-way glass? Must be. Overlooking what?

"I can't believe I ever dated you." She's madder than he's ever heard her. "Does this have something to do with you screwing him over?"

"Who?" The cop frowns. "Your deadbeat boyfriend?" He laughs and shakes his head. "Nah, but he's useful. Not as useful as your kid, but it'll all work out."

Renee stiffens. "If you lay a hand on AJ, I swear to God, I'll—"

AJ?

The whoosh of blood mutes Matteo's rational thought. AJ's *here*? This is worse than he thought.

He draws a breath and prays they can't see his chest move. Okay, *think*. There's rope on the leg of the chair. It's enough for a garrote, so that's one more weapon. The chair is steel, good for swinging.

But all of that's too risky. Two guns in play, both of them with Reggie. Teo can't risk the crossfire.

"The *money*." Reggie sounds heated. "I knew Bello was after it the second I saw him sniffing around. Got the son of a bitch out of the way three years ago, but here we are again."

She folds her arms. "I heard how you screwed him over."

She has? Maybe she talked to Seb. Maybe they put the pieces together.

Reggie laughs. "Bello's smart. He knew he'd get it out of you."

"Get *what* out of me?" She sounds utterly baffled. "I still don't know what you're talking about."

But Matteo does. He prays to God she won't believe this scheming asshole.

"A million and change," he continues. "Your old man hid it well."

"You're talking about the Hanford job?"

"Hamdorf." He pretends to applaud. "Nice job pretending you don't know all about it."

"Because I *don't* know all about it." Renee folds her arms. "I only learned about it today."

"Right." Reggie steps closer. "You know that's not true. The money's been missing for years. With your old man dead, you're the only one who knows where it is." He laughs. "Well, you and Bello. Tougher to get it out of him. The man can take a beating. You, on the other hand…"

Renee moves back. "You don't know my dad. He probably chucked it off a bridge. Anything to keep the cops from getting it."

"Bullshit." Reggie's pacing again, fingers grazing the pistol at his hip. "Your boyfriend knows it, too."

Hurt flickers in her eyes, but she hides it fast.

Please, don't believe him, Renee.

"You're wrong," she whispers.

"Am I?" A taunt, not a question. "A known criminal dates the daughter of the Pacific Northwest's most famous thief, and you think that's coincidence?" He stops moving and laughs. "That's cute, Renee. Real cute."

"You have to believe me." She sounds incredulous. "Don't you think if I had the money, I'd have used it by now?"

"You?" He laughs again. "Nah, you're too good. Too emotional. You'd hold on to it for sentiment's sake. Nostalgia always gets you in the end."

Matteo flexes his fingers. They're looking at each other, not him. If he could just get to a knife—

"Look, I know you know." Reggie's agitated now. "One of you does. With all this leverage, we'll find out soon enough."

"Leverage?" Her voice wobbles. "Please—leave my son out of this. I'll do whatever you say—"

"Look at him in there." Reggie taps the windowsill and smiles. "Cute kid. Reading to the teddy bear? Fucking adorable."

Matteo grinds his teeth. He can't see from here, but her cry paints the picture. AJ on the couch, a stuffie in his arms. Sweet green eyes and a smile for everyone.

His fingers curl into fists. He has to move soon.

"All right." Reggie sighs. "Wasn't gonna start with the kid, but let's get this over with." He moves for the door as Renee grabs his arm.

"No!"

He shoves her, and she tumbles, falling at Matteo's side. "Leave him alone!" she sobs. "I swear I don't know anything. I didn't talk to my father for ages before he died."

"Not true." Reggie stops with his hand on the door. "Prison

records show your father called you every year on your birthday. Christmas, too. The last call was five minutes and thirty-six seconds. Plenty of time to tell you where he hid the cash in your house before he kicked the bucket."

"My house?" She shakes her head. "That's impossible."

"It's not, sweetheart. Want to know how I know?"

Renee doesn't answer. "I never answered his calls." She struggles to sit up. "They'd go right to voicemail. That last one, the Christmas call? AJ answered and put the phone on the coffee table. I didn't see right away and then—"

"Enough with the lies!" He kicks the wall. "I'm done playing around. Let's figure out who knows what. We'll start with the kid."

Bile burns up Teo's throat. He'll have to do this unarmed. He's running out of time.

"Please." She's shaking. He feels it through the floor. "I swear I don't know a thing."

Her hand rests behind her. It's inches from his, splayed on the floor beneath the fanned-out sweatshirt at her waist. He needs her to know he's okay.

Slowly, carefully, he slides his palm across the rough wood floor. Splinters spear his hand, but he keeps going. Another inch and he'll touch her.

His fingers brush her knuckles, and he taps the opening beat.

Hey, Jude...

She gasps.

Don't scream. Please don't—

"Achoo!" She wheezes. Throws an arm like she's coughing in the crook of her elbow. Her eyes meet his beneath her bicep.

Matteo blinks once. Again, so she knows it's real.

Renee stops coughing and drops her arm. "Can I get a glass of water?"

"Nice try." Reggie taps the glass. "Aww, look! He's staring right at us. The kid must've heard you sneeze." He laughs. "It's one-way glass, so he just sees a mirror. Once we bring him in here—"

"Reggie, I'm begging you." She shivers and hugs herself. "I swear, I don't know anything."

"Now why don't I believe you?" He flings an exaggerated hand to his chin. "Oh, I know! Because I've got your dad on tape talking to my brother."

"Your brother?" She stiffens. "I never met your brother."

"No, but he met your dad. Spent almost a year in the same cell block. Know what he learned?"

She's shaking her head, twisting the arms of the sweatshirt at her waist. "That my father was a pathological liar?"

"He learned," Reggie continues, "that your dad trusted you with his stash. Once the old man knew he wasn't getting out, he made sure you got the money. Said so in his letter."

"I never got a letter." She shivers again. "And I swear I don't have the money."

"It was mailed after you moved." He sounds almost bored. "But there had to be more. Even if I couldn't find you, Daddy always could."

She shivers again. "What did it say?"

"The original?" Reggie taps his fingers on his chin and pretends to think. "'Dear Renee: I know you can't forgive me, but I need to get this off my chest before I die. Please use what's left of my legacy and give your boy the life I couldn't give you.'"

The color drains from her face. "I never saw that. I swear."

"Oh, but you know what it means."

"I don't—" She stops, shaking her head. "He was bluffing."

"Doubtful. We did toss your house a few times. A real shit-hole. Probably why we couldn't find much. Or did you move it off-site?"

"I told you, I don't—"

"Enough!" The bark makes her jump.

Shivering, she hugs herself tighter. "Okay," she says. "Okay, let me think." Another shiver. "Can I at least put my sweatshirt on? It's freezing in here."

Reggie glares. "Hold it up. Show me the pockets."

Matteo holds his breath as she gets to her knees, unwinding the sweatshirt from her waist. Her body blocks him from Reggie's view, so he risks a glance at her back.

Oh.

Not her ass, though that's perfect. There's a dishrag poking from her pocket.

And protruding from *that*...the handle of a knife.

He shuts his eyes and fights a groan. Thank God for smart women.

"See?" She's moving again, flipping the pockets of her hoodie inside out. "Nothing but pocket lint and a scrunchie. Can I put it on now?"

"Don't push your luck," Reggie grumbles. "I'm only doing this because I'm a nice guy."

"So nice." She shoves her arms through the sleeves, muttering as she reaches behind her. "I can't believe you ripped my best T-shirt."

Her fingers find the knife handle, and she slips it from her pocket. Rests it in the dish rag on the floor behind her butt. Matteo palms the blade and drags it under his forearm.

"Hey!" Reggie stomps toward them. "What the hell are you doing?"

Matteo braces to fight. His knife against two firearms. He's faced worse.

Renee grabs the rag off the floor. "What does it look like I'm doing? Blowing my nose." She honks loudly. "Is that all right with you?"

He's eyeing her warily. "You carry a rag around with you?"

"Show me a mom who doesn't." She drops it on the floor. "Kind of crucial with a sticky-fingered toddler. Do you have any idea how many boogers—"

"Stop, okay? Jesus." Reggie's moving again, back and forth by the door. "I know you're bullshitting me. Let's bring your son in and see what happens."

"No!" She leaps to her feet. "Look, I'll take you to my house. How about that? We'll look for it together."

"No dice. You've got two Neanderthals staking it out."

Seb and Dante. Good.

Also *not* good. Reggie's thugs found her house. He figured as much.

"Neanderthals?" Renee huffs. "The only Neanderthal I know is the creeper you've had following me. The guy with the huge forehead?"

"Watch it!" Reggie snarls. "Carl can't help how he looks."

"Carl?"

"My *brother*."

Oh. A puzzle piece drops into place. Shifting the knife, Matteo measures the distance. A five-inch blade with a weighted handle. It's not big enough to strike the man's heart on a throw, but it's faster than stabbing. This angle, though...it'll be hard to get a good hit.

He's calculating odds when Renee takes a step. Her foot hits the rag, and she stumbles. Staggers right, to the chair, to her *purse*. She's falling in slow motion, ungainly with intent.

Matteo sees his opening.

"You clumsy b—"

Wham!

The knife hits its mark. The cop falls screaming as Teo rolls to his knees.

"Son of a bitch!" Reggie grabs his leg and howls. "I'll kill you."

Matteo's wobbly, but his vision's clear enough. He sees the blade speared through the cop's thigh. An inch from the artery, maybe less. Right on target.

"Fucking hell!" Reggie flails and grabs the knife's hilt. The gun falls from his pocket and spins across the floor.

"Matteo, catch!" Renee's got the purse in her hands. She tosses it to him. "Two knives in the center pouch."

She rolls and grabs the gun.

"Got it." Both blades in hand, Matteo's in his element. His vision's not perfect, and his side aches where he got kicked. But rage has powered him through plenty worse.

Reggie's still pawing the knife in his leg. "Son of a—"

"Don't pull it out." Matteo grips both knives. "You'll bleed out in seconds."

It may not be true, but Reggie lets go. Matteo pounces, kicking the injured leg. "Hands up!" he snarls as Reggie staggers. "Do it, or I'll slit your fucking throat."

The dirty cop doesn't go down. Puts a hand to his holster, but Matteo's quicker.

Wham!

The second knife finds its mark. Reggie shrieks and flails his impaled palm. "Fuuuuuck!"

Renee's got the gun in a death grip. "Hands up, Reggie."

The asshole curses, then obeys.

She'd never fire, not with AJ in the next room, but Reggie doesn't know that. Doesn't know *her*. Not like Teo does.

He'd kiss her if he didn't need this dickhead to die.

The cop throws his palms up with a snarl. "You know the penalty for killing a cop?" Blood drips from his impaled hand. "You'd kill me in cold blood, Matteo?"

Wouldn't be the first time. "I won't rule it out."

He knows the feel of his blade sinking through flesh. Knows the metal scent of blood, the wheeze of dying breath.

Reggie Dowling is a dead man.

Movement grabs his eye in the window. AJ on a blue sofa, the flutter of a page. Through thick concrete walls, the child has no clue what's happening ten feet away. His lips move as he reads. There's a gray bear with a red bow at its neck. AJ stops to set him upright.

Matteo looks at Reggie. "You're not worth it."

"What?" The cop licks his lips, tasting weakness.

He's mistaken.

"Nope." He grabs Reggie's hair and jerks his head back. Stares deep in his eyes. "I could kill you. If I wanted you dead, you'd be dead."

"Yeah." The cop's jaw clenches. "I figured."

Renee slips behind him as he slams Reggie's head on the chair. The man goes down with a wheeze. He's out cold.

Snatching the gun from Dowling's hip holster, Matteo pats him down. No more weapons. He lets the body drop like a bag of dirty laundry. Looks at Renee and feels his heart heave up his throat. "Are you okay?"

"Yes." Panting, she lowers the gun. "I thought you were dead."

"I'm hard to kill."

"You scared me." Her voice trembles as she flicks a look at Reggie. "Dead or unconscious?" She doesn't seem to care either way.

"Unconscious." He could change that.

"You saved us." Renee draws a breath. "Thank you."

"Me? You brought weapons. If it wasn't for that, we'd all be d—"

"Don't say it." She hurls her arms around his middle and hugs hard. The butt of the gun bites his spine, and his ribs creak where Reggie kicked him.

But the space around his heart is a happy puddle. "I'm glad you're okay."

Shutting his eyes, he breathes her in. Two seconds, that's all he lets himself take his eyes off Reggie. The citrus scent of her sends him a surge of strength. "I'm sorry you had to see that."

She draws back to look at him. "What was his plan, anyway? If I led him to my dad's money, he'd have to kill me, right?"

Yes. Without question.

He won't say that. "He told me the plan when he tied me up."

Matteo swipes blood from his forehead. "He'd stage it to look like I flipped out. Just drove off a cliff in the camper."

He doesn't say the last part. The part where she and AJ die screaming in back. Nausea grips him, and he grabs the back of the chair.

"Matteo—"

"I'm fine."

"Oh, God." Tears light her eyes as she puts a hand on his back. "I can't believe this."

He can't, either. Not the violence, the malice. He's used to those.

It's his luck he can't believe. He's here, and she's here, and their son is safe in the next room. They're alive and all together. "You're sure you're okay?"

"Positive." She shoves the Beretta in her pocket. "You're hurt. We should call an ambulance—"

"I'm fine." He's walked off worse than this. "It's not as bad as it looks."

"I could have lost you." A tear slips down her cheek, and she dashes it away.

"But you didn't." Thank God. *Thank God.*

Renee takes a breath and touches his cheek. "I need to tell you something."

"Okay." If she has the money, it won't change things. Not how he feels about her. If she's a money-laundering millionaire or a pauper, he'd still move mountains to be with her.

"Renee, wait." He should say this first. "Look, I love you. I love you even if you're hiding a bunch of stolen money."

She blinks. "What?"

"The money." He's botching this badly. "Wherever it is, whatever you've done—or not done—I promise I have your back no matter—"

"Not that, Matteo. You *love* me?"

He should have led with that. "I love you." Drawing her

close, he skims curls off her face. "I've loved you forever, but I was too chickenshit to say it. And then I thought it might be too late."

"It's not." Her throat moves as she swallows. "It's never too late."

He says it again to be safe. "I love you so much."

She draws back to look at him. "This isn't just because we have a kid together?"

"It is."

"Oh." A flicker in her eyes as she tips up her chin. "I guess—"

"No, that's not it." He cups her cheek. "I don't love you because of AJ. I love you because you're the smartest, kindest, most beautiful woman I've ever known. You're tough as nails and so sweet I can't stand it. I've loved you forever, way before AJ. It's because of him I had the balls to tell you. I love you, Renee. You and AJ. You're what matters. You're what I see when I picture the rest of my life."

"Oh, honey." A tear slips down her cheek. "I love you, too."

"Yeah?"

"Don't sound surprised." She laughs and wipes another tear. "Despite the prison record and the fact that you're a capricious sack of snot, you're a lovable guy."

He laughs, and his voice sounds rusty. He's seconds from shedding tears of his own. "We should go."

"Right, yes." She darts a glance at the window. Gasps as her eyes go wide. "Oh my God, where's AJ?"

He spins as the door opens. He's got one hand on Reggie's gun as AJ flies through.

"Mama!" He takes off his shirt and runs over. "Hi, My Tail."

"Hello."

"Gotta go, gotta go!" His sandals scuff the floor as he tugs his shorts. Skids to a stop beside Reggie. "Sleep?"

"Uh, yeah." Matteo steps between the boy and the bad cop. "Everyone needs a nap, right?"

"Right." Renee's voice fills with false cheer. "Naps are good for us."

The boy frowns. "No nap."

"Do you have to potty?" She cups his shoulder and guides him back from the body. "I saw a restroom down the hall."

"Potty." Hopping up and down, he grabs his fly. "Help?"

"Sure." For a split second, he thinks how it would feel to have his kid piss on a dirty cop. Payback. Poetic justice. Revenge.

Be the better man.

Besides, there's DNA evidence to think about.

"Go with your mom, okay?" He smiles at his son. "Be quick. We need to get out."

The boy frowns. "You hurt, My Tail?"

"I'm fine." He touches the wound at his hairline. It's hardly bleeding. His ribs don't even hurt now.

"Two minutes." Renee steers their son to the door, then turns and lowers her voice. "Should someone be tied up?"

Matteo looks at the slumped form. "You mean Reggie?"

"Yes, Reggie." She rolls her eyes. "You think now's the time for bondage?"

"I mean—"

"You're the worst." She slips out with AJ.

Maybe he *is* the worst.

He's done lots worth regretting. Meeting her isn't one of them. If he's the worst, she's the best. Hardly a Hallmark greeting, but maybe that's what balance looks like.

Wishing for gloves, he bends over the unconscious cop. The asshole's breathing, with an ooze of blood on his temple. They're a matched set.

Matteo finds cuffs and slaps them on Reggie's wrists. Sits back and studies him. "Know what they do to dirty cops in prison?"

Reggie doesn't answer. Just drools and snuffles.

"I'll forgive you for putting me there," he says. "For double-crossing me. But fucking with my family?" He grabs Renee's dish rag and wipes his prints off the cuffs. Off the butt of Reggie's gun. "You're goddamn lucky I'm a new man."

Reggie groans in sleep.

"Good talk." He stands and lets the cop slump back to the floor.

Footsteps in the hall drag Matteo to his feet. "That was fas—"

He stops as words snag in his throat. Baby Cop looms in the doorway. Matteo swallows. "It's not what it looks like."

The cop hooks a hand on his gun belt. "Turn around, Matteo Bello. On your knees."

Heart in his throat, he does what he's told. Links his hands behind his head and sinks to the floor. "My son and my girl— don't hurt them. They're innocent."

Baby Cop's silent as he pats him down. Takes Reggie's gun and the knives. Matteo says nothing as the officer rolls them in an evidence bag. Shutting his eyes, he waits for the clink of cuffs on his wrists.

So close. He came so close to claiming a normal life for himself. For Renee and AJ, too. He wouldn't mind prison so much if he hadn't tasted this perfect life.

Leaving her again—it'll kill him.

"Turn around."

Matteo opens his eyes. Drops his hands and spins on his knees to face Baby Cop. "I need to say goodbye. Please, just let me say goodbye before you haul me off." To prison. To whatever shady corner this cop might have. Who knows if this guy's more crooked than Reggie? "Please," he tries again. "I just need my family safe. You can do anything you want to me."

The cop opens his mouth. Footsteps near, and Matteo's heart flops off a cliff.

Renee appears like a sunray at the door. "Matteo, I—*oh*." She gasps. Looks from the cop to him and back again. "I can explain."

Baby Cop folds his arms. "I don't think you can."

CHAPTER 14

"*P*lease, Officer." She's begged more today than her whole life combined, but she's not stopping now. "It's not what it looks like. I swear—"

"Ma'am?" He gestures to the chair. "Have a seat, please."

AJ sticks a thumb in his mouth and looks at the cop. "Ossifer Dan?"

Renee pulls him close. "Not Officer Dan." He does look a lot like the cartoon cop in AJ's book. "Honey, come here."

She doesn't let him argue. Just lifts him to her lap and hugs him tight. "Officer, please. Before you arrest us—"

"You're not under arrest. Not for this, anyway." He looks at Matteo. "Lucky for you, I got suspicious."

Matteo stares. "Come again?"

"Always got a weird vibe from Chief Dowling." The cop nods at Renee. "Especially when he pulled up with you in the car."

She blinks. "You saw us?"

He nods. "Got halfway home when my gut told me to come back."

Matteo's eyes harden. "You watched it happen."

"Not your beating." His eyes soften. "I'm real sorry about that.

Dowling said he had you handled. Sent me on another call that turned out to be nothing. Another red flag, by the way."

Renee's heart's in her throat. "So you know this is all Reggie. That we were just defending ourselves."

"I caught enough to confirm that." He takes off his cap and hooks it on AJ's head. "Will you hold that for me, little man? And if you wouldn't mind, there's a teddy bear in the next room who needs company."

"Big bear?" AJ tries to wiggle off her lap. She doesn't want to let him go, not ever.

The cop holds a hand up. "You're not in trouble, ma'am." His gaze swings to Matteo. "This room is wired for sound. I heard what he said from the desk out front."

Matteo's still scowling. "And you didn't help?"

The cop's eyes follow AJ as he hustles from the room. They watch him settle on the couch with the gray bear. Her precious little boy.

"I heard." The cop looks back at Teo. "But it's not real smart to storm into a roomful of weapons when you don't take two minutes to assess the threat."

"But you know we're innocent." She darts another glance at the window. AJ's got the bear on his lap, plus a copy of *Officer Dan Looks for Clues*. She forces herself to face the cop. "You know he's crooked, right?"

"Dowling?" He nods. "Always had a weird feeling about him. His cousin, too—Ranger Harris?" The cop looks at Matteo. "You've had some bad blows today. Do you need medical attention, sir?"

"No." Matteo straightens. "It looks worse than it is."

The cop frowns. "Even so—"

"I'm not going anywhere until I see my family safely back home."

Home. She's not even sure where he means. But anyplace together sounds good to her.

The cop hooks his thumbs on his belt. "One of you have a license for that gun?"

"Yes, sir." Matteo's jaw clenches. "Paperwork's in the camper."

"I'll be needing to see that." One edge of the cop's mouth twitches. "Pretty impressive work, you two. You make a good team."

Matteo looks at her. She reads everything in his eyes. Love. Fear. Hope. "We do make a good team," he says.

"The best." She's afraid to hope they might walk out of here. "Maybe someday we'll have an emotional heart-to-heart without firearms."

The cop laughs. "Helluva declaration of love, Bello. Didn't have the heart to interrupt."

"Thanks?" Matteo still looks stunned. "You're not arresting me."

"Not for this." He looks at Renee. "There's still the issue of some missing funds."

Not again. "I swear I don't have that money." Why won't they believe her? "I don't care what Reggie said. I never even knew about the missing money until today."

"All right." The cop seems to hesitate. "Wouldn't it be nice to solve the mystery?"

"Sir?" She's not sure what he means.

The cop rocks back on his heels. "Case like that, it's dogged law enforcement for years."

"Sure. I mean—I guess?" This must be a trap. "You want us to help you get away with it?"

"What? No!" He laughs and shakes his head. "You've got trust issues. I get it."

Matteo's brow furrows. "What do you want from us?"

"Nothing illegal." The cop pauses. "But maybe if we find it, folks'll stop looking and leave you alone."

That sounds good to her. "What's the catch?"

"No catch. Just trying to close the case." His smile turns shy.

"All right, full disclosure—I want a shot at making chief." He nods at Reggie. "There's a job opening."

Matteo scowls at Reggie on the floor. "You couldn't do worse than the last guy."

"True enough." The cop bends and checks Reggie's pulse. "Need to get this one to the hospital. You sure you're okay?"

"I'm fine." Matteo gets to his feet and slides an arm around her. "I just want to go home."

"Home sounds nice." She thinks of her ramshackle house. The threadbare carpet. The battered desk where she works. The finger paintings on the fridge. Matteo on the sofa, an arm around each of them.

It's the closest thing to heaven she can picture.

Renee clears her throat. "When Reggie mentioned that letter from my dad? I thought of something."

Matteo looks at her. "You know where the money might be?"

"Maybe." This could be a wild goose chase. "I've got an idea, anyway."

"Well, then." The cop sweeps a hand toward the door. "How about we take a little drive?"

IT'S LATE when they reach the beige bungalow she's called home for less than a year. The white shutters she washed last week still look tidy. Her front porch petunias will be potato chips, so she's shocked when they pull up and see bright blooms of pink and white.

"Is that your friend Dante watering my flowers?" She squints at the big, bald figure on her doorstep as Matteo parks.

"Yep." He waves as Dante coils a garden hose. "Ten bucks says he weeded your veggie garden."

"I don't have a veggie garden."

"You do now." Popping the camper door, he offers her a hand. "Looks like tomatoes and zucchini, but I'm no farmer."

She stares at the raised bed on the east edge of her house. "That definitely wasn't there before."

"Come on." He crooks an elbow, and she takes it. "Baby Cop'll be here any minute with the bank guy. Let's hide anything you don't want seen."

She looks at him. "Like underwear?"

"Sure."

She's guessing Matteo would have more to hide than underwear. She tries to think of anything worth concealing but comes up blank. For the first time in years, she's done hiding.

Dante approaches with Dr. LaDouceur on his heels. The dentist holds a hammer. "Hey, guys."

Matteo nods at the tool. "Dental work, or you're practicing throws?"

"Neither, smartass." He flips the tool in one hand. "Just finishing the new swing set."

Her mouth falls open. "A swing set?"

"For AJ." He flips the hammer again.

"You can use it, too." Dante folds arms the size of tree trunks. "It's got solid cedar beams. We mounted the legs in concrete."

"Thanks, I—" She's not even sure where to start. "Thank you. For everything. Truly."

Matteo's fingers lace with hers. "We dropped AJ at the vineyard with Jen and Nicole. He needed a break."

The dentist brightens. Nudges Dante. "Nic's at your place?"

"Not an invitation." The bald man scowls.

"What?" He's trying for innocence, but Renee doesn't buy it. "Just thinking it's been a while since I did some wine tasting."

Matteo gives an icy stare. "You're pathetic."

Dr. LaDouceur's smile fades as his attention shifts to the street. A muscle twitches in his jaw. "How many cops did you invite?"

She watches them crawl to the curb. Three squad cars, an unmarked SUV, and a black sedan that must be the bank examiner. "Guess they don't want the money walking off."

"If it's even here." Matteo squeezes her hand. "They might be barking up the wrong tree. You've moved enough times that you'd have found a million bucks sitting around."

"I like to think so." Secretly, she's not sure. How long has she clung to those hand-me-downs? Just moving them from place to place, holding tight to old furniture and a family she never knew. Maybe she thought she didn't deserve nicer.

Sebastian's scowling at the parade of cops. "Let's get out of here."

"Wait." Dante stops as another police SUV glides up. The logo doesn't match the others, and neither does the couple getting out. A man dressed in cop gear and a pretty brunette beside him.

"Hello, Dugans." Dante's as taciturn as ever, but the curly-haired woman isn't having it.

"Shut up and hug me, Dante." She launches herself hard enough to make the big man stumble back. "It's good to see you. Izzy sends love."

Renee tries to blend in as more cops start spilling from their cars. The brunette's eyes zero in on her. "You must be Renee."

"I am." She extends a hand, but the woman grabs her in a bear hug.

"Bree Bracelyn-Dugan," she says. "Chief Dugan back there is my other half."

Voices swell at the end of the driveway. "...not your jurisdiction, Dugan."

Bree's husband shows an *aw shucks* smile with an interesting edge. "You're forgetting the Hamdorf job happened in Deschutes County. They might've fled west, but it started on our side of the mountains."

Bickering erupts, and Renee realizes how an unruffled cop

like Dugan could end up friendly with Dante. Bree touches her arm. "Your little boy and ours are already the best of friends."

Renee blinks. "AJ?"

"We're close with Jen since Ponderosa Resort buys wine from Bello Vinyards." Bree's brow furrows. "I hope it's okay. We dropped off Brian so Austin could sort things professionally here." She lowers her voice. "And I came so you'd have someone in your court who's not a cop."

"Thank you," she whispers. "AJ's been wanting more play-mates." And Renee's been wanting more friends. "Maybe we can hang out when I'm not accused of hiding stolen money."

Bree grins. "I'd love that."

The cop knot down the driveway starts breaking up. Sebas-tian and Matteo scowl at the sea of blue uniforms. Dante claps Teo on the arm. "We're out of here. See you at the vineyard?"

Renee's not sure who he's talking to, but Bree jumps in. "We brought two trays of Sean's honey jalapeño chicken sliders. There's plenty for everyone."

"Sold." Sebastian elbows Dante. "Let's go get some sliders."

"Who invited you?" A grumbling Dante ambles down the driveway after the dentist. Both men give the cops a wide berth as Bree returns to her husband's side.

"You okay?" Matteo touches Renee's arm.

"I think so." She's honestly not sure. "I'm glad you're here."

"Same."

"And I'm glad we might get this over with so I can move on." She has her doubts about that one.

But there's no time to voice them as the cops swarm up her driveway. The one in the lead wears a blue necktie and walks like he's in charge. "Appreciate you waiting 'til we got here before you went in." He flips out a badge and waits while they scan it. "You can enter the premises now."

She needs permission to go inside her own house? Pulling out her keys, she dons her happy hostess smile. "Right this way."

Renee flips the lights on and breathes the smell of old wood and the vanilla candle by her door. Her living room looks dingier than she remembered. Was that armchair always so...*brown*? And that side table, it leans to one side.

Scanning her space through strangers' eyes, she sees its flaws. The lumpy couch in its shabby slipcover. The scratched wooden armchair where her dad swore her mother rocked her when she came home from the hospital. Was that even true?

Maybe it doesn't matter. She's found comfort in these scraps of family history. Maybe she won't need them after this.

Renee looks at the cops. "Sorry about the mess." She moves a stuffed rhino off the dining table. "Wait! Don't sit on that."

The cop sinking onto a dining room chair shoots upright. "Ma'am?"

"It's got a shaky leg." So does she. Her body trembles as she leads them to the living room. "I've been meaning to fix it, but the repair place wanted six hundred dollars, and we only need two chairs anyway, so..." She trails off, conscious of everyone watching her. "Can I get anyone a glass of water?"

"Ma'am." The cop with the necktie gestures to the room. "See anything out of place?"

Nothing's broken, so Seb and Dante must have tidied after Reggie's men tossed the place. She takes her time scanning her living room. Her grandma's old afghan on the footstool. The vase she splurged on from a thrift store. The grandfather clock her dad swore was worth money.

Eyes follow her as she walks to the clock. "Nothing out of place." She opens the case and peers inside. "I'm not even sure what I'm looking for."

"Take your time, ma'am." Necktie moves behind her. "Bricks of cash, stray bills, even a key."

"A key?" She pulls her head out to peer at him. "Like for a safe deposit box?"

A brusque nod. "Anything's possible."

She considers her dad's claim about the clock's worth. "Too obvious." She shuts it and moves to the sofa.

Matteo's standing beside it. "It's kinda uncomfortable. Maybe that's a clue?"

Her cheeks warm as she recalls their night on her couch. "You think it's stuffed with cash?"

He shrugs and grabs the slipcover at one end. "Might as well check."

Renee grabs the other end and tugs. "Hang on." She drops to her knees. "The fabric's stuck under the foot."

Chief Dugan helps her move it, and she peers beneath the sofa. So many dust bunnies. There's the race car AJ lost last week. Has it only been that long? "Let's try turning it over."

Four cops move to the corners as she gets to her feet. The guy Matteo calls Baby Cop grabs the far edge. "On three?"

One, two, three...

"God, it's heavy." A thick-chested officer wipes his brow.

Everyone crowds around the overturned sofa. Necktie scowls. "What do you see?"

She peers at the underside. Springs. Dirty foam. Dust. So much dust. "Nothing unusual."

Necktie frowns. "We'll have to cut it up."

"Cut up my furniture?" She steps to block his view. "It's a family heirloom. It's vintage."

He frowns at the faded floral fabric. "You're telling me that's worth money?"

"It's sentimental." She crosses her arms. "*I'll* decide when I'm ready to let it go."

Matteo touches her arm. "Let's try the coffee table."

Always the oddest piece in her collection. "Good idea."

They study the kidney-shaped melamine on brass legs. Mid-century modern, it's meant to look like marble. A cigarette burn scars one edge. A glue blob marks another. The low ledge around the rim—designed to hold drinks—sports a smattering of crayon marks.

Necktie shakes his head. "That's the ugliest—"

"It's an *heirloom*," she says, and he shuts up.

Baby Cop shuffles around it. "It's a really unique piece."

Renee runs a finger over a rose AJ drew with blue crayon. She hasn't had the heart to scrub it off. "My grandma gave it to my parents when they moved in together." Her father said so, anyway. Who's to say what's true?

"I think it's cool." A female cop named Laura moves beside her. "Come on. We'll lift together and be gentle."

Renee grabs one end, and Laura grabs the other. For once, the men shut up. The table doesn't weigh much, but it's sturdy. They flip it like a turtle, sending spindly legs in the air.

Matteo peers beneath it. "Is that pudding?"

"Let's hope." She winces. "AJ likes to wipe his hands under it."

"Better than his pants." Matteo moves to the other side. "What's Nay Nay?"

"My nickname as a kid." She shuffles her feet as she scans the scribble marks. "My dad used to call me that before...before he went away." She swallows a wad of melancholy. "I used to lie underneath with my crayons and coloring books."

Before. Way before her first foster home. Sometimes after, those rare times the courts let her dad have her. "I wrote my name so I'd know it was real. That I really was here."

Necktie clears his throat. "While this is a nice walk down memory lane, we haven't found the money."

Matteo glares. "Show some respect." He tucks her under his arm. "She'll take the time she needs to do this right."

Chief Dugan moves beside them. "I'm in no rush."

Bree slips to a space beside her husband. "No hurry here."

"Same." Baby Cop steps closer.

Necktie frowns. "Just hurry it up."

With a deep breath, Renee turns to the table. "What about unscrewing the legs?"

Matteo squats down. "They come off?"

"Maybe not." She spins the metal tip on one spindly brass leg. "This piece might."

"Hmm." He pulls out a pocket tool. Nods at Baby Cop as he flips out the screwdriver. "Thanks for getting this back to me."

"A man needs his tools."

There's silence as he unscrews a leg. Renee twists her hands in her sweatshirt pockets. "It's hollow?"

"Looks like it." He holds up the leg to show her. "See anything?"

"Not really." She peers inside and shakes her head. "Just dust."

Matteo puts the leg back on and tries the next one. "This one's more banged up." He hands it to her without looking. "Still nothing?"

She shakes her head. "Maybe this is silly."

"Third time's the charm?"

"Maybe." She eyes the other furniture and wonders what they're missing. How much cash could her father stuff in an ottoman?

She's bending to look when Matteo hands her the next leg. "Anything?"

"I don't see—*oh*." A slender, bronze key slips out. Clatters to the floor at her feet.

Matteo stares. "That's something."

Necktie swoops in and grabs it. The bank guy peers at his palm. "Definitely not a safe deposit box key. I don't recognize it."

A sniff from the skinny cop with a slight overbite. "Maybe it goes to one of those time capsule things you bury under statues?"

Baby Cop stifles a snort. "Not seeing any statues around here."

Matteo's not looking at them. He's watching Renee with curiosity. "You look like you have an idea."

"Maybe." She looks at the stairs. "Just thinking about my father's letter."

Necktie folds his arms. "The one you claim you never got?"

"The one I *know* I never got." She grits her teeth and ignores him. "But think about what Reggie quoted."

Matteo's got it memorized. "'Dear Renee,'" he recites. "'I know you can't forgive me, but I need to get this off my chest before I die. Please use what's left of my legacy and give your boy the life I couldn't give you.'"

"'*Get this off my chest.*'" A lightbulb blinks in her brain. "Come on."

She heads for the stairs, hoping they follow. If she's right, she'll need that key.

At the edge of AJ's room, she hesitates. Mama bear instincts catch her by the throat. It feels wrong to lead a pack of cops into the space where her baby sleeps.

"Wait here. There's not room for everyone." She holds out her hand. "May I have the key, please?"

Necktie wants to argue, but Laura stares him down. "For God's sake, Dick. Give the girl some space."

"Yeah, Dick." Matteo glares. "If there's a trap door under the race car bed, I promise you'll get her before she escapes."

Dick grumbles as he hands it over. "We're watching."

Resisting an eye roll, she carries the key to the corner. To the chest of drawers turned changing table. A waterproof pad lines the top with the wipe warmer tucked in one corner. She felt so proud of transforming it into something useful. Something for her son.

"The top drawers have diapers and clothes." She drops to her knees and scans the bottom drawer. "You can check if you want."

"We will." Suspicion dents Dick's forehead. "What's in that one?"

"The bottom's been stuck as long as I remember." She jiggles it to show them. "See? Won't budge."

Baby Cop cocks his head. "You never tried to find a key?" A glance at Matteo. "Or someone who picks locks?"

She ignores them and feels around the edges of the drawer.

"No keyhole," Matteo points out.

"None I ever saw." She taps the side and wonders what she's missing.

"Huh." Dick's only mildly appeased. "How many times have you moved this? You'd have noticed a million bucks in cash. The weight alone—"

"Ten kilograms." Matteo folds his arms.

Dick frowns. "How much is that in American?"

Chief Dugan moves beside him. "About 22.045 pounds. That's if it's in hundreds."

"I want to know how you have that information at the tip of your fingers."

Dugan shrugs. "Doesn't everyone?"

Dick's back to watching Renee. "Find anything?"

"No." There's got to be a keyhole somewhere. "It's always been heavy. Old oak is like brick, but maybe it's not solid everywhere."

He still looks skeptical. "And you never noticed a whole drawer didn't work."

"I noticed." She crawls around and pats a side panel. "I'm used to my furniture having character."

"Character." He mutters like she's said *feces*. "Well, come on. Let's move it out from the wall."

She's already pushing when Matteo reaches her side. "On three." He sends a pointed glance at the cops hustling to help. They scuttle back to the doorway. "Ready? One, two, *three*."

The chest lurches, squeaking as it scrapes the floor. There's a three-foot gap behind it, and Renee squeezes through.

"A lot of dust." She doesn't spot it right away. Glides her fingers down the wood, searching for something. Anything. Disappointment digs into her chest. "I was so sure this—" She stops as her fingers find brass. "Do you have a light?"

Matteo flicks one on his keychain. "What do you see?"

"Maybe a keyhole."

It's hidden in a carved oak flourish. She's never noticed it before. Her heart pounds as she slips the key inside. Fingers shaking, she twists. There's a ping from the front of the chest.

Then the drawer pops open.

"Holy shit." Dick moves forward. "Jackpot."

Baby Cop joins him, whistling low. "That looks like our stash."

Chief Dugan snaps a photo on his phone.

Renee gets to her feet. Wobbles with nerves and fatigue and emotions she can't name.

Matteo's there to steady her. "I've got you." He's not looking at the money. Not at the cops. His eyes hold hers like they're the only two in the room. "You okay?"

"Yeah." She tests the word to be sure it's true. Stares at the bundles of bills. Dozens of them. Hundreds, maybe. "I'm really okay."

He brushes curls from her face. "Do you need a minute?"

Renee shakes her head and steps back to let the cops do their thing. "I thought I'd feel something, but I'm just…relieved."

Matteo smiles. "That's something."

"It is, isn't it?"

He holds her as the cops load stacks of bills into evidence bags.

"So that's it," he says.

"Yeah."

"It's really over."

Closing her eyes, she burrows into his chest. Breathes him in, the father of her child, the man she adores, the best teammate she knows.

Her family.

"Not over." She draws back and smiles at him. "It's just starting."

CHAPTER 15

"*W*hat are we *not* doing today in class?" Matteo's got a hand on AJ's back as he guides him to the classroom door. His son's shoulder feels small and sturdy in his palm.

His son.

This will never not be amazing.

AJ smiles, and that's amazing, too. "I wear my shirt."

"Exactly." Renee stoops to zip his hoodie. "Even when you go potty."

"Love you, Mama." He hugs her hard enough to squeeze Matteo's heart. Then he turns and throws his arms out for his daddy. "Love you."

And *that*—well, that's the most amazing of all.

"Love you, kiddo." He pulls the boy in for a nice, long hug. "Be good at school."

"Okay, Papa."

Papa.

He earned that badge when they sat him down and explained things. AJ took it in stride. "Like in *Nelly Gnu and Daddy, Too?*" AJ's green eyes searched his. "Are you a Gnu?"

"Sure." Matteo paused. "I—don't actually know what that means."

"A wildebeest." Renee tousled his hair. "Daddy's definitely a wildebeest."

Daddy. Will this never stop dazzling him?

They read the book together and afterward, AJ asked for a pet Gnu.

"Gnus need bigger yards." He winked at Renee over their son's head. "But maybe a goldfish?"

She's smiling again as they climb the steps to the school. Nicole greets them as she hugs their son. "You two have big plans today?"

She knows damn well they do. Sisters are a pain in the ass.

"It's my birthday." Renee's smile seems bashful. "I've never been big on celebrating, but Matteo's taking me to brunch."

She says "brunch" like "France." Like he's flying them to Paris for croissants. In truth, they're hitting her favorite café. The one where they talked at the start of all this. It seems like a lifetime ago.

They say their goodbyes and turn to the sidewalk. "Want to walk?" He laces their fingers together. "I could use the fresh air."

"I'd love that."

"Have I mentioned you're gorgeous in that dress?"

"Since we left the house, you mean?" She laughs and tucks her other hand in the pocket of the pink sundress. "Only six times. Say it again, though."

"You look gorgeous in that dress."

"Thanks."

He watches her hips and wants her again. "You look even better out of it."

"You're the worst." She taps him with her sandal. "You have to buy me waffles first."

"Deal."

The weather's nice, but that's not why he wanted to walk. Life outside prison is still a marvel. For as long as he lives, he won't take fresh air for granted. Not sunshine or grass or the bright orange marigolds next to Seb's clinic door.

The dentist steps from his black BMW as they walk by. "Nice day for a walk."

Matteo glares so the bastard stops smirking. Safeguarding this secret has been like hitting a bullseye in high winds. "Sure is."

Renee's unsuspicious as Seb smiles like a dickhead.

"I almost forgot," she says. "I need to make an appointment with you."

"Dental cleaning?" He toys with the bullet on his keychain, and Matteo wants to punch him.

"That's the only service you offer, right?" He glares at Seb, pretty sure the asshole still takes contract jobs. Not the kind with dental floss.

Sebastian's still twirling that damn keychain. "I also do gum grafts, root canals, laser teeth whitening, dental implants, even sleep apnea treatment for—"

"See ya, Seb." He shoulders past his pal and leads Renee down the sidewalk. "We'll call later for the appointment."

"Hungry, huh?" She squeezes his hand as they drift down the block. "I've been craving Eggs Benedict all week."

"Same." He's not even sure what that is. It's been weeks of distraction, of planning and preparation. Today, he'll ask for what he wants. It's not Eggs Benedict.

He squeezes her hand. "Did I tell you they scheduled my orientation?"

"I'm still stunned you'll have a regular office." She laughs and kicks a pebble down the street. "Never thought Matteo Bello could be domesticated."

Neither did he. "I bought a three-hole punch."

She tilts her head to look at him. "You'll be punching lots of papers?"

"Beats me." He just liked the sound of it. "Seems like something I should have with an office job."

"Oh, Matteo." She squeezes his hand. "I love you."

God, he loves her. He never knew he could love anyone this much. "Love you, too." Why does his voice sound weird?

They're almost to the stop, so he clears his throat. "Let's go in here."

"This place?" She reads the sign on the door. "A furniture store?"

"They've got old stuff and new stuff and..." Crap, he's botching this. "I thought you might like to look around a little."

"Okay." She's humoring him but seems curious as they push through the glass doors. It's a huge showroom, filled with dressers and dining tables, and she spins slowly to see it all. "Oh, wow—how have I never noticed this place?"

"Not sure." Maybe she never thought she deserved to? He still doesn't grasp her attachment to the family's old stuff. It's homely and battered and bristling with not-great memories.

But he doesn't need to understand. It's his job to support her, to love her no matter what. He'd live in the drawer of her broken nightstand if it meant being close to her.

The clerk scurries to the front of the store. "Welcome, Ms. Lorenson." He nods to Matteo. "Mr. Bello. Where should we begin?"

Renee lifts an eyebrow. "You've been here, Matteo?"

"A time or two." Try fifty times. He wants this to be perfect. Even had the clerk rehearse with him yesterday.

Teo points to the right half of the store. "Over there is new furniture. Couches, bedroom sets, dining room stuff." He sweeps a hand to the other half. "That's all used stuff. Vintage, antiques, secondhand furniture with a story."

She touches the top of a dining room table. "I like the story."

"I know you do." He squeezes her hand.

"We also have a restoration department." The clerk steps back to let her survey the end table behind him. "We specialize in restoring old furniture to its glory. Vintage farmhouse tables, antique sideboards, mid-century Eames chairs—you name it, we spiff it up. I understand you have some vintage pieces?"

"I—yes." She looks at Matteo. "You're thinking we'd restore some of the old stuff?"

"Whatever you want." He looks into eyes filled with equal parts joy and confusion. "It's your call."

Her fingers stroke the fringe on a silk throw pillow. "I—guess I hadn't thought about it."

"You don't have to decide now." He slides a hand in his pocket and pulls out the envelope. "The gift card's good for any of it. Old stuff, new stuff, restora—"

"Holy cow, Matteo!" She blinks at the dollar amount. "I could outfit a whole house for this much."

"I know." That's his hope. "Or you could keep your old stuff. Clean it up, make it shine. Make it your own."

"Wow." She stares at the slip some more. "Do I want to know how you can afford this?"

"Maybe not." Okay, it's not mysterious. "My starting bonus was higher than I thought."

A lot more. Like, three extra zeros more. He still can't believe he's got a nine-to-five job. Tech work, just like he studied for. "Anything you want, Renee—whatever you pick is great with me."

She lowers the paper and looks at him. "Is this your way of suggesting we live together?"

"We kinda do already." Not officially. But it's been months since he slept somewhere without her. "We've talked about finding a new place. Something together, maybe closer to AJ's school."

"Wow." She laughs and shakes her head. "I know I sound like a broken record, but I'm in shock."

There's more shock coming. He takes a breath and drops her

hand. Nerves squiggle in his chest, but it feels good. Right, even though his hand's shaking as he stuffs it in his coat pocket.

"Renee Marie Lorenson." He watched a dozen Hallmark movies for practice but didn't think his voice would shake. "I love you more than anything."

"Oh my God." She claps both hands to her mouth. "Is this happening?"

He's not sure how to answer. "Do you want it to happen?"

"Yes." A tear slips down her cheek. "Yes, please. *Oh God.* Keep going."

Not the first time she's said those words. Sex clouds his brain, and he needs some time to get it together. "Renee Lorenson." He opens the ring box, and she gasps. "This belonged to my grand-mother. Nondi left it in the safe at the beach house. I grabbed it that day we went there because I knew then—" despite dodging bullets and hiding from thugs and potty training—"I knew even then I wanted to spend the rest of my life with you. And I hoped you might eventually feel the same."

"It's beautiful." Another tear slips as she touches the diamond. A two-carat round stone with small pink sapphires. "My favorite color."

"And you're my favorite person." He swallows again and fights to recall the words he practiced. "I love waking up with you every morning and falling asleep with you at night. I love our adven-tures in between. Trips to the park with AJ. Sharing popcorn at the movies. Camping at the lake."

All normal, family things. Things she deserves.

"Renee." He clears his throat. "I never hoped to get lucky enough to meet someone like you. If you marry me, I promise I'll spend every moment busting my tail to deserve you."

"My Tail." She laughs and pulls him to his feet. "Yes! Abso-lutely, I'll marry you."

"Thank God." He slips the ring on her finger before she changes her mind. "Wait. I forgot to ask the question."

"Ask me, then." Laughing, she holds her hand to the light. "Let's hear it."

"Renee Marie Lorenson—will you marry me?" He cups her cheek with one hand. "Please?"

"I want that more than anything."

For the first time ever, he kisses his fiancée. It's slow and sweet and gentle but heats up in a hurry.

The clerk backs away. "I'll give you two a minute."

He drifts to the restoration area while Matteo admires her hand. "The ring looks great on you."

"It's stunning." She flutters her fingers so it sparkles in the light. "A perfect fit."

"We are, aren't we?" That sounded way less cheesy in his mind. "I'm glad you said yes."

"Was there any doubt?" She twines her hands behind his neck. "You did sweeten the pot with furniture."

"Your hand in marriage for a coffee table." He kisses her temple. "A fair trade."

"You're crazy if you think I'm not getting a new couch, too."

"Whatever you want, for the rest of our lives." The lump's back in his throat. "I'll make it my job to give you everything you deserve."

Talk about a job change. No violence. No illegal activity. Just the woman he loves and a lifetime of family and shared dreams. How did he get this lucky?

"I love you, Matteo."

"I love you, too." He kisses her again. His bride. His soulmate. The mother of his child. "I've got it all planned out."

"You've got what planned?" She's skeptical for the first time since they got here.

"Not sketchy, I swear." He kisses her hand. "We'll do a family-moon at Ponderosa Resort."

"Family-moon?"

"With AJ." Another thing he saw on Hallmark. "A family trip together, post-wedding."

"And then?" She knows him well enough to guess there's more.

"A trip to Cabo. Margaritas on the beach. Guacamole. Sex in the sand and—"

"Sounds itchy." She grins and draws him close. "I'm in."

"Good." He draws back and takes her hand. "Should we start with furniture shopping or brunch?"

She smiles her coy, flirty smile and wraps her arms around him. "Maybe back to our place."

"You're not hungry?"

"Oh, I am." She grins. "I suddenly feel like celebrating. *Alone.*"

He can take a hint. "We'll get takeout." He swoops an arm around her. "Breakfast in bed with my bride."

"Perfect." Flashing the ring, she starts for the door. "Sounds like the right start for the rest of our lives."

He couldn't agree more.

***

In case you missed free series prequel for **Assassins in Love**, I'm giving away *Killer Looks* for zero pennies when you subscribe to my newsletter. Here's where to nab that:

https://BookHip.com/XWJJVFH

Enjoying the Assassins in Love series so far? Not sure about you, but I've looked forward to Sebastian's story since day one. That's up next in *Killer Smile*, and here's an exclusive peek at chapter one...

YOUR EXCLUSIVE PEEK AT KILLER SMILE

Target: Code name Rogue

Assignment date: Thursday, October 5

Job details: Target to be eliminated for the slaying of Danny "Duck Toes" DeCosta. Female subject will wear a red dress. Considered armed and dangerous. Location and details provided upon acceptance of contract.

*D*r. Sebastian LaDouceur, DDS, stares at the incoming memo. He's on his encrypted tablet, which he won't normally check at work.

Work at the *dental office*, which is just one of his jobs. The Dentist is a busy man.

He reads the words again, surprised The Union pinged him. He's taken fewer contracts lately to focus on pediatric dentistry. Who knew there were so many kids needing checkups and tartar scaling?

As he scans the note again, two words catch his eye.

Female target.

Interesting. They know he doesn't typically target women, so this one must be big. He heard of the hit on Duck Toes DeCosta. Doesn't know much besides the shooter used an M24 sniper rifle from 900 feet. A clean shot, one Seb admires in principle.

He types a message back.

MORE DETAIL REQUIRED. Time? Target profile? Price?

THE LAST ONE doesn't matter. Seb doesn't do this for money. His covert work for Uncle Sam's Army left him with a disdain for terrorists and rapists and other lowlifes he's asked to eliminate. These side jobs are a hobby.

Not like Dante and Matteo, who've mostly done dirty work for the Dovlanese government. Seb's a freelancer. A gig worker, as the cool kids say.

His front door chimes, and a guy walks in, gripping his jaw. "You've gotta help me, man!"

Sebastian taps the tablet into lock mode. "What's the problem?"

"Oh, hey—you're the dentist." The guy drops his hand. "Saw your billboard on Eighth and Main. Can you squeeze me in?"

Seb's not taking new patients today, but the guy looks desperate. "What's going on?"

"I've got this big hole in my tooth." He bares his front incisors like a spaniel subjected to non-consensual butt sniffs at the dog park. "See?"

"First bicuspid?"

The guy runs his tongue over his teeth. "Whassssat?"

"Left top. Three back from the central incisor." Sebastian peers in the guy's mouth. Solid, sharp cuspids. Some enamel discoloration indicative of a coffee habit. He scans the suspicious spot and nods. "That'll require an extremely specialized extraction technique."

"Extraction?" The man uncurls his lips. "I've got a date in three hours. I can't have her thinking I've got rotten teeth."

Sebastian slips a hand in his desk drawer. Finds a pack of plastic toothpicks with soft, bristled ends. "Congratulations, sir." He hands off the pack of picks. "I declare you an honorary dentist."

The guy stares at the packet. "Is that some kind of pill I should take?"

"Toothpicks." Has he never seen them not made of wood and stacked in a pink box? "That's pepper on your tooth. Use the mirror over there to get it off."

"No shit?" He pivots and stares at the mirror. "Huh." He pops out a pick and starts on his teeth. "I swear I brushed."

"Pepper's stubborn." A glance out the window gives Seb a second glimpse of stubborn. Matteo and Dante in Teo's 1973 Alfa Romeo Spider. They've got the top up and their eyes glued on Sebastian's guest.

Flipping them the bird, he checks his patient's progress. "All good?"

"You're a lifesaver, man." The guy pockets the pack of picks and makes for the door. "If I get laid tonight, I owe you."

"Wonderful." He leans back in his chair and waits for the guy to go away in his Tesla. The second he's gone, his buddies have their car doors open.

"Afternoon, gentlemen." He hooks his hands behind his head as his pals stride through the clinic entrance. "You here for a complimentary tongue scraping?"

Matteo leans on the counter. "A fucking comedian."

Dante scans the waiting room. "Where's your receptionist?"

"Terri's at lunch." Seb drops his chair legs to the floor. "Which means she can't slap me for calling her Terri." It's her name, but not one he gets to call his grandma. "Need her to schedule you for a denture fitting?"

Matteo glares. "You can stop the comedy routine any time."

Not really. It's kind of his thing. He's mulling another crack when Dante leans in and lowers his voice. "Last chance to join the Svenson job. Shouldn't take more than an hour."

"I thought you'd gone straight." Dante's a farmer now, and Teo took a job for some computer firm. "No more killing bad guys for money?"

"No killing." Dante cracks his knuckles. "Just talking."

A talk from big, bald Dante could scare anyone to death, so it's kinda the same. "Good plan."

"And we're not making money." Matteo hands him a ski mask. "It's a pro bono job."

The mask is a nice touch. Necessary, since Seb's face decorates billboards all over town.

"While I appreciate the anonymity, I'm out." He shoves the mask back. "I've got a gum graft at two."

Teo lifts a brow. "Performing or receiving?"

"Performing." He does a lot of that. "Maybe the next job?"

"Later this week." Dante scrubs his bald scalp with one big hand. "Drinks with a guy who sticks kittens in a sack and throws them in his pond instead of getting his cats spayed."

Grounds for murder in Dante's book. Seb can't blame him. The big guy loves animals.

As usual, Teo will pull the reins, insist they *talk* instead of slipping cyanide in the target's beer.

It's nice how his pals complement each other. "Which night?"

"Depends." Dante looks at Matteo. "Which night were Jen and Nic doing that fancy charity thing?"

Teo shrugs. "I'll ask Renee. They're all going together."

Sebastian rests a hand on the darkened tablet. It buzzed ten seconds ago, so The Union must've answered. "Can I let you know? I might have something going on this week."

"Busy guy." Dante thumps the counter with a meaty fist. "I'm making elk chili next Friday night. Come by at five."

His week's perking up already. "Will everyone be there?"

Matteo shares a scowl with both of them before jerking a thumb at Dante. "Just because this asshole's marrying one sister doesn't grant you permission to date the other."

Seb stifles a snort. Nicole Bello needs no one's permission for anything. "One of these days, she'll stop hating me. Then I'll be at all the family dinners."

"Dream on." Teo heads for the door. "Let us know which night you're free for the kitten guy."

"Will do." He watches his buddies march out. One bald and brooding, one dark and scowling. Both big as hell. If anyone's casing his clinic, they look like the weirdest couple to ever book a tandem cleaning.

Grabbing the tablet, he taps in his passcode. Waits for the message to appear.

TARGET IS **a female operator with 48 confirmed kills. Further details forthcoming only with signed contract.**

SEBASTIAN SNORTS ALOUD THIS TIME. He's been at this too long to take a job without more intel. He taps his favorite poop emoji, followed by a blue tyrannosaurus, a balloon bouquet, and a smiley face with oversized teeth.

It's meaningless crap and not code for anything, but The Union guys will spend hours deciphering its hidden message.

NO SHAREY, **no signy.**

HE'S BARELY SET the tablet down when his door bangs open. He looks up, and his heart heaves into his throat.

"God, you're a jerk."

As his heart simmers down, a different part of him wakes up. "Afternoon, Nicole." He gives her his best dentist grin. "You look lovely today."

It's true, though her scowl suggests she doesn't like hearing it from him. "How many times do I have to ask you *politely* not to let your patients park in my lot?"

"Politely?" He pretends to ponder. "Once would do it."

She huffs out a breath. "Seriously, LaDouceur. My families need to get in and out of my building as quickly as possible. They can't trek across the lot every time some douche in a Porsche shows up late for his teeth whitening and parks in front of my daycare."

Nicole Bello runs a childcare facility for families in hiding. Moms fleeing abuse or dads in witness protection. A remarkable gig, and she's remarkable for running it.

Doesn't mean he won't mess with her. "Much as I'd love to be the first dental clinic in Oregon to have valet parking, that's not in the cards. I put up a sign. What else do you want?"

"They're not getting the message from your stupid sign." Nic blows blonde hair off her forehead. "Make it *bigger*."

This bickering sends conflicting signals to his libido. "You want it *bigger*, huh?"

"God, you're a pig." Nic folds her arms. She's wearing one of her teacher dresses with a thick cardigan, but he sees the swell of her breasts behind the fabric.

He'd see them if she wore a suit of armor.

"Seriously, Minty Fresh." Her eyes soften, but her voice stays sharp. "It's a safety issue. I need you to take this seriously."

The fact that she said "seriously" twice means he shouldn't joke around. "*Seriously* seriously, or just *sorta* seriously?" He tips back in his chair. "Because there's a difference between—"

"Between me speaking plainly to you—business owner to business owner—versus me involving the police?" She grits her teeth. "Is that serious enough for you?"

Yeah, that'll do it.

He sets down his chair. "You know I'm just messing with you." He ordered the new sign last week. "M'lady wants it bigger, she'll get it bigger. It'll be up by the end of the week."

Her face softens like her eyes. Green eyes the color of sea glass or ocean waves or the little jade roller Terri uses for her face cream.

Thinking of his grandma helps make his hard-on go down.

"Thank you." Nicole rests her hands on the counter, and he does his best not to look at them. Not to wonder what they'd feel like trailing down his chest. "I don't mean to be a hard-ass. It's just really important."

Sebastian nods gravely. "All asses are important. Particularly yours."

Nic flings her arms up. "You're hopeless."

"Not true." He lifts one brow. "I'm very hopeful you'll go out with me tomorrow night."

"No."

"Wednesday night?"

"Sebastian—"

"Okay, okay." He rests his arms on the counter.

Is he seeing things, or did her eyes just flick favorably to his biceps? "Thursday night, and that's my final offer."

"Well, *that's* a relief." She backs toward the door. "Even if I wanted to—which I don't—I have plans Thursday."

"What sort of plans?"

"None of your business."

"Tuning your harp to play hymns with the angels?" He dials up the wattage on his grin. "Renewing your license to drive me wild with desire?"

Nicole snorts. "Do lines like that ever work for you?"

"Dunno." He grabs a paperweight off the counter. He's got no papers to anchor but wants to watch her ogle his arms as he throws it from one hand to the other. "I save all my best stuff for you."

"Please." Nic's eyes flicker.

He tosses again.

Another flicker.

She licks her lips. "If that's your best, God help the women who get your lousiest."

"There's only you, Nicole."

Another toss.

Another flash.

A roll of those green eyes. "Goodbye, LaDouceur."

She shoves out the door, and he sits up to watch her walk from his clinic to her car across the lot.

Wait. Not to her car. To the dry cleaner two doors down. He stares through the window as she hands them a ticket, then waits while the clerk shuffles in back.

Seb's not kidding about the date. From the instant he laid eyes on Nicole Bello, he wanted her. The fact that she hated him on sight may be a motive.

Sebastian loves a challenge.

But he loves her fiery personality more. Her beauty, her brains, her fierce love of family. He even loves how she tells him off. It's a game he enjoys, and deep down, she enjoys it, too. He's almost sure.

The dry cleaner comes back with a plastic-wrapped garment on a hanger. Sebastian squints to see it. A dress? Not one of her teacher dresses. This one looks slinky. Something long and curve-hugging and...

Red?

She swings through the door with the bag over her arm, and he follows her with his eyes. Stares as she slings the dress into her sensible Volvo. She checks the mirrors and buckles her seatbelt like a fine, upstanding instructor of young minds.

As she drives away—hands at perfect ten-and-two on the wheel—Sebastian feels his arms prickle.

Dragging his eyes to his tablet, he shoves it aside. Wiggles the mouse for his desktop computer and toggles past the patient portal. In the search bar, he plugs in "charity benefit events." Three clicks later, he's on the website for the chamber of commerce.

It's the silliest hunch he's ever had.

But as he scans the listings, he can't lose the tingle in his gut.

***

Want to keep reading? Click to grab *Killer Smile*.

https://books2read.com/b/menDnl

Did you read the free series prequel for **Assassins in Love**? In case you missed it, I'm giving away the *Killer Looks* prequel novella for zero pennies when you subscribe to my newsletter. Here's where to nab that:

https://BookHip.com/XWJJVFH

ACKNOWLEDGMENTS

I'm over-the-top grateful to the best street team ever, Fenske's Frisky Posse. Thank you for lending your names, your eagle eyes, and your support to this wild journey we've been on together all these years. I'm especially thankful to Erin, Regina, Judy, Becky, Tina, and Cherie for your fierce battles against typos in the ARC.

Thank you to Susan Bischoff and Lauralynn Elliott for your editing expertise, eagle eyes, and eternal patience with my pleas for "just one more week" on deadlines. Thanks also to Meah Cukrov for keeping me sane and on-track (as much as it's possible, anyway).

A million thanks to my awesome family, Dixie & David Fenske; Aaron & Carlie & Paxton Fenske; Cedar & Violet Zagurski. Your love and support means the world to me.

And thanks eternally to my partner in crime (mostly legal), Craig. This series took a lot out of me, and I'm grateful to you for putting it back in. Er, that wasn't meant to be dirty (it totally was). Want to mount a gun turret on the camper?

DON'T MISS OUT!

Want access to exclusive excerpts, behind-the-scenes stories about my books, cover reveals, and prize giveaways? You'll get all that by subscribing to my newsletter, plus **FREE** bonus scenes featuring your favorite characters from my rom-coms and erotic romances. Want to see Aidan and Lyla get hitched after *Eye Candy*? Or read a swoony proposal featuring Sean and Amber from *Chef Sugarlips*? It's all right here and free for the taking:

https://tawnafenske.com/bonus-content/

ABOUT THE AUTHOR

When Tawna Fenske finished her English lit degree at 22, she celebrated by filling a giant trash bag full of romance novels and dragging it everywhere until she'd read them all. Now she's a RITA Award finalist, *USA Today* bestselling author who writes humorous fiction, risqué romance, and heartwarming love stories with a quirky twist. *Publishers Weekly* has praised Tawna's offbeat romances with multiple starred reviews and noted, "There's something wonderfully relaxing about being immersed in a story filled with over-the-top characters in undeniably relatable situations. Heartache and humor go hand in hand."

Tawna lives in Bend, Oregon, with her husband, step-kids, and a menagerie of ill-behaved pets. She loves hiking, snowshoeing, standup paddleboarding, and inventing excuses to sip wine on her back porch. She can peel a banana with her toes and loses an average of twenty pairs of eyeglasses per year. To find out more about Tawna and her books, visit www.tawnafenske.com.

ALSO BY TAWNA FENSKE

The Sugar & Spice Erotic Romance Series
Eye Candy
Tough Cookie
Honey Do

The Ponderosa Resort Romantic Comedy Series
Studmuffin Santa
Chef Sugarlips
Sergeant Sexypants
Hottie Lumberjack
Stiff Suit
Mancandy Crush (novella)
Captain Dreamboat
Snowbound Squeeze (novella)
Dr. Hot Stuff

The Juniper Ridge Romantic Comedy Series
Show Time
Let It Show
Show Down
Show of Honor
Just for Show
Show Off (coming soon!)

The Assassins in Love Series
Killer Looks (prequel novella)

Killer Instincts

Killer Moves

Killer Smile

The List

The Test

The Last

<u>Standalone novellas and other wacky stuff</u>

Going Up (novella)

Eat, Play, Lust (novella)